The Roses Remember

In Tumblebrook, even roses have secrets.

Tumblebrook Mysteries
Book 6

Ellen Le Teace

Bradford
Press

Chapter 1

Midsummer Calm

The aroma of fresh coffee drifted through the Tumblebrook Inn's dining room, mingling with the buttery scent of warm scones on their trays. Morning light slipped through lace curtains and caught dust motes spinning above the polished floor. Amelia Farnsworth moved between tables with the ease of someone who had made innkeeping both her profession and her art.

She carried a steaming carafe in one hand and a basket of muffins in the other, her smile ready even as her mind ticked along. Carafe low at table two. Muffins dwindling at table five. Oven timer in four minutes. Directions request in three...two—

"Miss Farnsworth?"

A gray-haired man in a fisherman's cap raised his hand. Amelia pivoted, setting the coffee at a corner table where a young couple bent over a trail map.

"Another pot to fuel your adventures," she said.

"You're a lifesaver," he grinned.

His partner, adjusting a wide-brimmed sunhat, lowered her voice. "We heard about wildflower fields south of town. Worth the trek?"

"Absolutely. Take the loop trail, not the shortcut. Better views, and your boots stay clean."

The couple shared a pleased look. Guests loved a local secret. Amelia left them satisfied and crossed to the fishermen angling for refills.

Midsummer filled the inn to the rafters. Families rolled up in station wagons packed with bikes and coolers. Retired couples settled to chess by afternoon and fireflies by evening. Artists carried sketchbooks. Hikers tucked sandwiches into daypacks. The house thrummed with the season's rhythm, each guest weaving into Tumblebrook's tapestry.

She had stocked flour, eggs, butter—and patience. Patience was the true currency of innkeeping, she thought, setting a tray of muffins near the fishermen. One muttered thanks without looking up, already deep in an argument about lake levels.

Across the room, Mrs. Cranston held court. She had come since Amelia's aunt ran the inn and maintained the scones were "more authentic" here than anywhere. On her second one now, she buttered with gusto while discussing three topics at once: her grandson's engagement, the fickle weather, and the supremacy of rhubarb pie over strawberry. She could fill a room without raising her voice.

By the window, two sisters in their seventies clicked away at their knitting. Yarn baskets overflowed with colors bright as the flowerbeds outside. Scarves or socks for winter—debate ongoing—soft as background music to the morning bustle.

At another table, artists compared sketches of the lakeshore. Watercolor, one insisted, caught truth; charcoal, another countered, turned beauty into shadow. In Tumblebrook, even art sparked argument.

Cutlery chimed. Laughter bubbled. Voices braided and unbraided. It was the kind of music Amelia loved best.

And yet—

Even inside the warmth she felt the thin line that separates peace from disruption. Spring's storms—weathered and otherwise—had taught her not to trust calm for long. She treasured it. She did not expect it to last.

She carried blueberry muffins to the sisters. Agnes, the elder, inhaled.

"Divine. Do you use lemon zest?"

"Just a touch," Amelia said, pleased.

The sisters traded a look. "That's why they're the best on the North Shore," Ruth said, already reaching for seconds.

Pride warmed Amelia. Moments like this paid for early mornings and late nights—proof that people felt cared for here, seen.

The peace fractured, as it often did, with Clara Henderson.

"Amelia!"

The front door banged wide. Clara bustled in, arms overloaded with flyers. A gust sent them skittering across the floor like startled pigeons.

"Oh, bother," she muttered, dropping to scoop them up.

Amelia hurried over, balancing a tray of dishes. "Good morning to you too. What's on fire?"

"Festival preparations," Clara said, braid half undone, cheeks pink. "Chaos. Doris is about to pull her hair out. Mr. Larkin has me cataloging shipments until my fingers ache. And don't ask about booth assignments."

"The Summer Arts & Antiques Festival is a week away."

"Exactly. Seven days to do the impossible." She plunked the flyers onto an empty table with a sigh. "Do you know how many people call their work 'antique-inspired'? Old chairs with a coat of paint. Doris nearly threw one man out of the square."

"Sit before you collapse," Amelia said, fetching a teapot. "Tea before tantrums."

"Bless you," Clara breathed.

Guests glanced up, curious, then returned to breakfast. A family with two small children tugged at Amelia's sleeve for directions to the lakeshore. She handed them a folded brochure. An elderly gentleman in a linen jacket paused at the counter.

"Seen any digging near the north ridge?" he asked.

"Digging?" Amelia frowned.

He chuckled, embarrassed. "Probably nothing. Odd marks in the soil. Never mind."

He shuffled off. The question tugged at her for a breath—then jam was wanted and the oven chimed again.

From the porch, a familiar chirrup carried in. Lady Grey, Amelia's British Shorthair, sprawled along the railing, silver coat bright in the sun. Her amber eyes tracked sparrows scavenging crumbs; her tail drew a lazy question mark.

"You'll frighten them," Amelia called.

Lady Grey blinked, unimpressed. The sparrows scattered anyway.

"She looks like royalty," Clara said, sipping her tea.

"She thinks she is," Amelia replied, setting down a plate of muffins.

Lady Grey pounced—not on birds but on a stray flyer skating along the porch. She batted it under the railing, where it wedged half-hidden. Later, when Amelia stooped to retrieve it, the edges showed a faint smear of dirt, as if it had been dragged across the ground before Clara dropped it.

Odd. No time to dwell. A guest needed change; the timer rang again.

The room filled to capacity. Conversations swirled. From a neighboring porch came the easy strum of a guitar, notes drifting across the garden. Outside, the lake lay tin-bright under the sun. A breeze carried lilac, cut grass, frying bacon.

Amelia paused by the door, tea towel slung over her arm. She breathed it in—the contentment, the pulse of a town thriving under summer's hand. The inn felt alive, and for a moment her heart felt light.

Deep down, a chord tightened.

It was tempting to believe the darker days were behind them. Tempting—never wise.

Tranquility in Tumblebrook never lingered without a catch. Somewhere beyond the laughter and lilacs, something shifted, waiting its moment to disturb the calm.

When it came, Amelia, Clara, and Lady Grey would meet it at the door.

Chapter 2

The Café Garden Find

The morning rush had ebbed at Tumblebrook Café, leaving behind the lingering perfume of cinnamon rolls, brewed coffee, and the faint tang of mint from the planters Doris Finch kept beneath the front windows. Sunlight striped the wooden floorboards, catching dust motes that drifted lazily above neatly arranged tables. The café always seemed most itself at this hour—neither silent nor chaotic, but breathing like a creature at rest.

Behind the counter, Doris Finch surveyed her small kingdom with the satisfaction of a general after battle. Her floral apron was tied in a no-nonsense knot, her bun miraculously intact after the rush. Two part-time high schoolers cleared plates with less efficiency than she liked.

"Stack them properly, dear," Doris called as one boy wobbled beneath a leaning tower of dishes. "You'll chip the edges if you slam them about. This isn't a lumberyard."

The boy flushed crimson, muttered an apology, and adjusted the stack. Doris sighed, her sternness softening at the corners. She wanted them to do well—not just for the café, but for themselves.

Responsibility had to be taught early; she'd learned that long before she poured her first pot of coffee.

With the last customers drifting out, Doris wiped her hands, checked the counter twice, and slipped out the back door.

The garden greeted her with the hum of bees in the lavender, sunlight already pressing down heavy. The scent of basil, mint, and thyme rose in waves as she brushed past the planters. Here she felt most herself—not behind the counter, but with her hands in the soil, coaxing life from the earth.

The thyme patch had grown ragged, its leaves curling brown at the edges. She knelt with a grunt, knees protesting, and pressed her trowel into the soil. The ground gave more easily than expected, roots yielding too quickly. She dug again. This time the blade scraped something hard.

Doris frowned. She knew this garden like her own pantry shelves —roots, worms, rocks, yes. But not a sound like that.

"Rocks don't shine," she muttered as a tarnished glimmer winked up at her. Carefully, she dug around the edges, fingertips brushing metal, and tugged the object free.

A spoon. Long-handled, heavier than her café flatware, dulled by decades underground. She rubbed the grime with her thumb. A crest emerged: a crown poised above a sailing ship.

Doris's pulse quickened. She wasn't fanciful; she didn't believe in omens or curses. Yet the spoon carried weight, not just in her palm but in the sense that it held stories long buried.

"Well, what on earth?"

Footsteps crunched behind her. Clara Henderson hurried down the alley, tote bag of books bumping her hip, braid slipping loose against flushed cheeks.

"Morning, Doris!" she called, breathless. "Mr. Larkin had me sorting index cards until my fingers went numb. I thought I'd treat myself to lemon bars—oh!" Her eyes landed on the spoon. "What's that?"

"Dug it up with the thyme. Doesn't belong to me, that's certain."

Clara leaned closer, all thoughts of lemon bars gone. "That crest... it looks like something out of heraldry. A crown and ship. Colonial, maybe?" Her voice trembled with excitement, as if she'd stumbled into the middle of a research puzzle.

Before Doris could answer, the café's side door swung open.

"Clara, I thought I'd find you here." Amelia Farnsworth stepped into the sun, flour dusting her apron. "Doris, I came hoping for a scone—oh!" Her gaze dropped to the spoon. "What have you unearthed this time?"

"Not a potato." Doris handed it over. "Feels heavy enough to be silver."

Amelia turned it carefully. Despite the heat, the metal was cold, the crest glinting faintly through its tarnish. "Not a family monogram," she murmured. "This looks... official."

The way she said it gave Clara gooseflesh.

Against her better judgment, Doris carried the spoon inside to rinse at the sink. Within minutes, word had spread as though someone had run through the square shouting. Neighbors began drifting in—not for coffee, but for a glimpse. Tumblebrook never could resist a mystery.

Mrs. Cranston bustled in first, spectacles sliding down her nose. She peered over Doris's shoulder. "Still looks cursed to me. Digging up buried silver? Bad luck clings to things left underground."

"Cursed?" scoffed Gus Phelps from his usual corner. He slapped his newspaper against the table. "More like pirate treasure. My granddad swore smugglers used North Shore coves. Could be they buried loot here."

"This isn't the Caribbean, Gus," Mrs. Cranston sniffed.

"Smuggling, then," Gus said. "Or Prohibition hoards. That's no ordinary spoon."

Voices layered over voices.

A young artist suggested noble family scandal. One of Doris's waitresses whispered about shipwrecks—Lake Superior kept its secrets, after all. Another patron swore he'd heard of silver passing hand to hand in Prohibition taverns.

Clara scribbled notes on the back of a flyer, determined to catch every theory. Amelia, seated nearby, listened more warily. She recognized that gleam in townsfolk's eyes—the mix of curiosity and fear. It could bind a community together. Or tear it apart.

Then Lady Grey arrived.

The silver-furred British Shorthair padded through the doorway as if summoned, tail high, amber eyes sharp. She leapt onto the counter, ignoring Doris's squawk.

She crouched, gaze fixed on the spoon. Muscles coiled, she extended a paw.

"Lady Grey—" Amelia started, too late.

Clink.

The cat tapped the silver. A resonant note rang through the café, startling the crowd into silence. She tapped it again, then gave a low chirrup, as if pronouncing judgment.

"She's never done that over cutlery," Clara whispered.

"Instinct, perhaps," Amelia murmured, stroking the cat's fur. But Lady Grey's tail lashed, her fur bristling despite the touch.

Doris folded her arms. "Wherever it came from, it's not going back in my thyme patch. First gossip, then feuds, then police. Mark my words—that thing will bring trouble."

A nervous chuckle rippled through the café. No one disagreed.

The crowd swelled. The mayor proposed displaying the spoon at the Arts & Antiques Festival. A retired teacher insisted the library should catalogue it. A fisherman declared it belonged right where Doris found it. Teenagers whispered about treasure maps, eyes shining.

The café had become courtroom, museum committee, and gossip mill all in one.

Amelia watched uneasily. Less than an hour since the spoon surfaced, and already the town had divided into camps: treasure, history, curse. Clara's pencil raced across paper, eyes bright with discovery.

Lady Grey stayed sentinel on the counter, amber gaze unblinking, as if daring the silver to yield its secrets.

Amelia's eyes lingered on the crest. A crown. A ship. A story waiting to be told—or perhaps a secret that should have stayed buried.

Trouble indeed, she thought. And in Tumblebrook, trouble had a way of arriving on silver platters.

Chapter 3

Clara's Curiosity

The bell above the door of Gossamer Fables chimed cheerfully as Clara Henderson stepped inside, tote bag slung over her shoulder. The sound was comfort itself—announcing her arrival into a place where the world slowed, and order waited patiently among the shelves.

The scent greeted her next: old paper mingled with rosewood polish and the faint trace of lavender sachets tucked between volumes to ward off mildew. It was a perfume she never tired of—soothing, grounding, familiar. To Clara, the shop was not just a book-shop. It was sanctuary.

Here, the hum of silence wrapped around her, a balm after the chaos of Doris's café the day before. There, the silver spoon had turned chatter into clamor. Here, truth might be uncovered in ink and margin notes rather than rumor.

Mr. Larkin, the bookshop's elderly owner, had retreated to the back office as usual, muttering about invoices. He trusted Clara to mind the front during slow hours, a responsibility she carried with quiet pride. She slipped behind the counter, set down her tote, and unfolded the crumpled flyer she'd scribbled on at the café. She smoothed it against the wood.

At the top, underlined twice: *Silver spoon. Crest: crown + ship.*

Her pencil hovered. Heraldic crests weren't unusual in Tumble-brook—several founding families had them. But this one felt differ-ent. It carried weight, whispered secrets that begged pursuit. Her pulse quickened.

Dragging the step stool to the tall shelves, Clara tugged down a tome with a satisfying *thump*: *Silver and Heraldry: Symbols Through the Ages.* She brushed her hand reverently across the cracked leather binding before opening it. Dust rose like incense as she flipped past lions, griffins, fleurs-de-lis, and anchors.

Crown and ship. Crown and ship.

She lingered over entries: a Dutch guild with a galleon crest, an English family whose emblem was a crown above an anchor, a light-house topped with a starburst. Close—but not right.

The combination she wanted was absent. As if someone had plucked it from history, excised it deliberately.

"Clara!"

Mr. Larkin's voice drifted from the back room, reedy with age but edged with authority. "If you're pulling the heraldry volumes again, mind the spines! They're older than I am."

"I'll be careful," she called back, suppressing a smile. "I promise I won't topple the monarchy of silver."

A harrumph answered her. She pictured him hunched over his ledger, spectacles sliding down his nose. He'd check on her eventu-ally, but for now the shop was hers.

By midmorning, the counter resembled a scholar's den more than a shop. *North Shore Families: A Heraldic History. Colonial Crests of the Midwest. Symbols of the Sea.* Volumes sprawled open in every direction, reference cards and scribbled notes scattered like leaves in a brisk wind.

Clara sketched the crest as she remembered it from Doris's café: crown arches precise, sails angled into an invisible gust. She shaded the ship's prow to imagine how it might have gleamed when new. Nothing matched.

The absence itself felt like a clue.

The bell jingled again. Clara glanced up, half expecting a tourist. Instead, in shuffled Ezra.

The hermit-artist was a rare sight. He carried the smell of pine sap and turpentine with him, clothes daubed in paint, beard wilder than the last time she'd seen him. He clutched a sketchbook stained at the corners, shoulders hunched as if bracing against air too crowded.

"Ezra," Clara said warmly, masking her surprise. "Looking for something?"

He didn't answer. His fingertips drifted across book spines, pausing as though listening for whispers. At last, his gaze landed on her sketch of the crest.

"Silver," he murmured, voice soft but carrying, a ripple through the still shop. "Old silver doesn't shine without a shadow."

Clara blinked. "What does that mean?"

Ezra's smile was faint, enigmatic. "Means what it says." He tapped the sketch with a charcoal-stained finger, leaving a smudge. "Where there's silver, there's shadow. Always has been."

Before she could press him, he wandered off toward local-lore shelves, head cocked like a bird listening for unseen songs.

Clara jotted his words into the margin of her notes: *Old silver doesn't shine without a shadow.*

It glared back at her like a warning. Or an invitation.

The morning stretched. Customers drifted in and out—tourists buying postcards, a teenager trading allowance for a comic, an older man thumbing through bird guides. Clara served them all politely, but her mind never left the spoon, the crest, or Ezra's phrase.

She copied her sketches neatly, underlining details: the crown's arches, the sails' curve, the prow. She pictured a long table gleaming with silver, each piece etched with the same crest. Who had owned such a set? Who had lost it? And why had a spoon ended up buried beneath Doris Finch's thyme?

Her notes branched like roots across the page:

- Smuggler's mark?
- Secret society?
- Erased family line?
- Prohibition token?

The possibilities thrilled her.

By the time Clara restacked the books, they seemed heavier than when she'd pulled them down, as though knowledge had thickened inside them. She whispered a promise to return.

Slipping her sketches into her tote, she adjusted her braid and murmured: "I'll find where you came from."

Because in Tumblebrook, secrets always surfaced. And Clara Henderson meant to catch this one before it slid back into shadow.

Chapter 4

Speculation Over Tea

By midafternoon, Doris Finch's café buzzed again. The lunch rush had left crumbs on saucers and teapots cooling in their cozies, but the air was anything but calm. Word of the silver spoon had spread through Tumblebrook faster than jam on a hot biscuit.

Doris emerged from the kitchen balancing a tray of steaming teapots, sugar-dusted scones, and a plate of shortbread. She carried herself with her usual brisk efficiency, though the faint glow in her cheeks betrayed both satisfaction and nerves. Half the town had managed to squeeze into chairs. Elbows brushed, teacups rattled, and the air itself seemed steeped in bergamot, cinnamon, and anticipation —as though the café braced for drama.

"Now, now, don't all crane your necks at once," Doris scolded, though her lips twitched with pride. She set the tray at the central table where Mrs. Cranston, Gus Phelps, and several other regulars leaned forward like jurors awaiting a verdict. "If you want tea, you'll get tea. And if you want a look at history—well, you'll get that too."

With a flourish, she drew the tarnished spoon from her apron pocket and placed it on a folded napkin as though revealing a crown jewel.

Gasps rippled through the café. Even those who'd glimpsed it before leaned closer, eager for another look. The afternoon sun slanted through lace curtains, striking the crest so that crown and ship gleamed faintly despite their tarnish, as though insisting they had endured longer than the people staring now.

Mrs. Cranston adjusted her spectacles. "Still looks cursed to me."

"It looks valuable," countered Edwin Harper, the antiques dealer up from Duluth. He leaned forward in his corner seat, rings flashing. "Wouldn't surprise me if it fetched a tidy sum at auction."

"That spoon isn't leaving Tumblebrook," Doris declared. Her chest puffed, though her eyes flicked nervously around the crowd. "It was dug up in my garden, which makes it part of this town's story." She folded her arms, daring them to argue.

They did, of course.

The debate flared like dry kindling.

"Appraise it," one urged.

"Display it," suggested another.

"Donate it to the library!" cried a retired teacher.

Gus Phelps slammed a hand on the table, rattling saucers. "A museum would lock it away where locals couldn't touch it. That silver belongs here."

"And who's to keep it safe?" Mrs. Cranston shot back, narrowing her eyes at Doris. "You? Carrying it about in your apron? Suppose someone with sticky fingers takes a fancy?"

Doris bristled. "I can keep track of a spoon, thank you." She set a teapot down so firmly the saucer rattled.

The voices rose and tangled as more townsfolk squeezed in from the square. The mayor proposed displaying it at the Summer Arts & Antiques Festival "to draw visitors, of course." A carpenter suggested it might have come from a shipwreck. Two teenagers whispered of pirate treasure, already mapping chests in their imaginations.

The café had transformed into courtroom, museum committee, and gossip mill all at once.

Amelia sat at a side table, hands wrapped around her teacup. She watched the debate with unease. She'd seen how curiosity sharpened into greed, how speculation hardened into suspicion. The spoon had been above ground less than a day, and already it divided the town: treasure or trouble.

She sipped slowly, letting bergamot sting her tongue. It did little to settle her.

Beside her, Clara scribbled furiously in her notebook. "Every theory is a clue," she whispered, pencil racing. "Even the wrong ones show what people believe."

"Belief can be as dangerous as fact," Amelia murmured back. She knew too well how quickly whispers grew teeth.

At that moment, Lady Grey arrived.

The café's chatter softened as the silver-furred British Shorthair padded in, tail high, amber eyes gleaming. She moved like a queen surveying her subjects, paws soundless on the floor. Children gasped. Even grown men instinctively shifted to give her space.

Without hesitation, Lady Grey wove through chair legs, leapt onto an empty seat at the central table, and fixed her gaze on the spoon.

"Well now," Gus chuckled. "Looks like the cat's casting her vote."

Lady Grey leaned forward, whiskers twitching. She lowered her chin close to the crest, then settled into a sphinx-like pose, amber eyes unblinking. She looked less like a lounging pet than a sentinel, guarding the silver.

"That cat knows something," Mrs. Cranston whispered, knuckles whitening on her teacup. "Animals sense curses."

"Animals sense nonsense," Doris countered, though her tone softened, almost approving of Lady Grey's vigil.

Amelia's stomach tightened. She knew her companion too well. Lady Grey's stillness wasn't idle—it was warning.

The arguments swelled again, louder, sharper.

"Polish it and display it!" cried one.

"Don't polish it—you'll ruin its authenticity!" argued another.

"Call a historian!"

"Call the police!"

A young mother swore she'd seen the crest in her grandmother's attic. A fisherman claimed it was smuggler's silver, passed in coves at night. A tourist suggested a noble scandal.

Clara's pencil flew across the page, eager to capture every theory. Amelia, though, felt only dread.

Through it all, Lady Grey remained motionless, amber eyes fixed on the spoon. Once, she flicked her tail—a sharp punctuation. The room hushed instinctively, then resumed.

Finally, Amelia rose. She crossed to the central table, resting her hand lightly beside the spoon. Her voice was calm but firm.

"Perhaps we should remember that this spoon is still an unknown. It may be valuable, or it may not. It may tell a story, or it may hide one. Either way, fighting won't help."

The room quieted, though mutters lingered. Some stared into their teacups, chastened.

Clara looked up from her notes, eyes bright. "She's right. We need facts. Until then, speculation is just—well, tea without sugar. All steam, no substance."

A ripple of laughter eased the tension, but Amelia caught the undercurrent of unease. Tumblebrook was shifting. She could feel it.

Her gaze slid to Lady Grey, still sentinel, gaze unbroken.

Trouble was coming. And the spoon—gleaming faintly in its patch of sun—had only just begun to speak.

Chapter 5

An Unwelcome Guest

The café still hummed with speculation. Teacups clinked, voices overlapped, and the air was thick with bergamot, cinnamon, and gossip. At the center table, the silver spoon lay on its napkin like a relic at a shrine, drawing eyes as surely as a flame drew moths.

Then the bell above the café door gave a sharp jangle. Not its usual cheerful chime, but a clang that sliced through the room. Conversations faltered. Cups hovered midair. Even the kettle in the kitchen seemed to hush its hiss.

The man who stepped inside carried presence like a weapon.

Tall, broad-shouldered, and overdressed in a city-cut wool coat far too heavy for July, he seemed to darken the doorway. His shoes shone like mirrors, his slicked hair gleamed with precision, and the faint musk of cologne clung to him—sharp, foreign, wrong among Doris's lavender and cinnamon. His small, calculating eyes swept the room, scanning faces until they fixed on Doris.

A slow, deliberate smile spread across his face—polished, practiced, and utterly devoid of warmth.

"Well, if it isn't cousin Doris," he drawled. His voice slid over the room with the ease of someone who had spent years commanding attention. "Still running this place with your iron fist and gingham apron, I see."

The spoon gleamed faintly at the corner of his eye. He studied it the way a banker studies coins—not with affection, but with calculation.

Doris froze mid-pour, nearly spilling boiling water into a saucer. Her knuckles whitened on the teapot's handle.

"Vernon." Her voice was flat, clipped, as if the name itself left a bitter taste.

The café held its breath.

Whispers rippled across the tables. *Vernon Finch.* The name swept in murmurs like a gust of wind stirring dry leaves. The cousin no one mentioned. The one who had left town under clouds of rumor —debts, disputes, disgrace.

Amelia stiffened in her seat. She hadn't even known Doris had a cousin, let alone one who looked as though he'd stepped out of a stage play titled *Villain in the Parlor.* Beside her, Clara leaned forward, notebook forgotten in her lap, eyes narrowing with naked curiosity.

Lady Grey, ever the intuitive sentinel, leapt silently from her chair and padded closer, tail flicking like a metronome. Her amber eyes locked on the stranger.

Vernon removed his coat with exaggerated care, folding it neatly over his arm before striding in as though he owned the place. He didn't ask for a seat; he claimed one.

"I heard whispers," he said loudly enough for all to hear, "about a little discovery made right here. A spoon, wasn't it? Silver, no less." His gaze darted to the napkin. "Imagine my surprise. I believe that belongs to me."

Gasps rustled across the café. A teaspoon clattered to the floor. Someone muttered, "The nerve of him."

Doris slammed the teapot onto the counter. "Yours? Don't be ridiculous. I dug it out of my garden."

"Our garden," Vernon corrected smoothly, each word dipped in condescension. "The Finch family property, divided though it may be, still belongs to us both. Inheritance isn't so easily tilled away as thyme and rosemary." He cast the room a knowing look, clearly expecting chuckles.

"You've never lifted a finger in that garden," Doris snapped, her cheeks flushed. "You wouldn't know thyme from weeds if it bit you."

Vernon chuckled low, the sound curling through the café like smoke. "Maybe not. But I know heirlooms when I see them. That spoon is Finch history. *My* history."

Clara tilted her head, pencil tapping against her notes. Her tone was mild, but her eyes were sharp. "That's odd. If it's truly your heirloom, shouldn't you recognize the crest?"

All eyes turned to Vernon.

For a heartbeat, his smile faltered. Then, slick as oil, it returned. "I hardly memorized every trinket. Heirlooms come and go. What matters is the bloodline they passed through. And that bloodline"—he spread his hands—"is mine as much as Doris's."

Amelia caught the lie instantly. His gaze lingered too long on the spoon, studying rather than remembering. He wasn't recalling an heirloom. He was calculating an opportunity.

The crowd shifted uneasily.

Mrs. Cranston pursed her lips. "Well, he does have the Finch nose," she announced, as though genetics alone proved ownership.

"Finch nose, my foot," Gus grumbled. "What he smells is opportunity."

Near the window, a pair of tourists whispered excitedly. "This town really is like a novel," one said.

Doris folded her arms, apron rustling. "You never cared for this family or this town. You left without a glance back. Why come sniffing around now?"

Vernon spread his hands in mock innocence. "Can a man not return to his roots? Especially when those roots yield treasure?"

His words were airy, but his eyes clung to the spoon.

Lady Grey leapt onto the table in one fluid motion. She planted herself between Doris and Vernon, amber eyes blazing. A low growl rumbled in her throat—steady, resonant, like distant thunder.

The café stilled.

"Keep your beast under control," Vernon snapped. His polished veneer cracked; irritation bled through.

Amelia rose, her voice calm but cutting. "Lady Grey isn't a beast. She's an excellent judge of character."

Clara, pencil poised once more, added, "And she doesn't growl unless she has reason." She underlined something in her notes, never looking away from Vernon.

His smile returned, brittle at the edges. "Believe what you like. But mark my words, Doris—this spoon is Finch property. I'll be speaking to a lawyer in Duluth about securing what's rightfully mine."

He reached for the tray, plucked up a scone without asking, and bit into it noisily. Crumbs fell onto his lapel. "Still dry," he muttered with a smirk.

Gasps and mutters swept the room. Some patrons sided with Doris, branding Vernon an opportunist. Others whispered about inheritance law. A few leaned toward treasure theories, eyes shining with the thought of more silver.

The café swelled with noise until it rattled the windowpanes.

Amelia stayed silent, studying Vernon. His mask of charm had begun to slip: his anger at Lady Grey's growl, his evasiveness about the crest, his fixation on possession. They told her more than his words ever could.

She leaned toward Clara. "He's lying."

Clara's pencil scratched. "And I intend to prove it."

Vernon swung his coat over his shoulder and strutted to the door as though he'd won. The bell clanged sharply behind him, his cologne lingering unpleasantly in the air.

Lady Grey remained by the spoon, her gaze locked on the door. She flicked her tail once—sharp as a warning.

Amelia followed her stare, a chill settling over her despite the summer heat.

Trouble had just walked in. And it carried the Finch name.

Chapter 6

Tense Supper at the Inn

The lamps threw a honeyed glow over the Tumblebrook Inn's dining room, turning the long table into a ribbon of light. Amelia would have wished for gentle chatter and second helpings of casserole. Instead she set one extra place and felt her sigh rattle the silver.

From the kitchen came Jonas' careful clatter; in the pantry, peach cobbler cooled to a burnished gold. Everything in order—except the man at the head of the table.

Vernon Finch had chosen that seat as if it called him by name. His cufflinks winked; his smile skimmed. Conversation about vendors and the morning's catch tapered to a watchful hush.

"Charming," he said, stretching the word. "Provincial, but quaint."

Doris had insisted he stay at the inn—*better to watch a snake in a jar*—and Amelia had agreed. Now, setting his plate, she regretted it.

Clara slipped into the chair at Amelia's left, notebook at her elbow, a graphite smudge on her hand. When Vernon glanced away, Clara's small headshake said, *Breathe. Observe.*

The table filled with familiar faces: Agnes and Ruth with knitting under their chairs; the Bertrams of Milwaukee; Edwin Harper, antiques dealer up from Duluth; Laurel Weston, the mayor, pearls neat as a private moon. Lady Grey entered last, silver coat catching lamplight, eyes filing the room.

"I've reached out to legal contacts in Duluth," Vernon announced, cutting across Edwin's remark on hallmarks. "Inheritance will be resolved quickly in my favor. These things require finesse."

"Legal contacts?" Clara asked, mild. "So you've worked in law?"

"Not directly." A flick of fingers. "Property portfolios."

"What kind?" Amelia asked before she could stop herself.

"Diversified. Dull to explain, dazzling in profit." He drank, satisfied with vagueness.

Edwin tilted his glass. "Who would you ring for late-eighteenth-century silver with... unusual symbology?"

"Let's not pretend a crown and a ship are unusual," Vernon said, spearing a green bean. "You antiques types love drama."

"And lawyers love vagueness," Edwin returned. Laughter loosened shoulders.

"Curious," Clara murmured, pencil poised, "that someone so familiar with heirlooms didn't recognize that crest yesterday."

Vernon's fork clattered, then was retrieved with a thin chuckle. "One doesn't memorize every doodle on silver. What matters is bloodline, not baubles."

Amelia circulated, focusing on plates and the soft drag of linen rather than his voice. Still, she noticed what he avoided: specifics. He watched spoons more than faces—the way a crow studies a picnic.

A whisk of fur and Lady Grey leapt to the empty chair beside him. Vernon stiffened. The cat's gaze slid past him to the leather suitcase by the sideboard—the one he'd refused to leave upstairs. Delicately, she scratched the leather. From inside came a faint metal clink.

Vernon jolted. "Keep that creature away from my things."

"She doesn't bother luggage," Amelia said evenly, "unless something inside interests her."

He snapped the clasp with more theater than necessary. The clink came again—then silence. "Cats are fickle," he laughed, brittle.

Lady Grey's tail made one sharp punctuation. *There is something in that suitcase,* Amelia heard as clearly as speech.

Jonas returned with cobbler; cinnamon and peach calmed the room. Agnes complimented the crust; Edwin eyed the béchamel. Vernon chewed as if grading.

"You mentioned portfolios," Clara said lightly. "Which markets?"

"Diversified," he repeated. "No free seminars."

"You might like Duluth's maritime museum," Edwin offered. "Crests in surprising places."

"Museums bore me."

"Odd," Laurel murmured. "They thrive on donors."

The table gratefully drifted to festival booths. Vernon held forth on "contacts" and a Hargreeve who owed him a favor. His story was a paper house—walk around it and you saw daylight through the seams.

The suitcase sat like a glossy period beside the sideboard.

After coffee, the lobby phone rang—a bright peal that tugged Amelia from the room. "Tumblebrook Inn, good evening."

Static, a breath, then a rough male voice: "Is Mr. Finch registered with you?"

"We don't disclose guest information," she said. "I can take a message."

A pause, a click. Gone.

Back at the table, Clara lifted a brow. Amelia gave the smallest shake: *later.*

Cups emptied. Edwin requested a wake-up call. Laurel gathered shawl and pearls. Agnes and Ruth chose peppermint tea over casting on. Vernon pushed back his chair with a squeal and rose as though taking a bow. "Charming meal," he said, and palmed the suitcase handle, checking the clasp with his thumb like a habit.

"Shall I show you to your room?" Amelia asked.

"I can find my way," he said, and waited to be led anyway.

On the landing, lake air slipped under the sash. In Room Seven, the suitcase bumped the doorframe. On instinct, Amelia glanced at the seam where Lady Grey had scratched. A crescent of fresh dirt clung there—not dust. *Recently set down outside,* she thought.

"Breakfast at eight," she said.

"I don't keep farmers' hours," he smiled. "Tell your cook not to burn the bacon."

"We don't burn bacon," she said blandly. The latch clicked with the satisfaction of a man who likes hearing things snap shut. Something slid inside the suitcase; springs creaked.

Back downstairs, conversation had softened. Lady Grey had installed herself at the head of the table and blinked at Amelia, one eye at a time.

"Well?" Clara asked.

"Just a phone call," Amelia said. "A man asking if Mr. Finch is registered."

"Name?"

"No. 'Business matter. Time-sensitive.' Then he hung up." A beat. "The suitcase chimes when it moves. He wouldn't leave it."

They filed the facts and let conclusions wait.

"Let's move the spoon," Amelia said. "Not here overnight."

"The office safe," Clara agreed.

In the little office, the safe crouched beneath the desk. Amelia spun the dial; the door yawned. Petty cash. Ledger. A tin of receipts. Her aunt's brooch awaiting a new clasp. On the desk, the spoon lay in a napkin; the crown and ship stared back like two small moons.

"Crown with five arches," Clara murmured, angling her sketch. "Three-masted ship. Official and anonymous."

"Doris says it's heavier than it looks," Amelia said, feeling its compact weight before settling it inside. The lock grumbled, then agreed. Lady Grey tapped the napkin once as if to bless the decision.

Evening thinned. Jonas, damp-haired, said good night with gratitude for leftover cobbler. Doors clicked, heels counted down the hall, knitting bags swung. Amelia slid the front bolt; her lungs released.

"Careful," Clara said, as Lady Grey butted Amelia's knee. "She'll keep you up pacing."

"She loves timing," Amelia said, scratching velvet ears. They parted.

Night rearranged the inn: wood-scented, clock steady, wind whispering in the eaves. A loon called somewhere out on the lake. Sleep circled Amelia, thoughtful.

Just past eleven, a floorboard murmured. Not Lady Grey's skitter, not Jonas's gallop: a careful weight. Amelia slipped into the hall. In the night-lamp's seam, a broad-shouldered figure paused—Vernon, shirtsleeved, suitcase in hand. He listened, then went not toward the front stairs but down the narrow back steps to the service door and the garden path.

Lady Grey pressed a paw to Amelia's instep—grounding. Amelia counted to sixty after the soft click of the back door, then followed.

Moonlight pooled on kitchen tile. The door stood ajar by a hand's width. Outside, the garden lay hushed. The path to the side gate held dark, fresh boot prints, the heel nicked into a small triangle she could recognize again. Near the hedge, metal clinked softly—set down, then set down more carefully. Silence.

She waited, let the night hold its breath, then closed the door and returned to bed with a heart a shade faster than thoughts could keep up. Sleep came like boat-sleep—aware of every sway.

Morning washed the inn gray-blue; coffee took the air by gentle coup. Without interrogating the impulse, Amelia checked the safe. The dial turned; the door released. Petty cash. Ledger. Brooch tin. The spoon in its napkin, crown and ship catching a thread of light. Relief surprised her with its weight.

Jonas whisked, hair static-tossed. The lobby bell jangled—crisp, polite, insistent.

Two men stood there, damp with weather undecided about rain. One wore a suit too hot for the season; the other wore the suit's expression. The taller flipped an identification wallet just enough to show a crest Amelia didn't know and the word **Collections** where she'd have preferred **Library**.

"We're looking for a Mr. Vernon Finch," he said. "Time-sensitive paperwork."

Upstairs, a faint clink sounded—as if a suitcase had been set down a touch too quickly.

"Of course," Amelia said, steady as a plate in a practiced hand. "I believe he's just... finishing breakfast."

She looked into the dining room and Vernon was gone.

"I'm sorry," Amelia said with practiced sincerity, "it appears Mr. Finch is not here at this time."

The men promised to return and left as quickly as they had arrived.

Lady Grey appeared in the office doorway and sat, tail neatly wrapped, amber eyes saying what no one else would: *The calm is over. Mind your footing.*

Amelia smiled the smile she'd earned and, in lake-colored light that smelled of coffee and rain, did what she did best—kept her voice gentle, her eyes open, and her questions ready.

Chapter 7

Lady Grey's Instincts

The Tumblebrook Inn settled into its evening hush—lamps glowing, the mantel clock ticking, lemon oil faint in the air —but tonight the quiet felt stretched thin. The timbers listened. The house held its breath.

Lady Grey patrolled the upstairs hall like a sentry, pacing and pausing outside Room Seven—Vernon Finch's door—with a low rumble in her chest. Every few passes she glanced at Amelia as if to say: *Here. Watch here.*

A latch clicked. Vernon stepped out, jacket over his arm, his face cut in half by the hall lamp's shadow. Lady Grey's growl snapped into a hiss; her back arched, tail puffed. A moth startled from its lazy orbit.

Vernon halted, scowled. "What's wrong with this animal? You'd think she'd seen the devil." He tried a chuckle that didn't land and edged on, heavy steps softening halfway down as if he'd remembered to tread lightly.

"She doesn't hiss without reason," Amelia said, "by the way, some men came by to see you this morning. Something about 'time-sensitive paperwork'."

Vernon scowled and headed toward the front stairs.

Lady Grey settled only when his footfalls faded. Amelia carried her to the bedroom, but the cat slipped back and lay sphinx-still at the threshold, guarding the hall with narrowed eyes.

When the lamps had burned low and Vernon's door stayed shut, curiosity tugged. Amelia eased into the corridor. A closet near the landing stood ajar; inside, a leather suitcase rested with a thin crescent of red dirt along one seam—fresh, not the inn's gray dust. Lady Grey nosed the leather, paused, then chirped once—verdict.

The odor reached Amelia a beat later: acrid tobacco—not pipe-sweet—and beneath it, the metal-sharp ghost of gun oil. She wiped her fingers on the towel she'd brought as pretext, though no stain marked them, and closed the door softly. *Legal contacts. Influence.* Vernon's dinner boasts frayed in memory. His story smelled like a firing range.

Back in her room, Amelia watched the lake ripple in the moonlight and thought of Clara's pencil and tidy questions. Lady Grey curled at her feet, eyes half-lidded, ears awake. Sleep came in choppy pieces; twice Amelia woke to footsteps—one familiar, one not. Each time Lady Grey tensed, then loosened as the tread moved on.

By dawn Amelia knew: Vernon hadn't just unsettled her; he'd unsettled the inn's bones.

Morning washed the lobby blue-gray. Coffee staged its daily coup; bacon lifted spirits on contact. Before anything else, Amelia checked the office safe. The dial clicked; the door eased. Petty cash, ledger, her aunt's brooch—and the spoon, folded in its napkin, crown and ship catching a sliver of light. She hadn't expected it gone; she'd needed to see it safe.

At breakfast the Bertrams plotted booth routes; Agnes and Ruth knitted; Laurel Eddison read the paper with cool attention. Vernon arrived last, just as two damp-at-the-edges men lingered by the front desk. One flashed an ID wallet—crest unknown, the word **Collections** visible.

"We're back to see Mr. Finch. Time-sensitive paperwork."

"Of course," Amelia said lightly.

"No need," Vernon said, appearing with a practiced smile. He shepherded them to the parlor. Lady Grey padded in and sat squarely on his shoe, immovable. As he tried to shake her loose, the sole flashed: a small triangle missing from the heel. Amelia mapped it onto the boot print she'd seen on the garden path. Puzzle pieces met.

The men spoke in soft, bureaucratic measures—accounts, vehicles, deadlines. Vernon's voice slid velvet to steel and back. He signed nothing, promised "this afternoon," saw them out, and declared the morning "charming." Amelia offered coffee; he accepted but didn't drink.

Clara arrived midmorning, wind-pinked and intent. Lady Grey led her straight to the office. Behind a closed door that smelled of pencil shavings and ledger ink, Amelia told her: suitcase, tobacco, gun oil, boot print, the heel's nick.

Clara's pencil scratched. "Gun oil," she repeated, then, "He went out at night. To meet, move, or hide something."

Amelia opened the safe and unfolded the napkin. They angled the spoon to the light.

"There," Clara murmured, tapping near the neck: a faint maker's mark beside a tiny numeral—**4**. "Numbered. Part of a set."

"Four of... twelve?"

"Or six. Old families, guilds, institutions—numbered pieces to track loans or ceremony. And the crest—crown and ship—reads merchant more than royal. Trade, not war."

Amelia refolded the napkin. Lady Grey tapped it once, tidy as a clerk.

"Two men from Collections came at breakfast," Amelia added. "Paperwork. Deadlines."

"Then somebody's desperate," Clara said. "And if there's a four, there may be a one, two, three."

"We'll tell Doris about the gun oil," Amelia said. "Gently. Tonight we watch. Locks, eyes. No heroics."

Lady Grey blinked solemnly: *Noted.*

Word of the visit toured town by noon. Doris swept in soon after with muffins and fury. "He's up to his neck. Always was." Amelia told her about the suitcase; Clara showed the mark and numeral. Doris's brows pinched, then lifted. "Then more are out there. Keep that spoon locked. If he asks, tell him it's at a spa he can't afford."

The afternoon stacked itself: the Bertrams returned with three clashing shipwreck tales from the historical society gift shop; Agnes and Ruth argued *cables or lace* for a hypothetical baby blanket; Edwin reappeared with a crinkling, non-clinking parcel; Laurel sent a small bouquet with a note—*To steady a table and a town.* Vernon moved like a draft: a call in the foyer, a murmured message for "Hargreeve," a box from the docks smelling faintly of machine oil. He collected it without thanks. The nicked heel mapped his route up the stairs.

"Tonight we do it properly," Clara said, appearing in the kitchen doorway.

"You go home on time," Amelia told Jonas. "Come early for pancakes."

Jonas squared his shoulders. "Yes, ma'am." He nodded to Lady Grey with superstition and respect.

Dusk laid mauve over the lake; festival booths in the square tested griddles and playlists. Amelia and Clara latched doors, checked windows, spun the safe dial, and made their rounds like people tending ordinary work—which tonight included guarding a town from a story gathering speed.

At eleven-fifteen, Vernon's door opened. He didn't look around; men who expect the world to mirror their wants rarely do. He carried the suitcase with the balanced weight of someone who had added to its contents. He took the back stairs; the nicked heel tracked him like a signature.

Amelia counted to sixty—twice—and followed with Clara. The kitchen held the clean hush of dish soap and dill. The service door stood ajar. The hedges cut the dark into soft blocks. Boot prints—heel nick precise—punctuated the gravel.

A soft clink near the far hedge—metal touching metal; a muffled latch; a quiet exhale. Then stillness.

Clara squeezed Amelia's arm and pointed at a small square of waxed paper face-down beside the thyme row. Even in the dark it glistened with oil. Clara slid it into a sandwich bag she conjured from a pocket. "Tomorrow," she whispered.

They waited, learned nothing from waiting except patience, then closed the door and climbed the silent stairs. Lady Grey held her post by the hyacinth lamp, tail ticking like a metronome. They slept as well as people sleep who have put their hands on a wheel and asked the road to behave.

Morning carried its tin pail of light. Jonas cracked eggs like a surgeon. The phone rang; Clara promised a dash to Gossamer Fables for references. The spoon lay where Amelia had left it—steadying, singular.

Vernon came down late, moving like a bruise. He accepted coffee but ate only a dry slice of toast. The men from Collections didn't return—yet.

Lady Grey stationed herself between lobby and parlor like a customs officer. As Vernon passed, she set one paw on his trouser hem. When she withdrew it, a thread drifted down—what looked black until it turned in the light: a deep, uniform blue. Clara arrived in time to see it land, pinched it between finger and thumb, and tucked it into her notebook like a pressed flower.

"Tea later?" she said aloud.

"Of course," Amelia replied, pulse settling.

By midmorning, Vernon argued into his phone on the porch—*deadline, transfer, damages*—and, caught on a gust, "the spoon is—" before the wind smudged the rest. Ezra wandered past like weather, turned his face toward the inn, and kept walking. It was enough that he'd seen.

Clara returned with a reference volume whose spine had surrendered years ago. "Merchant marks, Great Lakes, 1890–1920. Not our exact crest, but look—crown over lighthouse for a Duluth trust; a ship for a merchant banking house. Partnerships combined marks for one-off commemoratives."

"Like a numbered set," Amelia said. "Spread, lost, buried."

"If you wanted to hide them, you'd separate them," Clara said. "If you wanted to assemble them, you'd follow rumors to gardens."

Lady Grey hopped down from Amelia's chair, trotted to the hall, and sat neatly in front of the radiator at the bend. Her look said *This way.*

Amelia knelt. Beneath the radiator: dust, an earring back, a shy curl of brass. She fished out a small key on a brittle tag. The purple-stamped words were faint but legible: an address Amelia didn't know and a number she did—**Locker 14**.

Clara inhaled. "Storage," she said. "Deposit. Harbor."

"Or all three," Amelia answered.

Lady Grey tapped the tag twice, then looked up: *Well?*

Amelia closed her fist around the key. The lobby clock coughed out the half hour. Beyond the square, a hammer set the rhythm for festival booths.

"Tonight," Amelia said—to the inn, to Clara, to the cat—"we find where this opens."

"And how many spoons," Clara said, eyes bright, "make a story heavy enough to sink."

Chapter 8

The Finch Feud

Morning painted the café tables pale gold. Doris moved briskly from kettle to counter, her tidy choreography edged sharp: measuring spoons clicked, cups met saucers a touch too hard. She kept patting the pocket with the café safe key, then stopping mid-reach, as if scolding herself. The inn held the silver spoon in its office safe, yet worry walked with her like a shadow.

When the rush thinned, Clara slipped in—quiet as a bookmark—and ordered a lemon bar with a penciled note. Amelia lingered at a corner table, hands around a mug. Lady Grey, elegant parenthesis on the windowsill, watched them all.

Doris set the kettle to hum, crossed to their table, and sat as if her feet had finally given permission. "You asked why he's here," she said. "Vernon. Why now." She drew breath. "The Finch family hasn't been whole since the '30s—little to go around, cousins turning enemies. Heirlooms went missing piece by piece: a ring, a ladle, my grandmother's garnet brooch between a wake and a will in 1958. Each theft came wrapped in a tale called 'safekeeping.' Rumors trellised on a little truth until the branches wouldn't share shade."

"And the spoon?" Amelia asked.

"Vernon was raised on stories of 'stolen Finch wealth,' trained to sniff for it. So when silver rises out of my thyme—crown and ship stamped clear—he hears trumpets. He doesn't want truth. He wants proof he can pocket."

"What else?" Clara's pencil waited.

"Dessert forks engraved 'FG' from a bad wedding. A harbor painting, *The Crowned Gull*—ugly, with a frame heavy as a sermon. A christening cup someone swore proved pedigree." Clara underlined *crown* again; Lady Grey blinked like she agreed.

"I resent him," Doris said. "But I resent the feud more. You think you've stepped out of the mud—then it remembers your name."

Amelia covered her hand. "You're not alone. We'll stand at the truth and let the wind do the rest."

The bell jingled. Edwin Harper breezed in, surrendering to blueberry scones and gossip. "Your crest—crown over ship—reads trade mark, not English heraldry," he said. "Great Lakes merchant houses loved commemoratives. Small numbered sets gifted to principals."

"Numbered," Clara echoed. "We found a '4.'"

"Then it has sisters," Edwin said.

The bell clanged harder. Laurel Eddison swept in, pearls and purpose. "Vernon just filed to 'preserve chattel,'" she said. "He'll bark a public claim by noon."

"Courts like paper," Edwin murmured.

"Courts like posture," Laurel corrected. She slid an anonymous kiosk notice onto the table: **THE CROWN COMES HOME**, a crude ship beneath. Lady Grey's ears tipped. "I'll speak to the clerk— quietly," Laurel added, and left.

Doris fetched a shoebox from the office: yellowed clippings, a wedding photo, three handwritten inventories. "I thought I'd thrown these away." Clara bent over the lists. "Six dessert spoons, numbered 1–6," she said. "Only place numbers appear. Note: *crest unknown.* So the set came from outside."

"Merchant consortium, 1910s–'20s," Edwin said. "Celebratory."

"Or a Finch borrowed and never returned," Doris said tightly.

The bell clanged again. Vernon entered, suit and smile polished. "Cousin," he purred. "Good morning to your reputation. I've petitioned to secure the item pending *rightful* ownership. I'm willing to resolve this privately—a fair sale, generous to both branches."

"Would you recognize the crest without it?" Clara asked mildly. "Or need to borrow a memory to tell it from a soup ladle?"

His mask slipped—hunger—then reset. "Choose your alliances carefully," he said, and left, certain the last word would meet him at the door. Lady Grey curled a lip, then yawned.

"He'll push hard," Edwin said.

"We won't," Doris answered, reaching for the register—then stilled. "Where's the key?" A pat, a frown, a too-small circle. She found the café safe key, warm in her palm, but not the old cash-box key. "Maybe I left it on the desk."

In the narrow office, the cash box sat square to the blotter, latched —and double-latched. Doris touched the side slide. "I never use this."

"Someone did," Clara said, eyeing the scuffed seam. "We need the inn. Not panic—move."

Back in the café, Doris issued brisk instructions—"Scones at ten. Don't pour bergamot like whiskey. We're off to the post."—and Agnes materialized to nod. Lady Grey bounced to the floor and trotted ahead like a nurse late to rounds.

Outside, the kiosk had already gathered new notices. Under the morning's anonymous boast, someone had stamped **TONIGHT**. Clara snapped a photo and tucked her notebook close.

"Locker Fourteen," Amelia murmured. The storage key in her pocket—found beneath the inn radiator—felt heavier than brass. "And now *tonight*."

"Let them stamp until the ink dries," Doris said, chin up. "We'll meet them where the locks live."

On the corner, a slim boy in a North Shore Storage cap pedaled by. "Ms. Farnsworth! Old depot by the ferry road—lockers start at ten, right side of the aisle!" He was gone before thanks could form.

Clara met Amelia's eyes. No words needed.

"After we check the safe at the Inn," Amelia said. "We go."

"And if we find one spoon," Doris said, steady now, "we'll find four."

"Or six," Edwin called.

By the inn door, Lady Grey turned her head and gave them a single, cool blink.

Chapter 9

Library Ledger Trail

The Tumblebrook Public Library was a hush stitched from paper and light. Morning poured through its arched windows, laying soft ribbons of gold across oak tables. Dust motes drifted through the beams like they, too, were deep in thought. Built in 1898 of sturdy brick now laced with ivy, the building had watched generations come and go, the way an old friend watches without judging. Inside, history waited patiently on its shelves: scuffed ledgers, newsprint bound into fat, fragile volumes, and microfilm reels gleaming like stacked coins.

For Clara Henderson, the library was a second home—the only cathedral she'd ever needed. She arranged her tools beneath the tallest window: notebook open to a fresh page, two pencils lined like cutlery, a thermos of strong tea balanced on a coaster so Mrs. Winthrop wouldn't cluck at the rings. The table bore its own history —names carved by long-graduated students, faint stains of mug rings, and a gloss worn smooth by elbows leaning into thought.

Outside, the park was alive: children's laughter, the squeak of a seesaw, a dog barking with self-importance. Clara barely heard it.

Her mind was set on something older—the kind of mystery that left fingerprints in paper and whispers in ink.

She began with bound newspapers that smelled of dust and linseed oil. Headlines marched across the pages: fishing reports, Prohibition raids, harvest dances, sermons, society weddings. She skimmed until one phrase caught her eye: *estate sale—Finch name.* She jotted notes in her precise shorthand, arrows threading between dates and surnames like fine stitching.

Then her pencil stopped mid-line.

Silver Spoon Affair Hushed Up — 1932.

The headline crouched near the bottom of page three, shy and half-apologetic. Yet it pulsed like a heartbeat. Clara leaned closer, tracing each word with her fingertip.

Several pieces of silver had gone missing from the Finch estate during a "private supper" attended by "prominent families and gentlemen in shipping and finance." The incident was "resolved quietly," police involvement "minimal." The article's tone trembled between discretion and guilt, hinting at smuggling, at secrets kept for the town's good.

Her pulse quickened. She copied the headline twice, boxed **Finch**, circled **smuggling**, and arrowed toward the margin: *crown + ship crest?* The spoon unearthed in Doris's garden suddenly felt less heirloom, more evidence—a ledger entry from a debt no one had settled.

Mrs. Winthrop ran the copier while Baldwin, the ginger library cat, yawned like a weary monarch. "Ghosts again, Clara?" she asked.

"Not ghosts," Clara said. "History pretending to behave."

She climbed to the mezzanine and pulled the 1932 city directory. **Finch, Harold (Mena), Crown Point Road.** Her breath caught at the word *crown* until she realized it referred to the bluff's shape, not the family's ambition. In the business listings, her finger stopped at **Crown & Anchor Merchant Society (Aux.),** 96 Harbor Lane. The advertisement below mentioned *secure bays and lockers for members.* In fine print: **Lockers 10–20, Right Aisle.**

A perfect echo of the number etched on the brass key Amelia had found.

Clara grinned. The puzzle was starting to hum.

Downstairs, the man in the low hat who had slipped in unnoticed still loitered by the periodicals, turning a single page too slowly. Baldwin cracked an eye. Mrs. Winthrop's stillness said *I see him too.*

Clara threaded a microfilm reel into the reader and scrolled to spring 1932. Photographs blinked past: wool suits, a cake iced like a ship, a paper crown passed from head to head. Caption: **C&A Auxiliary Dinner, Celebrating the Season's First Crossing.** Donors listed beneath: **Finch, Eddison, Harper, Phelps**, and **North Shore Storage (in-kind).**

A line at the bottom snagged her breath: *Commemorative items to be catalogued and deposited with the auxiliary secretary until permanent disposition.*

Later that year: *Auxiliary storage moved to North Shore Storage, ferry road; items placed in locker fourteen.*

Locker 14. Right aisle. Ferry road.

She printed the frame before excitement could make her clumsy. The room's silence seemed to tilt, as though even the air leaned closer to read.

On instinct she scrolled forward to 1958—Doris's year. Two terse notices blinked by: **Auxiliary concludes; items to be returned or disposed.** A week later: **Unclaimed item(s) held in Locker 14; key acknowledged to Finch (H.).** Clara's hand trembled as she wrote. The chain held: silver commissioned, stored, forgotten, and finally inherited by Harold Finch.

Mrs. Winthrop appeared beside her, ledger in hand. "You'll want this," she said. "North Shore Storage index. A widow's donation. Paper outlasts memory."

Inside, careful handwriting traced decades of payments:

1932–36: **Locker 14 (Aux. Sec. M. A. Vellum)**, moved to ferry road.

1948: **Finch, H. (holdover)**.

1958: **key acknowledged.**

Later, a penciled rumor: *'Crown set'—see Finch file.*

The name *Vellum* glowed on the page like a forgotten password.

Clara hurried to the historical society drawer. The Finch file yielded brittle clippings, a photo of Harold Finch beside the harbor light, and two letters:

"Dear Mr. Finch, per the dissolution of the Auxiliary, we remind you of Locker 14's contents."

— *M. A. Vellum, Secretary*

Followed by Harold's curt reply:

"Hold them, then. We're not done measuring. — H.F."

Always measuring, someone had scrawled beneath in another hand.

The phrase gave her chills. She copied everything, heart drumming in neat ledger time.

By evening, the library's gold had turned pewter. The man in the hat finally left, tipping his brim as if closing a scene. Clara exhaled, packed her copies, and thumbed a message to Amelia:

Locker 14 confirmed; key with H. Finch in '58. C&A dinner photo. Silver Spoon Affair, 1932. At inn in ten. We have a map.

Amelia's reply came quick:

Come. Doris here. Laurel stopping by. Lady Grey stationed. TONIGHT stamped again at kiosk.

Clara lengthened her stride through the square, past festival banners flapping like restless secrets. The kiosk wore that same purple stamp: **THE CROWN COMES HOME — TONIGHT.**

At the inn, Amelia opened the door before Clara reached the handle. The lobby smelled of beeswax and coffee; Doris stood anchored by pride and worry, Laurel's pearls gleamed in the lamplight, and Edwin hovered with his satchel. Lady Grey, silver and certain, sat like a sentinel.

Clara spread her notes on the counter: the dinner photograph, donor list, and locker documents. "The auxiliary stored commemoratives in Locker 14, moved them to the ferry road in 1932, and the key stayed with Harold Finch in 1958. The silver spoon affair—it started here."

Doris studied the photo of the ship-cake. "We thought it was a birthday," she murmured. Laurel's brow furrowed. "Not just family. Civic. Shared guilt means shared leverage."

Edwin traced the locker numbers. "Right aisle, ten through twenty. That matches the depot layout. And I have a torch."

"The manager's nephew gave directions," Amelia said. "Fourteen should be the fifth door on the right. And"—she lifted the brass key—"we have this."

Lady Grey tapped it twice, approving.

Doris's voice steadied. "If that locker holds anything, we'll set our story first—before Vernon prints his."

Silenced consumed the air. They exchanged knowing glances.

Soon they would have answers. Amelia hoped those answers would not come with receipts due.

Chapter 10

Festival Preparations

By midmorning, Tumblebrook hummed like a town wound tight to a cheerful metronome. Blue-and-gold pennants fluttered from lampposts, kettle corn perfumed the air, and laughter spilled across the cobbled square. Even the storefront windows gleamed, as though the town itself had decided to dress up for its annual portrait.

Amelia made her rounds, ledger tucked under her arm, greeting vendors and volunteers as they set up for the Summer Arts & Antiques Festival. The Bertrams were polishing their hand-turned bowls, Agnes and Ruth were stringing knitted bunting the color of lake glass, and Jonas struggled with a tent pole taller than his patience. Around her, the town pulsed with twin rhythms: the bright drum of festival cheer and the quieter undertone of gossip. Words floated through the breeze—*Finch heirloom... worth something... cursed, maybe.* Tumblebrook could never resist a mystery.

Doris's café had transformed overnight into both gathering place and exhibit hall. Geraniums overflowed the window boxes; lace curtains fluttered like gossip held in check. A chalkboard out front read **TEAS & TATTLE—SERVED ALL DAY.** Inside, the air smelled of coffee, lemon polish, and something faintly metallic—the spoon itself, perhaps, giving off the scent of history.

"Hold that corner," Doris ordered as she and Amelia maneuvered a glass display case into position near the counter. Jonas held, Doris polished, and Amelia braced until the thing sat square. There was reverence in the work—ritual disguised as practicality.

"There," Doris said, stepping back with satisfaction. "Safe, visible, dignified. The spoon deserves a place of honor."

Clara, perched on a stool with her notebook, arched an eyebrow. "Safe is relative," she said, pencil tapping. "You're displaying it in the busiest café during the busiest week of the year."

"If it's hidden, they'll think I'm ashamed," Doris replied, stubborn as granite. "Better to face whispers than pretend they don't exist."

Amelia checked the latch. "We'll need a lock—and a sign. Laurel will insist on approving the font."

Doris retrieved the cloth-wrapped bundle from beneath the counter. When her fingers trembled, she disguised it with a practical frown. She laid the tarnished spoon on a square of velvet, and the crown-and-ship crest caught the light with quiet pride. Clara's pencil darted again, recording everything.

Before anyone could comment, the café door jangled and Vernon Finch strode in, grin buffed to unnatural brightness. "Ah, I see we're displaying my family's heirloom," he said, voice pitched for attention. "A fine gesture. I assume the label will read *Finch Family Silver—on loan courtesy of Vernon Finch*?"

Doris stiffened. "It will say no such thing. I found it in my garden, and that makes it mine."

"Your soil, perhaps," Vernon countered smoothly. "But our inheritance. Family ties run deeper than flowerbeds."

Amelia stepped forward with calm authority. "Labels can wait. Right now, security matters more."

The door jingled again—Laurel Eddison this time, crisp as a comma. "Indeed," she said. "One: the case stays locked. Two: no touching, no photos without permission. Three: if the crowd swells, the spoon goes back to the safe. And four: no mention of ownership. The sign reads, *On view for the Summer Arts & Antiques Festival, courtesy of the proprietor.*Full stop."

Her tone brokered no debate. She slid the placard into place and turned the lock. The faint *click* seemed to ripple through the café; even the chatter softened.

A crowd formed within minutes—locals, tourists, and a journalist sniffing for headlines. Vernon lingered too near the case, his smile sharpening whenever cameras flashed. From the windowsill, Lady Grey leapt among the geraniums and fixed him with amber eyes that said *Try it, and you'll regret it.*

By late afternoon, the café pulsed with voices and clinking cups. Doris served shortbread and lemon bars beside her unlikely exhibit while Clara jotted overheard theories—*merchant English... smuggling tokens... family feud.* Amelia's calm steadied the room, though her eyes flicked often to the door.

Laurel bent close. "The kiosk message reappeared," she murmured. "*THE CROWN COMES HOME—TONIGHT.* We go after dusk. Quietly."

Amelia's nod was slow, measured. "Quiet," she echoed, though unease shadowed the word.

At five o'clock, the extraction began with the precision of a practiced performance. Clara drifted toward the door, engaging tourists in cheerful distraction while Laurel intercepted Vernon's next approach. Edwin Harper, pretending to rearrange napkins, offered a loud joke about velvet ropes. Meanwhile, Amelia lifted the glass lid just enough for Doris to remove the real spoon and slip it into a plain bakery box beneath the counter. A velvet-wrapped decoy took its place. To anyone watching, nothing had changed—except Lady Grey, whose tail flicked once like a signature.

Vernon studied the case. "I'll return after sunset," he said. "With counsel."

"You do that," Doris replied. "We'll be closed."

By twilight, the last of the festival guests had gone, leaving the café steeped in the scent of coffee and polish. The spoon now lay locked in the back-room safe, beside ledgers and a brooch that caught the light like a secret.

Outside, the town glowed under strings of warm bulbs. The band rehearsed in the gazebo, and kettle corn snapped like applause. Across the square, the kiosk sign gleamed: **THE CROWN COMES HOME—TONIGHT—AT DUSK.**

At the Inn, history waited like a restless child. Lady Grey, perched on the windowsill, guarded secrets from those who would bury them forever.

Chapter 11

An Ominous Warning

Evening settled gently over Tumblebrook, a hush stitched from lantern glow and lake breeze. Festival music drifted up Main—brass, a guitar's easy strum, children arguing cheerfully over cotton candy. Behind the inn's desk, Amelia traced neat columns in the ledger, thoughts slipping to the glass case in Doris's café, Laurel's placard, and Vernon Finch's smile—like a lock picking its own teeth.

She closed the ledger, locked the door, reached for the lace curtain—and paused. A bright square lay on the mat, folded too precisely for a flyer. She picked it up: eucalyptus-scented stationery pretending at gentility.

SOME TREASURES BEST REMAIN BURIED.

Block letters, gouged hard enough to emboss the page. No signature. The words landed like a small weight tied to breath.

Lady Grey padded from the parlor, peered, chirruped, and snagged the note, dragging it beneath the runner. She sat on the edge as if sealing a jar.

"You'd rather not look either," Amelia whispered, smoothing the cat's back. But hiding isn't removing. Lids leak.

The back-hall door sighed. Clara entered with her satchel, clocked the posture and the cat's paperweight pose. "What's wrong?"

Amelia handed over the note. Clara's eyes sharpened. "Vernon?" she said reflexively, then shook her head. "Too jagged. He signs as if sketching a coat of arms. Cheap ballpoint, too—he favors fountain pens."

"Someone else," Amelia said.

"The handwriting says hurry," Clara murmured. "Pressure. Could be local, could be a festival ghost." She turned it, testing angles that might reveal meaning. "I can compare signatures tomorrow—logs, vendor forms—but it may be the only sample."

The mantel clock chimed. They drifted to the parlor by habit as much as chill. Lamplight gentled wingbacks and water-ringed tables. Amelia fed a birch log to the coals. "Whoever wrote it thinks the spoon points to something that should stay hidden."

"Or wants us to," Clara said, pencil scratching block letters and arrows. "Fear is leverage. Vernon uses performance; someone else may prefer costume."

Lady Grey loafed by the hearth, ears angled toward the door. Guarding.

"We go to the depot at eight," Amelia said, testing the sentence.

"Then the note aims to delay us—or push us into haste," Clara replied. "We refine, we don't retreat. Two lights, not one. No bolt cutters. The manager opens any lock. And we don't split up."

"No heroics," Amelia said, a vow they'd made—and tested—since spring.

A shadow crossed the frosted pane. Paused. Moved on. Music hiccuped into laughter and steadied. Amelia's jaw loosened a notch.

The side door whispered. Doris filled the kitchen arch, cheeks flushed, apron bow skewed, a bakery box that might hold anything or nothing. "Jonas has the café," she said. "Emma escaped before alphabetizing the sugar." She slid a twin note from her apron, eucalyptus ghost and all. "Under the back door. I'd have missed it if Lady Grey hadn't halted patrol and stared at air until I stared with her."

Clara set the two slips side by side. "Same pen, same rush. Our writer wanted one of us to read it."

Laurel arrived on that line, pearls catching firelight. She locked the second bolt, shrugged off her coat. "Edwin's on his way with a clipboard, which apparently confers legitimacy within fifty miles." She read the notes, expression tightening. "Cute. A Greek chorus with cheap stationery. We proceed."

"We're not foolhardy," Doris said.

"We're methodical," Laurel answered, ticking off points. "Amelia carries the key. No tools that scream breaking. We document: photos, notes, chain of custody before and after. Manager accompanies or watches. If anything looks tampered with, we stop. We remain clerks of the truth, not protagonists."

"Speak for yourself," Edwin said lightly from the doorway, brushing dew from his sleeve. He sobered at the notes. "Anonymous literature. I prefer threats that rhyme."

"No cutters," Laurel said.

"I brought them to show the night air," he promised. "They'll stay leashed."

The mantel clock sighed the quarter hour. The inn sounded like a place pulling on gloves. Outside, the festival swelled and dipped—busker guitar, ring toss thunk, a child's delighted squeal.

Amelia fetched a small velvet-lined pouch from the desk: the brass key, stubborn in the hand. "I'll carry it," she said.

Clara added a second pencil and a rubber band to leash the first, tested a flashlight's obedient white circle. "I left velvet decoys at the café," she told Doris. "If anyone sniffs for an easy snatch, they'll get buckram, not silver."

"Bless you," Doris said.

Lady Grey looped once around Amelia's calves and tapped the bakery box—doilies and pretense—with an approving sound.

"Five minutes," Laurel said, checking her watch. "We leave at eight."

Rituals steadied hands. Doris folded her apron over a chair, fabric keeping order in her absence. Edwin swapped torch batteries. Clara retied her braid, each pin a quiet decision. Laurel wrote their names and **8:00 – North Shore Storage** on an index card and a spare line for **Returned**—paperwork as prayer.

Amelia paused at the window. The square shone like a low sky. Ezra stood by the kiosk, charcoal flicking; he never looked up when he knew he was already drawing you. A figure in a dark hat paused opposite the door—new-shoe careful—then moved on. Not Vernon; Vernon's shoes tried to escape. Amelia filed the silhouette under *Later*.

"Let's go," she said in her cake-come-out-now voice.

They crossed the foyer. The warning slip rode back beneath the runner; Lady Grey set a paw on its edge, claiming custody. Amelia nodded to the cat like an equal.

Night met them warm. Booth lights pooled. Laughter braided and unbraided. Walking toward tin doors and old dust felt like stepping offstage. But stories ask for choices.

Ezra detached from the linden's shadow and held out a sketch, charcoal smudging his hand: a locker door, a cat's eye, a crown ringed like broken teeth, and beneath—a shallow grave scribbled with **water** until the paper bruised. "Old silver doesn't shine without a shadow," he said softly. "And shadows like company."

Laurel accepted, returned, and nodded. "We'll bring a lantern."

They moved. Amelia locked the inn with a twist that said trust and caution can share a hand. Edwin swung his torch like a baton. Clara matched Lady Grey's stride, the cat's tail a small metronome. Laurel set their course as if the square were a meeting that must end in good order.

At the kiosk the stamped notice glowered: **THE CROWN COMES HOME. TONIGHT. AT DUSK.** Purple bled around the letters. Clara snapped a photo; facts don't stay because you stare.

"Do we tell the manager about the notes?" Edwin asked as the square's warmth fell away.

"We show him the ledger copy and key," Laurel said. "We show a list, not fear. If we need help, we ask with names and paper."

Amelia felt the key's profile through leather and the inn at her back, the café turning from lemon-and-tea to coffee-and-sugar. In her mind: the runner, the paw, that sentence humming like wire.

The ferry road cooled the air by a degree—the lake's hand on night. North Shore Storage rose bluntly useful—corrugated walls, a roof that tried not to remember storms. The office window bore the old emblem: anchor looped by crown, friendlier by day than now.

Inside, the manager—thin, bespectacled, intention-worn—looked up from figures. "Evening," he said, as if four townspeople and a cat were ordinary after eight. Laurel slid copies across: the 1932 move notice, the ledger line for Locker 14, the 1958 key acknowledgment. "Verification only," she said. "No removal."

He studied, then nodded. "Right aisle. Fifth door. Lights are twitchy," he added, like a man calming a horse that's already decided.

They entered the hall. The air shifted—less festival, more iron. Lights hummed, obliged, flickered. Doors passed: Ten. Twelve. Fourteen waited, as if leaning there all day for warm hands at eight-oh-five.

Lady Grey sat before it, straight-backed, pupils wide. One ear flicked toward the far end. *Listen.*

They did. The square laughed faintly. A pipe pinged. No footsteps. Only dust, oil, the faint trace of eucalyptus traveling in pockets.

Amelia slid the key home.

Clara's hand hovered over her notebook. Edwin angled the torch low to keep the first look honest. Laurel steadied the frame with her palm.

The lock turned—reluctant, then willing. The door clicked. A draft slid over their hands, breath kept too long. Amelia eased it inward.

From the office a mild voice called, "You'll need this," and the corridor lights fluttered, then steadied. In the beat between dark and bright a figure shifted at the far end—perhaps only shadow rethreading itself, perhaps more—and Lady Grey's growl rolled low across the floor, velvet and warning.

"Some treasures best remain buried," Clara whispered—not surrender, a note in the margin she refused to close.

"Let's verify," Laurel said, crisp as a page turn.

Edwin lifted the beam, and Amelia carried its lanterned oval into the locker's dark.

The past breathed back.

Chapter 12

Lady Grey on Watch

The moon rode low over Tumblebrook like a polished coin, its pale shine lacquered across shingles, cobbles, and the lake. From the inn's parlor the night looked harmless—lanterns guttered to amber, laughter a warm murmur, embers humming. But peace is a surface thing.

Lady Grey slipped through the kitchen window the way fog moves through reeds. She dropped to the flagstones, crossed the lane, and ghosted along the hedge toward Doris's café garden.

By day the garden was a cookbook illustration; tonight it breathed earth and chlorophyll—and a metallic tang that didn't belong. She flattened, listening past owl and moth and the lake's slow roll until another rhythm stuttered through: shovel into earth, shovel into earth, urgent breath.

Near the thyme bed, a figure hunched. Moonlight rimmed a small spade. Soil rose in clods, fell with panicked thuds. Not planting —searching. Menthol threaded the tobacco on the air: cigarette, wintergreen, eucalyptus—human anesthetics. The spade struck metal with a bright ping. A sliver flashed.

Lady Grey hissed.

The head snapped. Eyes met—amber and human—and then the figure bolted through the gate. The spade clattered against stone and thyme and stopped. Night tightened again, but the seam showed.

Lady Grey held still until the air settled, then stood over the churned bed and set a paw on the handle. Mine. She turned toward the inn and let out the rare, low sound that always brought Amelia.

Amelia jerked awake, lit the mantel lantern, and moved. The lane seemed too loud with its emptiness. The garden gate creaked; the lantern found Lady Grey poised on the low wall, eyes like coins.

The thyme bed was scooped and messy. The spade's handle felt warm, the blade roughened by a burr—metal meeting metal. Menthol lingered, thin and cool. Not Vernon.

Amelia pressed a palm to the earth: not cold, not calm. The alley beyond was the usual jumble of crates and a bicycle and places to vanish. The lantern made the dark behave only within its circle.

She carried the spade to the inn and set it on the counter like a letter that couldn't be burned. Clara arrived on that sound, hair mussed, robe belted, eyes quick. Amelia's account came fast—hiss, figure, digging, flash, flight, menthol, spade.

Clara's pencil flew, then steadied—burr, odors, footfalls hurried. "So it isn't just Vernon," she said. "He blusters in public; this one burrows in private." Lady Grey anchored the spade's neck with a deliberate paw.

The note under the rug glowed in Amelia's mind—Some treasures best remain buried. Dug earth answered it.

"We ring Laurel," Clara said. "And Doris. And Haines. But first —preserve what we can." She laid the spade on a clean towel, sniffed. "Menthol, and oil—maybe lighter." She boxed the thought on her page.

"Footprints?" Amelia said, already reaching for flour and twine. "We can dust the stones."

"Bells," Clara added. "A line across the gate."

They crossed back to the garden with the quiet urgency of conspirators whose only conspiracy was defense. Amelia sifted flour over stepping stones in a thin veil; Clara strung twine three inches above the latch and tied on three tin bells, then added a second line an inch higher. Silly and perfect.

Laurel arrived with pearls steady; Doris with apron strings flying; Deputy Haines with a notebook. They listened without interrupting, then crouched. "Clever," Haines said at the flour. He bagged the spade. Doris stood by the thyme, very still. "Someone's hunting," she said.

"Or planting," Clara said. "If they wanted to rattle us, they'd dig and leave signs. Make us imagine treasure." Heads tilted; the idea held.

"No depot tonight," Laurel decided. "We did right by the ledger; we'll do right by sleep. Investigation is a morning animal. We'll watch." Haines advised: "Call me before you call out."

They rotated watches. Amelia with tea and quiet steps; Clara with a pencil and the habit of lists; Doris with a general's jaw. Lady Grey chose the windowsill with the most sky and least glare, a felted comma facing the gate. Twice the bells trembled at moths; twice her tail twitched and the moths reconsidered. A raccoon tried philosophy on the roof and gave it up. The flour lay untroubled. Thyme tried and failed to forget hands in its roots.

A little after two the alley breathed differently. A shape eased down the spine and paused at the hedge like a promise deciding whether to keep itself. A hand lifted the gate, found the twine, touched a bell, stopped. A whispered curse. The hand withdrew. Menthol came and went like a draft.

Doris didn't move. "I know you," she said to the dark. "You wear courtesy like a coat over a knife."

Morning reset the town. Bulbs went gray; birds made lists. In the flour, near the gate, a partial tread: heel chipped at one corner, a sole once patterned, now smudged with miles, a faint diagonal scar across the ball.

Clara crouched, delighted and sorry at once. "No full cast," she said, "but a story: a shoe that thinks it's invisible, and isn't."

"And the menthol?" Amelia asked.

"Fainter," Doris said. "Was here. Isn't now." She flicked a private smile at Lady Grey. "Your cat runs a tighter ship than the aldermen."

Lady Grey pretended not to hear and placed a paw in the only unfloured gap.

"Two things," Clara said, standing. "We change the placard to temporarily removed for preservation and plant Edwin with his clipboard to remind the curious that curiosity isn't entitlement. And we hunt the menthol—pharmacy receipts, vendor rosters. Who buys eucalyptus oil by the case or menthols by the carton?"

"And three," Amelia added. "We look under the thyme again—but with a sieve and a brush." If metal met metal, it may have left a whisper.

They fetched a colander, a paintbrush, and—Doris's idea—a pie server that already knew how to lift treasure. Soil sifted in velvet avalanches; roots yielded; stones declared themselves. Nothing glittered—until a tiny resistance near the burr's lesson. Clara held her breath and then remembered to breathe. Amelia's fingers did what they'd done a thousand times—small turn, lift, hold. The brush coaxed out a disc no bigger than a match head. Not silver. Not stone. Thin tin or nickel, punched with a hole and stamped minutely.

They leaned. C & A, a crown looped with an anchor, and the number 7.

"Crown & Anchor," Clara whispered, writing as she spoke. "Seven." She drew a line to her earlier list: numbered tokens—shares, counters, chits people don't write down.

"A marker," Doris said. "Taking stock. Or dropping it."

Laurel appeared as if summoned by paperwork itself. She smiled —not at the find, but at the clarity. "We photograph, bag it, and lock it with the spoon. Then someone watches the gate day and night until the festival closes."

"Who?" Doris asked.

Laurel glanced to the windowsill and met a steady amber gaze. "We'll rotate. But the captain has appointed herself."

Lady Grey didn't blink. She allowed the smallest pleased ripple of fur, then faced the garden like a person to a desk. String, bells, flour, the tiny disc in a spice-tin lid, sunlight deciding to be kind—she took it all in, washed a paw, and drew it over one ear with the bright economy of a commander cleaning her blade after a first skirmish.

The inn, the café, the square stood under the same morning yet felt different, the way rooms do after a secret leans into light. The warning under the rug hadn't changed its sentence, but it had acquired a neighbor: a fingernail-sized token that said the past wouldn't stay quiet if called.

Amelia slipped the disc into a clean envelope, dated it with the care she reserved for wedding books and goodbyes, and sealed it. "We'll keep watch," she said.

"And keep looking," Clara answered.

"I'll keep my temper," Doris added, tightening the twine so a bell would kiss metal at the smallest insult.

Lady Grey resumed her post, tail aligned with the gate's line, eyes on the place where menthol had lived and might return. Try it, her stillness told the alley. If you come back, I'll be here. If you don't, I'll be here anyway.

The lake lifted under a light wind. The band struck a cheerful first chord. Laurel's phone began its daytime chime. Edwin arrived with two coffees and a theory; Haines with an evidence bag and patience.

In the middle of it, a cat watched a gate and a town breathed. The festival opened in full. The hunt that began with a scrape and a hiss began in earnest. And in a garden neat yesterday and not neat now, the future clicked twice—like bells when a string is tested and holds.

Chapter 13

Festival Day Frenzy

Morning snapped over Tumblebrook like a clean sheet—bright, brisk, buzzing. Flags rippled, bunting stitched lacey shadows, the square wore its best cobblestone grin. Scents stacked cheerfully: kettle corn, cinnamon-butter, beeswax, brass.

By eight, crowds swelled the lanes; by nine, stalls were an orchard: quilts like maps, jars tossing sun, lake paintings in pewter and steel. The band marched with brass bravado. Festival mornings usually rose in Amelia like dough—steady, pleasant. Today a taut thread pulled whenever "the spoon" clinked into conversation.

Outside Doris Finch's café, a striped dais held a glass dome and, beneath it on velvet, a silver spoon's replica. The crest—crown and ship—pricked light. Doris rapped glass as needed and aimed her famous look at foggy breathers.

"An heirloom of Tumblebrook itself," she told the third crowd, chin high. The placard read:

FINCH SILVER SPOON (CRESTED)

Discovered in the soil of Tumblebrook, June.

Temporarily removed for preservation.

Image and exhibition replica on display.

Getting that last line approved had cost Laurel five minutes and three eyebrows. Doris still bristled, but truth mattered. So did bait.

Lady Grey perched on the awning like a ship's figurehead, amber eyes on the dome, tail keeping time.

Under the awning, Clara turned a chair and planter into a field desk. Her notebook filled with arrows and sketches: Doris's chin tilt; a dealer's hovering hand; children squashing their own cheeks to resist touching glass.

"Note how he avoids smuggling," she murmured as Amelia drifted close. "It's inheritance and lineage all the way down."

Vernon Finch had stationed himself like a portrait come to life—waistcoat proud, hair glossed, one hand tucked in his vest. "Family inheritance," he told dealers and church ladies alike. "An artifact tied to generations. My cousin forgets her soil was shared."

"Shared when you want it," Doris said. "Private when there's work."

Laughter chimed, but the knot held.

Laurel, crisp in navy, patrolled and kept the dome shut. Edwin Harper, rings flashing, coached lines with his clipboard costume. Deputy Haines was there and not—present to those who needed him, scenery to the rest.

Amelia clocked a man who dodged notice: tall, too sharp for cobbles, shoes for marble, hair tamed with intent. He paused by Vernon; words traded; his eyes flicked to the dome and away—as if refusing to admire what he didn't yet own.

"Outsider," Clara wrote. "Quietly carnivorous."

Ezra drifted by, charcoal and pine, tilting his sketchbook: the dome, the cat, and—suggested behind the alley—an eye. Beneath: *shadow*.

By midmorning the square bloomed. Inside the café, Laurel signed the chain-of-custody line with a looping, unarguable hand. "Replica," Edwin sang for the fifteenth time. "Real is napping responsibly." Mrs. Cranston pronounced it cursed and bought a scone to sweeten the omen.

At eleven, Laurel swapped a larger replica placard. Vernon demanded "family loan" be added. Laurel smiled a tidy no. "Your claim is noted," she said, "and will continue to be noted until it's ignored."

Lady Grey hadn't shifted more than a whisker since nine. Twice her ears tipped toward the alley; twice her tail became an exclamation. Amelia followed her gaze—only crates and a tottery ladder—but filed the cat's certainty.

The outsider's first pass looked casual. He let the crowd float him to the rope, rested a hand as if steadying against music, studied the replica exactly long enough to confirm what he knew. Clara wrote: *wants to be seen not touching.*

He drifted away. Vernon drifted with him. They angled toward the alley—together, not; together again. Laurel's look found Edwin's, then Haines's, then Amelia's; Lady Grey's gaze cut to the same gap and stilled.

Clara slid to the alley mouth, feigning interest in macramé while catching three clean words: "title," "chain," "quiet." The outsider's vowels wore old cities; Vernon rasped with performance.

"No alleys," Laurel ruled on Clara's return. "Quiet goes in rooms with minutes and bad coffee, not lanes that pass rumors like bread."

Noon arrived with brass and sausage. The dome gathered dust and got wiped. In the library, the real spoon slept in borrowed velvet beside a tiny token stamped **C&A 7**, Laurel's signature a small oath.

A boy pressed his ear to the dome. "Pirates," he whispered. His sister called him dumb, then copied him. Doris softened—then hardened at a phone too near. Edwin produced a microfiber cloth like a magician.

At one, a lake gust nudged umbrellas. In that slice of distraction three things happened: the kettle-corn umbrella sagged; a handsaw bit a nail; and the outsider returned, sliding his left hand a deliberate inch beneath the velvet plinth—testing give—while looking at Lady Grey.

Lady Grey launched. She landed on the dome like a metronome's downbeat. Glass rocked and held. Fingers snapped back. The crowd exhaled oh. Doris steadied the table with oven-moving conviction; Edwin palmed the velvet smooth. Haines materialized.

"Afternoon," he said, pleasant as weather. "Enjoying the show?"

"Forgive me," the man said. "The workmanship—my hand drifted."

"It does that in crowds," Haines agreed. "Picks up what it didn't bring."

"Keene," the stranger supplied when Doris asked *on what* he was expert. "Provenance." A thread of menthol sighed from his cuff. Clara underlined *menthol* twice and thought of the spade's burr. Amelia's shoulders had already read it.

"Art wants eyes," Keene said. "Vaults are a shame."

"Artifacts want context," Laurel replied. "They get cranky without it."

"Scone?" Doris added. "You're undercooked."

"Another time," Keene said, slipping into the crowd. He looked not at the dome but the alley mouth, like a door he planned to open later.

"He'll try again," Clara said.

"Yes," Laurel said. "Not to steal—yet. To decide when ours becomes the world's."

Afternoon thinned; toddlers danced; Gus told the same story three ways. Two women sold paper crowns printed with anchors; children paraded past the dome solemn as saints.

In the alley, shadow recalibrated. Lady Grey felt it as a current at the base of her tail. Amelia and Clara followed the same invisible tug.

A figure—hat low, gait careful—slid past the fence and vanished. Menthol flickered. Clara noted: *hat, careful, menthol.*

The night's flour had been swept away; the twine bells remained. They gave a faint *tik*—not a ring, a taste.

Laurel shifted a half step, hand on the rope knot; Haines flowed toward the alley like a man fetching a cup for a drip. A gust glazed the dome; focus softened; Keene reappeared at the edge of vision; Vernon failed at lemon bar with dignity; a child crouched under the rope—and the bells rang, clear and small.

Not a taste. A strike.

Haines moved without moving. Laurel's mouth set. Edwin raised his clipboard like a shield. Doris rounded the table, apron strings snapping.

At the gate, a hand discovered twine is a thing and swore in the universal whisper of thwarted plans. The tongues clacked again as it withdrew. Same menthol thread.

"Enough," Laurel said. "Show's over." With Edwin, she lifted the dome, dropped the blackout cloth he'd stitched at dawn, and knotted it tight.

"You can't—" Vernon sputtered.

"We can," Laurel said. "We are." To the square, committee voice on: "Thank you for your interest. The artifact will be available later under conditions that safeguard it and the town."

Grumbles turned to applause—Tumblebrook, all in all, had a good day. Doris carried the false spoon inside like it could break and break the town. Haines checked the alley; Amelia's morning flour had left a fresh silk. A partial heel kissed the dust—same chip, same diagonal scar. Ezra sketched the bells' bright note.

Amelia finally sat on the café's back step, palms open to show the day she held nothing else. The alley wore a kinder shade. Clara leaned a shoulder, the intimacy of women who have done work together and will do more.

"We made it through the afternoon," Clara said.

"We did," Amelia said. Lady Grey installed herself on Amelia's lap to deliver her evening report. "Tomorrow?"

"Tomorrow we count what we caught," Clara said. "Menthol. Ink. A partial tread. A name that may not be. An appetite that dislikes *no.* And a town willing to be witness when asked to be spectacle."

"And the note," Amelia said, remembering the sentence under the inn rug: *Some treasures best remain buried.*

"We didn't bury anything," Clara said. "We uncovered a habit."

Cleanup became its own small festival—tents thumping, instruments tucked, lemon bars inventoried. Laurel's heels clicked: let me write this before it dissolves. Haines's radio murmured weather no one would heed. Edwin laughed like a man who had quietly helped.

Lady Grey rested her head on Amelia's wrist, eyes narrowing to hot coins. The line between what the town permitted and what it would not had been drawn again—with a cat's paw and a bell's thin cry.

By dusk, lights winked on, the lake dressed in pewter, the decoy wrapped, the real spoon asleep behind lock and ledger—and the outsider, if near, tallying his next move like coins by finger memory in the dark. Tumblebrook breathed between chapters.

The square glowed; the alley watched; the bells hung quiet for now; and above the café door a silver cat yawned, showing a small crown of teeth sharp enough to matter.

Chapter 14

A Shocking Discovery

Dusk poured over Tumblebrook in pewter folds. Festival strings winked out; bunting drooped; the square exhaled. Inside that hush, three women and a cat kept moving.

Amelia and Clara folded tablecloths with the intimacy of people who'd folded harder things. Doris packed bunting like boxing a quarrel, eyes tugged to the dais—the glass dome, velvet plinth, placard, and the replica spoon flashing modestly. The real spoon slept where Laurel had sworn—library safe, ledger, token—known to three people; two stood within arm's reach of the dome. Even knowing it was bait, Doris's gaze wouldn't settle.

"Successful enough," she muttered. "If Vernon hadn't hovered like a vulture, I might call it pleasant."

"He shadowed you," Clara said, pencil finally tucked behind her ear. "And Keene—more than chatter."

"Let him preen." Doris snapped a crate lid. "The spoon's on Finch ground. Even the pretend one. I'll put it away before bed."

"We'll walk you in, then lock up," Amelia said.

Lady Grey paced the booth lip, tail drawing velvet arcs. She tapped the dome once, then looked from Amelia to the alley. Not done.

When the café door closed, the square took its night shape. Amelia returned to the inn with the slow fatigue that follows a day held tight by purpose. Lamps doused, locks checked. Lady Grey curled at the bed's foot like a comma promising a clause.

The knock didn't belong to quiet. Fast, panicked—awake-awake. Shawl, stairs, door.

Clara stood pale, eyes bright. "Amelia. Quickly. Doris—"

They cut through the alley because panic cuts corners. Lantern light made poor theater of the garden: slicked thyme, lavender exclamation points, a kettle belly-up, rim blotched dark.

Vernon Finch sprawled where the ground refused him. Torn waistcoat, soaked shirtfront, evening sky in eyes that didn't see.

For one unkind beat Amelia thought he'd fainted with flair. But the jaw's angle and still chest said finished. "Oh," she breathed.

Clara knelt—close, not touching. "Haines," she said. Low to Amelia: "Kettle. There." Blunt rim spattered. "Not a fall."

Doris—white-lipped in the doorway—took one look and made a sound that broke the night's agreement about quiet. "No! We argued —" She lurched, then collapsed into Amelia's hold.

"They'll say it was me," she rasped. "My kettle. My garden. I'm being—" Framed stuck and fell out as a sob.

Clara's head snapped to the kitchen window above the sink. Ajar. Curtain breathing in and out. Lady Grey flattened, ears slicked, gaze fixed on the gap.

"Window," Clara said.

"Door was locked," Doris managed. "I locked it after the last tray. Went upstairs. Heard—a whump. A cry. And—"

"And you came down," Amelia steadied.

Clara and the cat flowed inside. Night made house shapes. The display dome sat a hair off. Absence was palpable even before the lantern confirmed it: the velvet lay empty. The replica spoon was gone.

Amelia and Doris staggered in on the realization. Doris made a thin wail—the sound a kettle makes yanked from flame, still boiling with nowhere to pour. "No. I was going to put it—"

"We put the decoy back," Amelia said, grounding herself with narrative. "Fewer questions." Said aloud, it sounded like invitation. *Come. Try.*

"The real spoon is safe," Clara said. "Library. Laurel has it. What's gone is theatre. But the gesture—" she flicked at the empty velvet "—is a note pinned to a door."

Footfalls—solid, measured. Deputy Haines in the doorway, Laurel on his shoulder, Edwin behind, Gus a murmur, Mrs. Cranston a gasp. Word runs downhill.

Haines swept the room: ajar window, dome a hair wrong, empty velvet; Doris white and wild, Amelia steady and shaking. "Stay back," he told the gathering, voice unraised and obeyed.

"Laurel?" Clara asked.

"The library's lock is untouched," Laurel answered. "Spoon and token where we left them." She held up the key. "Chain of custody intact." Notes went into her pocket book—the town's second memory.

Doris laughed, edges not humor. "So someone killed a Finch to steal a pretend spoon? They'll hang me for theatre."

"No one's hanging anyone," Haines said, the sentence sturdy as boots. "We'll collect. We'll call the coroner."

From the garden, Gus: "Heel mark. Same chip as this morning. Menthol." He sniffed for agreement.

Clara and Amelia moved to the back. Lady Grey paced the sill, pressed her nose to the latch. Scraped paint dusted the metal where something slender had persuaded it.

"Pry marks," Haines said, torch low. "Flatbar or long screwdriver. Old wood, new insult." To Doris: "When did you last open this?"

"Lunch," she said automatically. "Steam. Then closed. It sticks—then gives."

Haines wrote with slow neatness. "Everything—then slower."

They told him: end of day; resetting the replica; plan to tuck it away; knock; garden; kettle; window; case.

"And Keene?" he asked, pebble in a pond.

"Too interested," Clara said. The alley exchange: *title, chain, quiet.* The hand under the rope—left; ink at cuticle; menthol like a second shadow. The bells' rude ring before close; a retreat, not quite a run; the partial tread—heel chip, diagonal scar—caught in fresh flour that morning.

"So: a body, a staged theft, an opportunist, and a rumor with a breath mint," Haines said. To Doris: "And you—who did none of this and will carry it anyway if we let night do its favorite thing."

"What do you need?" she asked, chin lifting.

"Shoes—what you wore today and when you came down. Keys besides yours. Who had reason to want Vernon alive at noon and dead at ten."

Doris answered: sensible shoes; slippers upstairs; keys (hers; Emma's; Gus's for repairs). Emma left at nine-thirty. Gus lingered telling stories—comforting, and in retrospect convenient.

"And Vernon?" Laurel asked gently.

"He came at dusk," Doris said. "Asked if the spoon had gone to bed. Took a lemon bar without paying. Preened off to be a headline. If he had a friend, the friend wore expensive shoes and cologne that smells like dental offices."

"Keene," Clara said.

"Or someone trying to be," Doris said.

Haines's radio woke bureaucracy. He gave two facts and one polite request. Outside, the crowd sorted into a respectful mob. Edwin worked the line like a maître d' to tragedy; Laurel walked with phrases that comforted without promising. A young patrolman took the alley mouth with kind, unyielding orders.

"You're coming to the inn," Amelia told Doris. "Laurel sits on your safe. Haines on your door. I'll sit on you."

"I am all corners," Doris said faintly, but she stayed.

They made a small, stubborn camp: Doris back to the wall,

Amelia beside her, Clara with notebook and undrinkable coffee. Lady Grey took the counter, paws aligned, gaze fixed down the back hall as if holding it by looking.

In the garden, Haines and the coroner worked with quiet respect. The kettle into a bag; a thyme sprig too dark; a shred of linen with no business in dirt. Haines bent where Clara had at dawn and found what flour and patience offer: the heel with the chip; the diagonal scar; and a second, lighter tread—a half-step inside the heavier.

"The lighter stands within the heavier," Clara said. "Not following—correcting. A man laying his story over another's."

"Mr. Keene," Haines said neutrally.

"Or anyone wearing Mr. Keene," Clara said.

Back inside, Lady Grey lowered her chin to the empty velvet, inhaled twice, then tapped the join where glass met plinth—exactly where a hand would slide to lift.

Amelia bent. Something winked—the tiniest crescent. Laurel's tweezers lifted it: clear plastic film, the adhesive dealers lay over embossing to dodge fingerprints.

"God bless the cat," Edwin whispered, then, because he must, "and municipal funding."

"Bag it," Haines said. *Adhesive fragment—case edge.*

"When did you close the back door?" Laurel asked Doris softly.

"Ten. Ten-fifteen. Emma out at nine-thirty. Locked the back door, wiped the counter, turned the sign. Went upstairs. Heard the kettle like a loved name, then it hit the ground like my name in the wrong mouth." Her hands clenched. "So I came down."

"We'll write it," Laurel said. "Your way, not rumor's."

"Rumor has better paper," Doris muttered.

"We have better ink," Laurel replied.

Time found a new rhythm. The van took Vernon away with professional quiet. Haines ringed the kettle's last place with tape that fluttered like warning in carnival colors.

"Who tells the Finches?" Clara asked.

"I will," Doris said. "They won't hear this from a stranger. Not even the ones I don't like."

Laurel's phone brr'd. "Larkin is on the safe. The spoon sleeps. Keene's at the Lakeview Motor—checked in under Keene."

"Hubris or a message," Clara said, jotting: *Keene—Lakeview.* "Vernon's room?"

"Morning," Laurel said. "Consent or warrant. Tonight we keep Doris where kinder eyes can find her."

The town did one more good thing: blankets, two more awful coffees, a plate of lemon bars that had somehow escaped. Emma arrived, braid tight, fear making her older; she flung herself at Doris and wept. Doris, who rarely allowed such liquidity in public, patted her head and said her name like a spine-giving prayer.

"When you first dug the spoon—weeks ago—you were in the thyme," Clara said, glancing at the dark square of dirt. "If someone wanted this to rhyme—"

"—they'd put him where the story started," Doris finished, mouth trembling. "Use my kettle because the town knows it. Take the decoy because the town can be fooled even when it tries not to be." She stared at the bagged kettle. "I'm throwing that in the lake."

"We may need it," Haines said kindly.

Clara drew a line beneath her notes. The chapter closed—theirs, not the town's; the town writes longer books.

Amelia looked at Lady Grey, who had not moved except to blink like a creature thinking. "Well, captain?" she asked, soft enough for only cat and women. "Have we done what we could?"

Lady Grey's tail flicked once. She looked at the window, then the case, then the door, and rested her paw—very gently—where the adhesive had been. A benediction. A promise.

"Tomorrow," Amelia said. Not comfort; a vow.

"Tomorrow," Clara echoed, and her echo had teeth.

Lantern flame guttered, righted. Outside, the lake turned, dreaming older ships. The café breathed the long breath old buildings take when they decide to let a night pass without breaking.

Vernon Finch was dead—the kind that shifts a town's axis. The replica was gone—gesture over gain. The real spoon—the story's spine—slept behind a lock about to become a character. The kettle waited in a bag with a number. The alley kept its menthol secret, for now.

And in a front room turned watch-post, a cat kept vigil on a velvet square that held nothing—and everything—still.

Chapter 15

Whispers of Blame

By dawn, rumor had already lapped Tumblebrook twice.

From the inn's porch, Amelia watched the square form itself under milk-colored light. The lake breathed silver across the cobbles. Gulls wrote ragged cursive against a sky promising heat. Shop doors yawned open. A broom shushed flour dust into the street. And everywhere—under hats, in pockets, between people who rarely spoke—whispers ran like pickle brine: sour, quick, preserving what should have spoiled.

"Terrible business," one voice said, as though reciting grace. "Right in Doris Finch's garden."

"With her own kettle," came another, scandalized and satisfied. "I remember when she tossed that thing out back last summer and said it was too heavy for soups. Should've been a sign."

"Family feud," a third murmured as Amelia tightened her shawl. "Blood remembers."

The inn's steps felt less like a welcome and more like a witness stand. She descended anyway, list in pocket: eggs, ice, Laurel at the library, Haines for updates, find Emma, keep Doris fed. Small tasks steadied her, though every porch seemed to grow its own jury.

The café door stood open, spilling heat and voices. Inside, the air clung with worry, salted by echoes of lanternlight. Doris sat in a corner, apron rumpled, flour streaks chalked on her hands. She looked older, sharper—softness stripped away. Lady Grey perched beside her, tail curled along Doris's forearm, ears pivoting at each footfall with economical distrust.

"They'll believe it," Doris said to her empty cup, voice thinned by exhaustion. "They'll believe it was me. Motive, kettle, history. They'll braid it into rope."

"You didn't," Amelia said, dropping to eye level. Some mornings needed declarations more than comfort. "I know you didn't."

Doris's gaze snapped up, anger wet but not for Amelia. "That won't matter to Harlow."

The bell answered for her—an alarmed jangle. Chief Harlow entered with the morning heavy on his shoulders. His coat carried pipe tobacco, his boots creaked like courtroom benches. He scanned the room and found his target with the inevitability of loss.

"Mrs. Finch," he said evenly. "I'll need you to come with me."

Doris's palms flattened to the table, flour syllables blooming under her hands. "You mean to arrest me."

"Question you," Harlow corrected. On paper the word was harmless; in the café it clanked. "Your kettle, your garden, your quarrels with the deceased. You won't be held long if things point elsewhere. But I can't ignore what's in front of me."

"You've eaten here since you were twelve and thought coffee made you grown," Amelia burst out before she could stop herself. "You know Doris. She feeds this town at Thanksgiving whether it deserves feeding or not."

For a heartbeat, the man peeked out behind the uniform. Then Harlow adjusted his belt and was the rank again. "If it were any other kettle, you'd tell me not to ignore it. Let the process work."

Clara slipped in from the back, notebook in hand, pencil sharp as intention. "Process or not, you're reaching for a neat conclusion," she said, mercilessly polite. "Vernon Finch made enemies for sport. The kettle being here doesn't put it in Doris's hand."

"Facts first," Harlow said, mantra-like. "Conclusions later."

Lady Grey flattened her ears and produced a low, engine-like rev of disapproval. She slithered down, forming a narrow gray barricade between Doris and Harlow, glaring at his boots with theological disdain.

"See?" Doris whispered. "Even the cat knows court from mistake."

"Cats don't sway the law," Harlow said, mouth twitching despite himself.

"They sway me," Amelia said flatly. "And their record is good."

Harlow exhaled. His voice softened without slackening. "Mrs. Finch, please. You're not under arrest. I need you at the station for a long talk, in a chair, not standing in your café."

Doris rose stiffly. "Don't let them bury me in this," she said to Amelia, Clara, Lady Grey—to anyone listening. "Don't let them make me the tidy ending."

"We won't," Amelia promised.

Harlow moved carefully, as if Doris might break. At the counter he paused. "Permission to pass, ma'am?" he said gravely to Lady Grey.

The cat blinked, unimpressed, then stepped aside with the grace of one granting favor. She leapt to the sill and watched them go until the bell's last tremor.

By midmorning, the square had grown pulpits. Every stall preached its own rumor. The jam booth offered speculation in three flavors. The quilt table laid out old tales end-to-end. The air smelled of varnish and almonds, like a hymn that had lost its words.

"I knew Doris had a temper," Mrs. Cranston declared. "You can't bind a feud with lavender sachets. Sooner or later something snaps."

"Rubbish," Gus Phelps countered, though with little thunder. "Doris couldn't swat a fly. She'd talk it into leaving."

"The spoon's gone," someone whispered reverently. "She hid it."

"Hid it? She sold it," hissed another. "You think lemon bars bake themselves?"

"And curses," a young mother added, half weeping. "My grandmother said no Finch ever slept a night unpaid."

Amelia and Clara moved through rumor like fish through nets. They heard Doris braided to Vernon, kettle to garden, spoon to curse. Each repetition sanded nuance until the story slipped too easily into eager hands.

"They want to be finished thinking," Clara muttered, shorthand skating across her notebook. "Neat knots strangle."

"Then we cut," Amelia said grimly. "Start with the last at the café: Emma, Gus, Edwin. And Keene."

"Keene's shadow too," Clara said, writing the name with no apology.

At the square's edge, the dealer leaned against a post, suit too fine for dusty streets, shoes too clean. Keene's voice wrapped vendors like thread around a spool. His gaze slid over Amelia, lingered on the inn, then dismissed it like merchandise beneath him.

"Watch him," Clara said. "Stillness is theater."

"And the menthol?" Amelia asked.

"Half the town smells of menthol now," Clara said. "But his prints will stand out."

Laurel appeared with coffee that steamed responsibility. "Doris is at the station," she reported. "Harlow's by the book, Haines with her. She's not alone. The spoon's safe; Larkins is on the lock." She sipped, winced. "This coffee tastes like a burned sermon."

"Bless you," Amelia said.

On the porch rail, Lady Grey surveyed the square like a magistrate, then leapt to Amelia's shoulder and pressed her face into her cheek as if swearing an oath.

"We'll prove it," Amelia whispered. The purr rumbled like a small engine ready to move a town.

They divided the day.

Amelia walked to Emma's bungalow, where laundry soap scented the yard. Emma, pale and shaken, poured tea with trembling hands.

"I closed at nine-thirty," she rushed. "Miss Doris sent me home. I took trash to the alley and saw a man. A hat, not a cap. Standing still. When he turned—" Her nose wrinkled. "That dentist mint. Not gum. Cologne over smoke."

"Tall-ish. White cuff. Shiny shoes, scuffed at the toe," she added.

"You've told me now," Amelia said, jotting notes. "That matters."

On her way out, she caught Keene watching from the end of Willow, hat tipped like punctuation. She gave nothing back.

Later, she cornered Gus, whose hands trembled around undeserved coffee. He admitted standing near the café, hearing Doris scream. "It's the sound that makes all others small," he muttered. Amelia wrote his alibi with mercy and moved on.

Clara dug through slips at the library with Laurel. She spotted the kinked R in "Rogers Antiques," blocky and awkward. "Not Vernon. Not Edwin. But Rogers—someone trying to imitate another hand."

Laurel nodded. "I'll compare with Keene's registration at the motor court."

At the station, Haines slid her preliminary notes: kettle, pry marks, two shoe prints, adhesive fragment, menthol, tobacco, gun oil. Clara added Vernon's suitcase: gun oil, tobacco, lining suspicious. "Check Keene's shoes. And Rogers'."

Haines wrote without fuss.

Later, Mrs. Halvorsen told Clara: "I saw him. Hat. Jacket too warm. Walked with vanity, toe out, like watching himself in a window. People like that don't see who they step on."

"Keene," Clara whispered.

"I prefer 'culprit,'" the teacher said tartly.

By afternoon, Amelia and Clara regrouped with Laurel. Evidence spread across the café table: the glue fleck, tag backer, ledger samples, ominous note. Clara scrawled across the top: *Two plays run.*

Lady Grey pawed the case seam until Laurel pried free another tag backer. "Security adhesive," Laurel said. "Keene would know. Rogers, badly."

"Find them," Amelia said. "And prove Doris isn't their scapegoat."

At sunset, Harlow relented. "We're releasing her," he told Amelia, lemon bars in hand. "Glue. Shoes. Letters. And Laurel with her statutes."

Doris emerged looking wrung out but whole. She let Amelia steer her to the inn, Lady Grey wrapped like ribbon around her ankles.

"Tomorrow," Doris said. "We find the man with the hat. Or we make the town see truth."

"Tomorrow," Amelia echoed.

On the sill, Lady Grey kept vigil, amber eyes fixed on the lamplight's shadow.

Clever, the cat would have said, is not the same as safe.

Chapter 16

Lady Grey's Nose

Tumblebrook woke as if it had misplaced its courage. Mist knit the street into a muffled corridor; the lake lay pewter-flat. Inside the inn, clocks ticked too loudly. Amelia stood at the kitchen window with tea that tasted of tannin and worry. Under Clara's door, light had burned to dawn—pages, arrows, order against rumor.

Lady Grey had patrolled all night, pausing to stare at the café as if a last act insisted on being played. When dawn tried on color, she landed on the floor and gave a meow that was not conversational. A summons.

"Back garden," Amelia said as Clara appeared, dressed and pinned for battle.

Mist pearled their shawls. Yesterday's declaration of order was now a page angrily erased—thyme drooping, damp soil mounded where secrets were demanded. Lady Grey went to the churned spot Clara had labeled *impact*, whiskers vibrating. She inhaled in careful sips, then dug—no scrabble, just tidy, surgical swipes.

Amelia knelt beside her. Against her knuckles: resistance. She coaxed it loose. A dull gleam shifted under mud. She lifted a fork—

long-tined, slightly bowed, heavy handle—and there, shallow but definite, the crest that had turned the town into a choir: a crown above a full-sailed ship.

"A fork," Clara breathed, reverent, then brisk. "Same crest. A set." She sketched before the image could run. "Spoon, fork—perhaps knives, ladles. Courses hidden in thyme."

"A service," Amelia said. "Concealed—and not yesterday."

Lady Grey chirruped once, dug two more pawfuls, and sat back to wash as if to say: you have what you need.

"If Vernon dug," Clara said, eyes on the handle's cut, "he wasn't after a trophy. The spoon was a map pin, not the prize."

"And if he knew," Amelia whispered, "who killed him may have known—or guessed."

"Almost certainly."

They wrapped the fork in a tea towel—not because it was precious (though it was), but because carrying it bare felt indecent. At the counter, Lady Grey sat beside the bundle, tail tucked tight; each time Amelia moved it, the cat's pupils widened: precise alarm.

"We keep this quiet," Clara said, buttoning her satchel as if corking ideas. "Laurel and Haines. No one else."

Lady Grey thumped her tail: agreed.

"See the wear?" Clara went on, unwrapping once more. "Nicks where tine meets neck—regular. Crown flatter than British; hull deep, almost Dutch; sails simplified, American-proud."

"Smuggling," Amelia said—the minor key stepping to the front. "Prohibition. Silver as payment. Or a cache set aside as insurance."

Clara made two columns: **Heirloom** (Finch estate; 1932 theft) and **Currency** (liquor routes; hidden caches). An arrow between. "If heirloom became currency, that's motive with teeth."

"Show Laurel, then Harlow," Amelia said.

They locked the fork in the office safe. Breakfast ran on muscle memory; after the last guest left, Amelia phoned the clerk's office.

Laurel arrived in ten minutes, cardigan askew, folder under her arm. She listened, gloved up, turned the fork in the light like a jeweler, photographed angles and crest; Clara redrew with new certainty. "Not English royal," she murmured. "An American house mark, perhaps."

"You'll find it," Laurel said—less comfort than order.

Back in the safe the fork went. The click sounded too loud and not loud enough.

"Now the garden—with a sieve," Clara said. "Mapping, not mining. No big holes."

Haines arrived with evidence bags, sieve, and the face of a man who'd slept in a chair. He nodded to Lady Grey, enthroned on the fence post. "I hear you found a fork," he said, half a question.

"Found your next hour," Clara replied, showing photos.

String and stakes cordoned the thyme. They scraped in thin layers, bagging by depth. "Here," Haines said at the second square, holding a soft metallic chip. Under Clara's loupe: a silver shaving. Bagged, labeled. "If it matches the fork, we have a tie."

In the third square, Clara's sieve caught a tacky fleck. "Glue," she said. "Another tag-back bit."

"So," Laurel traced their path, "our thief prepped or disarmed a tag here, passed the dome, then the garden." Her mouth flattened. "Then used the kettle. Or someone else did."

"Order matters," Haines said, writing. "Theft as disguise—or coda."

Lady Grey padded to the alley downspout, pawed the storm-drain grate, then sat and looked at Amelia.

"What now?" Amelia asked, crouching. "Ditch treasure?"

Haines levered the grate. The drain was dry. On the lip: a menthol lozenge wrapper and a pale curved sliver.

"CoolMint," Clara read, sealing it. She sniffed the sliver. "Wood infused with oil."

"Gun oil," Haines said. "Someone stood here, worked a mechanism, popped a mint to smell like a dentist."

"Or cologne and a conscience to freshen," Laurel said.

Bagged; marked. Lady Grey flicked an ear, satisfied, and reclaimed her post—Justice without a blindfold.

"Where does this drain go?" Clara asked.

"Under the alley to the lake," Haines said. "Out by the old boathouse."

"The bait shop where Edwin absolutely did not talk to Keene," Laurel said, dry.

"Let's not give Edwin new material," Amelia said.

Back at the inn, Clara lined up envelopes and redrew the garden with a small rectangle at the alley: *grate—mint + oil.* "He stood here," she said. "Wrapper-droppers are nervous. Keene's a pocketer. Our hat-man—Mrs. Halvorsen's question mark—drops wrappers. Same song, different notes."

"Next," she added, "library heraldry; county archives for silver-smiths; church registries for 1932. If someone laundered conscience with a serving spoon, the Ladies' Aid wrote it down."

"And the boathouse," Amelia said. "When the bait shop is loud. You charm the clerk. I'll pet the dog."

"Deal."

Doris came down the back stairs—braid neat, skin sallow from a law-office chair. For a second she looked afraid of interrupting her own life.

"Come," Amelia said. "We're building you a bridge."

Doris sat. Lady Grey relocated to her lap with judicial authority. Amelia slid toast and honey across; Clara pushed Laurel's fork photos. Doris touched the paper's edge. "You found more," she said— grief meeting a new cousin.

"In the thyme," Amelia said. "Quiet for now."

"Good. This town turns holes into graves."

"We'll fill this one with facts," Clara said.

The library's high windows slicked noon sun into polite bril-liance. Mrs. Winthrop, resident cat draped sash-like, marched them to *Hartwell's Compendium of American Crests* and *Silversmiths of the Upper Midwest.* On page 412: regional privateers, crown-and-ship motifs—close but not exact. In the gossip book: Jonas K. Beller (Duluth) advertised a "North Crown Service" for lake merchants, 1898–99. Limited run; cash clients unnamed.

"North Crown," Clara breathed. "Crown and ship. Lake merchants. Someone could have commissioned a bespoke crest—Finch, or Finch-adjacent."

Minutes from 1932—six weeks after the "Silver Spoon Affair"—stilled her pencil: *Anonymous donation: one silver serving spoon, crown-and-ship, worn; accepted with thanks.* Pastor suggested prayer.

"Pieces left the Finch estate after the scandal," Amelia said. "Someone bled the set into town. Someone else cached a share—here. Why here?"

"Because gardens forgive," Clara said. "Or because this window watches the alley."

They thanked Mrs. Winthrop and walked to the bait shop. Behind it, the boathouse sagged; the drain discharged into riprap. A glassy bead caught light—ambered epoxy, half-peeled.

"Tag glue again," Clara said, sealing it. "Our thief sheds like a maple."

Back at the inn, Laurel waited with three triumphs. "St. Luke's says your chip matches the fork—coin silver, about ninety percent. The glue fleck matches two cheap alarm tags: Brogan's General or Marston's in Duluth. And the State Patrol pulled Mr. Keene at 10:20 on Highway 61; he's presently indignant, discussing the difference between provenance and felony."

"Bless that trooper's toe," Amelia said.

"Harlow wants you at six," Laurel added. "Shoe prints don't match Doris, Emma, Gus, or officers. He needs your notes on hat-men and toe-out walking. He's prepared to apologize with his eyebrows."

They went. The square tried on better posture. Harlow met them hat-in-hand. "Size ten, narrow, toe turned. Lab confirms glue. Keene had a tag disabler, but your tags are the cheaper kind. If he tagged anything, he did it competently. Your hat-man shops where glue tells on him. We're running down a name: Paul Reiner, Two Harbors."

Clara handed a page—the crest, Beller entry, Ladies' Aid line. "Not just a family squabble," she said. "A cache. Vernon was complication and advertisement."

Harlow read, eyelid twitching with effort. "Mrs. Winthrop will copy this," he said. "I'll pretend I found it when I talk to the county."

"Do," Laurel said. "We'll clap from the back row like cousins."

They walked home through silver evening. In the inn window, Doris sat with Lady Grey in her lap, amber eyes like lanterns. "Well?" she asked, not standing—a good sign.

"We're pushing the right stones," Clara said. "And one rolled onto Keene's foot."

"Good. I don't like his shoes."

"They don't like you either," Amelia said, and Doris's laugh fluttered like a bird testing air after rain.

They ate tomato soup and grilled cheese cut on the bias, because some rituals are empirically correct. The cat accepted one cheddar tidbit with liturgical solemnity and resumed guard. They told Doris about Beller, the minutes, epoxy and drains, the wrapper.

"Treasure under thyme," Doris said. "If you'd told me last month my garden held secrets, I'd have smacked the dirt and told it to share sooner."

"You did," Amelia said. "It listened."

When dishes dried and lamplight found its night strength, Clara spread her timeline: *Murder—9:45–10:15? Theft—10:30–11:15? Mint at grate → boathouse epoxy. Beller—North Crown. Anonymous donation '32.* Under both: *Who knew to dig? How?* Three question marks; a tiny crown-and-ship.

Amelia set a palm on the paper and closed her eyes. Pencil scratch, cat's breath, lake's shush, Doris's heart quieting. It felt like standing at a field's edge at night, hearing corn whisper about rain—nothing visible, everything coming.

She opened her eyes. Lady Grey stood on the table, forepaws on the timeline, studying the penciled crest. She sniffed it, looked up, and blinked, slow and certain.

"You're right," Amelia said. "We'll find the rest. And who wanted it enough to kill."

Lady Grey tucked her tail and purred—low and steady—like a promise being notarized.

Outside, the mist let go. Somewhere down the highway, a car carried a man in a hat toward a destination he had mistaken for safety. In Tumblebrook, under a roof that knew how to keep good people, three women and a cat set their faces toward morning. Tomorrow would need shovels and statutes, patience, and the tact of a cat's nose.

Tonight required believing that thyme keeps its secrets only until you ask the right way.

Chapter 17

Police Pushback

Morning had the gall to be beautiful.

Sun combed the birches; the bakery exhaled cinnamon; gulls scribbled rude punctuation across a too-blue sky. In Tumblebrook, good weather only carried gossip farther. Amelia locked the inn, slipped the key into her apron—ritual without comfort. Clara fell in with her notebook; Lady Grey trotted three steps ahead, tail-tip flicking: faster.

"Will Harlow listen this time?" Clara asked.

"We're not giving him a choice," Amelia said. "Laurel brings lab notes. Haines translates to Chief."

They climbed the two shallow steps of the stone-fronted "sheriff's" office. Lady Grey peered in like a shareholder. Chief Harlow—cuffs rolled, knuckles drumming—looked up with a sigh you could almost see.

"If you're here to... assist... make it quick."

"Good morning to you too, Chief," Amelia said, not sweetly. She sat; Clara stood as if testifying. Lady Grey brushed file cabinets, leaving a silver bloom of ownership.

"We have more," Clara began, opening to the crest, thyme grid, and Laurel's rulered photos. "A second piece—fork, same crown-and-ship, buried where Vernon fell."

Harlow didn't reach for the photo.

"And glue flecks," Amelia said. "From a cheap display tag—Marston's in Duluth or Brogan's here. Haines sent the memo."

"Mint wrapper and gun-oil toothpick at the alley drain," Clara added. "Epoxy tear at the lake outlet. Window → alley → lake."

"You're very proud of your treasure hunt," Harlow said.

"This is motive," Amelia answered. "If a set's hidden in the garden, the death and spoon belong to one story. Doris didn't bury silver. Someone else did—and dug."

"You've questioned Harper?" Clara asked. "He hovered like a buzzard."

"Insufferable and delighted, which isn't a crime," Harlow said. "Told Doris twice to use a safe. He'll happily repeat it. And Keene? St. Louis County has him—for speeding. Nothing ties him here. Parasite, not proof."

"The hat-man?" Clara pressed. "Narrow foot, toe turned out."

"We're trying on a name. I won't say it until the shoe fits."

Lady Grey hopped onto a visitor chair, tail tapping Harlow's wrist like punctuation. He glared at the tail-tip, then finally glanced at the photos.

"What's that smear on the kettle handle?" He squinted through a magnifier. "Not blood. Shiny."

"Glue sheen?" Clara tried.

"Or varnish," he deflected.

"You just did get ahead of yourself," Laurel said from the doorway, cardigan buttoned wrong and not caring. She handed over St. Luke's prelim and Haines's memo. "Silver shaving matches the fork. Glue fleck matches Marston's budget tags. Keene's kit doesn't use glue. Your hat-man buys cheap—or stole cheap. Also—Ladies' Aid entry, 1932: anonymous donation of crown-and-ship serving spoon weeks after the 'misplacement.' Say 'thank you, Laurel.'"

"Thank you, Laurel," Harlow said automatically, reading. His thumb made a crease he'd deny. "Not proof of outsider murder."

"No," Laurel agreed. "Motive that moves suspects."

He exhaled daylight admission. "Doris stays put. No cuffs, not yet. Inn or café. And you two don't dig more holes without Haines."

"We were doing stratigraphy," Clara said.

"If you find another piece, call Haines before unwrapping a towel," he finished.

"Done," Amelia said.

Lady Grey chirped once—contract signed.

* * *

The square tried new vocabulary in trios: prosecution, probation, postpone. News that Doris hadn't been charged—yet—made some generous, others indignant. Mrs. Cranston posted up near the bakery like a chief witness; Gus held court at the bait barrel; children played Don't Touch the Kettle on the fountain rim.

"Do you ever wish we let others untangle their knots?" Clara murmured.

"Frequently," Amelia said. "Then I remember they tie them tighter for sport."

They collected Doris from the café—she'd wiped the counter to surprise. Crossing took two seconds of resistance, then the inn exhaled her. Lady Grey escorted like a dapper uncle: serious, outwardly bored, secretly proud.

In the parlor they made a war table as some households set winter puzzles. Clara spread notes; Amelia set down the cloth-wrapped fork like an unspoken prayer.

"Two tracks," Clara said. "Crest origin and cache map. Beller's ads and ledgers in Duluth. And here—" she tapped the grid "—a finer sweep of the outer edge. Context, not treasure."

"Take Haines, my trowel, my blessing and rage," Doris said. "But not a shovel big enough to make a rumor happy."

The bell rang. Laurel entered with Haines and a neat suit with expensive hair: a man who considered climate an accessory. Dove-gray fedora in hand.

"Mr. Paul Reiner of Two Harbors," Laurel said. "Collects nautical silver and civic scandals."

Reiner smiled with his own cologne. "Charming town. I heard of your unfortunate incident."

"Pretty word for murder," Doris said.

"I'd hoped to view yesterday's piece. Crown-and-ship is a partic-ular interest."

"Spoken with Harper? Mr. Keene?" Clara asked.

"I don't know a Keene," Reiner said pleasantly. "Harper and I shared brief opinions about small-town markets."

"About ownership," Amelia said.

"About everything." He adjusted the hat crease to precision. "I also spoke with a Mrs. Halvorsen about bakery hours. Missed my roll."

The hat tugged Amelia's memory. Lady Grey made a low *mm*: we've met your kind. Haines tracked the shoes—polished, narrow, toe flaring like a dancer's. He made a small mark.

"What about North Crown silver?" Clara asked, mild. "Jonas Beller, 1898–1903, private commissions."

A flicker. "A taste, not a pedigree," Reiner said a shade too fast. "Merchants liked to look like houses."

"And like liquidity," Laurel said.

"Silver is portable history," he smiled.

"History is heavier than you think," Doris said.

"If I can help clarify provenance when it's recovered, I'm at the Two Harbors Inn until Tuesday," Reiner said. "References in Duluth, if you value such things."

"We value truth," Amelia said.

"Rare, even with references." He reclaimed the hat and left with the grace of a man convinced doors like him.

"Toe-out," Haines murmured. "Mint on his breath."

"Gun oil on cuffs?" Laurel said, catching herself. "Too neat. Let evidence decide."

Lady Grey placed one paw squarely on Clara's grid—C3, outer edge toward the alley. The room stilled.

"C3," Clara said. "Yes, ma'am."

Back to the garden they went: Laurel with a clipboard that could make a mayor behave; Haines with tools; Clara with historian's quiet fizz; Amelia with another towel—touching silver bare felt like touching a secret without an introduction. Doris nodded from the doorway: finish this.

They worked C3 like surgeons at a wound's edge. The sieve sang. At four inches: roots, a bottle cap. At six: Haines's trowel kissed something dull.

"Another chip," he said, joyless grin. Clara loupe'd; same scratch grain. Bagged, labeled; Laurel logged with choreography of competence. At eight inches the sieve held a cloudy, cracked plastic rectangle—the ghost of a price tag.

"Marston's style," Clara said. "Cheap. Brittle."

"So our thief tested the tag, then handled the kettle, then the man," Haines said. "If I pull one print with this glue that isn't Doris's, I'll buy Harlow a drink he'll pretend not to like."

They worked until light tilted. No full piece today. Enough chips, plastic, glue, and disturbed layers to prove the ground had held silver and impatience.

Back at the inn, the parlor reclaimed them. Laurel left with evidence and the satisfied bark of a woman who treed a raccoon. Haines promised to bully the lab kindly. Doris sagged into the sofa like someone relearning how to sit without apology. Tea did what law and physics wouldn't.

"Chief won't like being wrong," Doris said.

"He'll like being right later," Amelia said—Laurel's line, shamelessly borrowed.

Clara flipped to a clean page. "Beller's ledgers next. Reiner leaves

Tuesday—if he's in this, he'll hurry; if not, he'll perform innocence. We watch which way his shoes turn."

Amelia set the wrapped fork at center like a moon. Lady Grey settled beside it, eyes half-lidded in that not-sleep cats use when they want you to think they're not working. A lighthouse watch.

"I don't know what I'd do without her," Amelia said, surprised by the thickness in her voice.

"Borrow her from yourself," Clara said, not looking up. "That's what we're all doing."

Evening leaned in. Lamps warmed wood; the lake breathed. Their list stood:

Crest: Beller's North Crown; private commissions.

Cache: Multiple burials; silver chips; tag plastic; glue; disturbed layers.

Suspects: Harper (opportunistic); Keene (tools, stopped on 61); Reiner (toe-out, mint); Unknown helper.

Motive: Treasure-as-currency; inheritance-as-alibi.

Next: Marston's purchases; Brogan's stock; church minutes '29–'33; Mrs. Thistle's kin; boathouse watch; Reiner's movements; Beller archives in Duluth.

"If Reiner bought tags at Marston's two days ago, his card will tattle," Clara said. "If cash, the clerk will remember the hat."

"Everyone remembers a hat with that much self-regard," Amelia said.

Lady Grey made a sound some would call laughter, circled the map, then placed one paw lightly on the wrapped fork—signature.

A knock, not timid: Harlow. Bareheaded—a concession he'd never name. He looked at Amelia, Doris, the cat, then at the parcel like it might oblige him with scripture.

"I'm not here to apologize," he began.

"We'd faint; you'd fetch water," Amelia said.

"The county attorney wants me to hold charges until the lab finishes. He didn't say 'because your clerk and librarian will make a fool of you if you don't,' but that's the translation. Doris, don't leave town."

"I don't want to leave the room," she said.

"The hat man checked into Two Harbors under his own name. We're getting a warrant for his car. Keene is... cooperating loudly. Harper is composing a letter destined for the Museum of Audacity."

"Thank you," Amelia said.

"Don't make me regret this," he told them—meaning the pause, the listening, the new story trying its legs. "And if you find another piece—"

"We'll call Haines," Amelia and Clara said together.

He grunted—Harlow for *fair enough*—and left.

The latch settled; Doris exhaled a week. "He still thinks I could have done it," she said.

"He thinks many things," Amelia said. "He'll think better tomorrow."

They sat until tea cooled and lists absorbed intent. The fork returned to the safe; notes were tied with a ribbon like a writ. Doris went upstairs and let her lamp rest.

Lady Grey followed Amelia to the kitchen windowsill, surveying bakery light, a café ready to forgive tomorrow, a lake that had seen larger ships than crowns and smaller men than kings. Her tail flicked once, twice, then settled. Eyes closed.

"Tomorrow," Amelia said into the quiet, "we run faster than rumor."

From the sill came a small, certain rumble of a purr: *and straighter than fear.*

Chapter 18

Clara's Ledger Find

The bell at Gossamer Fables whispered Clara inside, trading the square's boil for paper hush and sensible light. Lady Grey flowed after her, scaled a chair, and settled like a lighthouse above the local history alcove.

"Back in five," Mr. Larkin called. "If that cat topples the 1892 atlas, I retire."

"She won't," Clara said, already at the Reference corner of stubborn shelves—pamphlets, church minutes, bound *North Shore Sentinel*, stray ledgers rescued from attics. She bowed—respect, not worship—and found a cracked spine: **F. Ledger**.

At the window desk the book breathed flour and cellar cool. Early pages were ordinary—wheat, lumber, eggs—then the numbers leaned. In 1928: **deliveries—night; shipments—lake;** odd round sums; a lone initial **B**. She copied:

May 12, 1928 — deliveries—night (3) — $180

May 19, 1928 — shipments—lake — B — $540

B for Beller, barrels—or family code.

July 3, 1929: *warehouse—back — repair on crate—false bottom sticks; talk to R. —* $8. False bottoms belonged to contraband. Clara wrote: **R = Rogers? Reiner too early.**

Lady Grey descended the ladder in queenly steps, bumped Clara's elbow: turn the page. 1932 bristled. Three days after the paper's coy "Silver Spoon Affair":

Apr 17 — transfer: **crest pcs.** *— parish fund? — TBA — —*

No money. In the margin, faint pencil: **move to garden — S.** South bed? Spoon? Someone's initial?

A pale blue ribbon—modern—marked later pages. The ledger fell open to 1979–82: neat tallies shared between **D.F.** and **V.F.**—Doris and Vernon. In 1982, a graphite aside: **crest pieces — kept safe.**

Clara sat. Lady Grey set a paw precisely on *crest pieces.* Essential. Clara built a quick timeline:

1928–31: night entries; lake shipments; B.

Apr 1932: transfer crest pcs.; margin *move to garden—S.*

Post-1932: Ladies' Aid receives anonymous crown-and-ship spoon.

1979–84: D.F./V.F.; margin *crest pieces—kept safe.*

Mr. Larkin arrived with donations, saw the spread, and softened. "We don't shelf living families' ledgers. They drifted in. I read just enough to see the Finches were better at sums than reckoning."

"We need copies—to protect Doris," Clara said.

"I'm lending my copier to a librarian and a cat," he sighed. Lady Grey parked on the lid. Copies hummed out: 1928's nights, 1932's transfer and S, 1982's *kept safe.* Larkin slid them into a manila folder: **FINCH—LEDGER EXCERPTS (REFERENCE HOLD).** "Originals get locked. When the town is kinder, daylight."

Amelia entered on a thread of lilac, took in the table. "You found something."

"A throughline," Clara said, laying copies like cards. "The set moved after 1932—one piece to parish, the rest to the garden. In '82, beside Doris and Vernon's figures: *kept safe.* Vernon—or someone— read this. That's why he dug."

"Doris never mentioned ledgers," Amelia murmured. "Vernon read *kept safe* as *mine*; someone else read it as *must stay mine*."

Lady Grey sniffed *move to garden—S*, then stared toward the café.

They added more thread: church minutes echoing the anonymous spoon; a 1946 note—*boathouse repairs; sanding false bottom; no squeak*—with the same looping S. Copies joined the packet.

Laurel arrived, cardigan corrected, pen already titling **ARGUMENTS FOR NOT INDICTING DORIS**. "Chief will pretend he isn't relieved; the county will pretend she thought of it first. This—" a tap to *kept safe* "—is heavy."

A gust. The bell jangled. Paul Reiner: suit that believed in itself, hat angled like a thesis. "Catalogues on regional silversmithing?" His gaze swept shelves, counter, ledger—quick, thorough.

"Essay '97, index of Great Lakes marks," Larkin said blandly. "Both out. Your name?"

"Two Harbors Inn. Paul Reiner. Tragic about the spoon." Minted breath; careful smile.

"Tragedy isn't collectible," Laurel said.

"I collect only the documentary kind." Tip of hat; exit. Laurel watched his toe-out gait. "Haines will want to know he shops for reading where he leaves shadows."

They moved the packet—Laurel's tote, then a municipal envelope: invisibility by boring. Larkin re-shelved the ledger; Lady Grey supervised to the exact drawer.

"Tell Doris?" Amelia asked.

"Yes," Clara said. "Truth that helps; hold the rest until it can."

Back at the inn, Doris stood at the window weighing futures. She sat without being asked. Lady Grey leaned in like a gray comma.

Clara spoke gently. "Your ledgers include more than accounts: night deliveries, lake shipments in Prohibition; *transfer: crest pieces—parish fund?* with no sum; *move to garden—S*; and in 1982 beside D.F./V.F.: *crest pieces—kept safe*. We think Vernon—or someone— read this and dug."

Doris held breath at *garden*; released it at *kept safe*. "No one told me that phrase existed. We reconciled petty cash in the early '80s; if I saw it, I didn't understand. We always said the garden grew our good luck. We meant thyme." A brittle smile. "Maybe we meant something else."

"You didn't bury it," Amelia said. "And you didn't kill him."

"What do you need?" Doris asked.

"Names," Clara said. "Who handled ledgers in '82. Tool keys. The boathouse back door."

Doris gave a clean list: Aunt May the cash-box dragon; Uncle Russell (talked big, paid small); the old church treasurer's Duluth grandson; a neighbor with an expansive idea of "emergency." Each sharpened the map.

Laurel took the packet to her clerk's safe. "If anyone asks, I'm balancing budgets and saving the world for paperclips."

They stayed with Doris until tea went tepid, then sweet again. Lady Grey patrolled and reported: no intruders, one spider, plan unmade. At six, Clara tapped **NEXT**: *Beller in Duluth; boathouse; hat-man.*

"Duluth tomorrow," she said. "Beller's commission book—who bought North Crown. If Finches didn't commission, they acquired. If they did, this wasn't Vernon's alone."

"And the boathouse?" Doris asked.

"Haines at dawn," Amelia said. "We'll ask the false bottom to squeak again."

Doris laughed—a hinge finding itself. "All right."

Dusk cooled the town. Clara paused outside Gossamer Fables; in the high window her reflection met Lady Grey's, eyes bright. Two fingers lifted; the cat blinked: compact signed—follow ink, honor earth, keep Doris safe.

At the inn, the wrapped fork lay like a moon. Clara placed the copies beside it—direction, not spectacle.

Outside, rumors tired; night softened the square. Inside—paper, silver, and a cat—three women built the next day.

Chapter 19

Inn Under Scrutiny

By the third morning after Vernon Finch's death, the inn felt like a listening device. Guests read newspapers while watching the room; spoons paused midair whenever anyone said *spoon*. Tumblebrook Inn had always been a place to be seen. Now it was where people came to be seen *seeing*.

Amelia moved with the veteran coffee pot. "Top up, Mr. Humphries?"

The traveling salesman angled his cup as if secrets poured too. "Heard he was digging at night," he told his eggs. "These lake towns —shore keeps what the lake won't."

"Cream?" Amelia asked, hand steady. He blinked, stirred rumor into his coffee.

At another table a girl mouthed *Prohibition,* her companion offering appetite disguised as theory. A retired couple competed to know more about Duluth collectors. On the windowsill, Lady Grey lay like a statue: neat paws, heavy-lidded stare, tail flicking sunlight.

Clara slid by with a tray physics shouldn't allow. " 'Old cargo' just came out of the porridge," she murmured. "Today's special: Shipping Manifest, 1932."

"Add a side of dangerous men in Duluth," Amelia said, laying down oatcakes. "Humphries says Vernon owed the kind who come due."

"Then our fork isn't just heirloom," Clara said. "Collateral."

They didn't look toward the counter drawer holding the wrapped fork with its crown-and-ship crest. The drawer had never felt heavier.

By late morning rooms were made, the pantry restocked, the parlor polished—and the inn still too full of eyes. Lady Grey patrolled the stairs like a customs agent. Outside Room Five she sat, while sharp tobacco crawled under the door—bar-stained, hurried.

"We don't allow smoking," Amelia murmured, passing with towels.

We don't allow murder either, the cat's look said.

Room Five belonged to Humphries. He opened to Amelia's knock with his smile already ironed. Tidy room, gleaming sample case, no ash—yet the smoke clung like an unserious apology.

Back on the landing, Lady Grey hooked a thin length of pale blue ribbon from under the linen cupboard.

Amelia turned the satin in her fingers. Not hers. Yesterday at Gossamer Fables a ledger had been marked with just such ribbon when Clara found *crest pieces—kept safe.* Something slid inside Amelia. She pocketed it. "We'll show Clara."

The bell chimed and admitted Chief Harlow with Deputy Haines. Harlow's shoulders arrived first; Haines carried his hat—hard outside, useful underneath.

"We're here to look around," Harlow said.

"Warrant?" Amelia asked, to keep order in the air.

"Consent spares your guests a spectacle," he replied. Silence fell so fast it blushed.

"Friendly," Amelia said evenly. "Where first?"

"The office. Then storage. Then rooms. Deputy—upstairs."

Lady Grey's ears went back as Harlow stepped behind the desk. Amelia opened the drawer with the reservation book, reached in, and pulled out the bundle she'd dreaded leaving. "I have something to declare," she said, calm. "We found this in Doris's garden the morning after. We meant to bring it to Laurel—and to you—when we weren't serving breakfast."

"A fork," Harlow said, surprise showing. Hunger, too. The crest caught the light.

"With the same crown and ship," Amelia said.

"And you kept it."

"I kept it from being passed from mouth to mouth like a snack," she answered. Harlow slid the fork into an evidence bag without fumbling. "We'll log it," he said. "It helps Doris that you brought it. It would also help if you didn't inventory scenes like estate sales."

"Duly noted," Amelia said, and did not add *If I'd left it, it wouldn't be there now.*

Upstairs, Haines walked with Clara, opening doors and windows while she asked the small, exact questions that make a deputy think. "When you lifted prints from the café window, did you lift the latch? Doris cleans with vinegar and lemon; ammonia would say otherwise."

"I'll re-run it," he said, ears pink.

At Room Five, Humphries performed likability. Haines checked the latch; Lady Grey sniffed the sample case, rubbed her cheek on the corner with such ease Humphries tugged it closer.

"Friendly cat," he said.

"She has standards," Clara answered, noting the quick twitch before his smile settled.

A quiet woman with a novel—one page in ten minutes—asked if this was necessary. "We're keeping the air breathable," Haines told her gently, and the answer worked.

From the linen cupboard: a faint scent of earth and river. Lady Grey pressed the door; Clara followed. Behind disciplined stacks of pillowcases lay a rolled café apron—Doris's kind, blue-striped cotton. Soil freckled the hem; a thin smear—coal dust? old grease?—ran along the pocket.

"Gloves," Clara said. Haines bagged it, labeled it neat as print:

Apron (D. Finch type) found in inn linen cupboard—3rd floor—10:42 a.m. Planted, their eyes agreed. By whom?

"Only staff and long-term guests know this latch," Clara said. "It sticks unless you lift first."

"Who was up here last night?"

"Everyone," Clara said. "An inn is a family and a train station at once."

They finished the "consensual walkthrough," what everyone else calls looking where you wouldn't if you trusted me. Harlow took desk log, rota, a copy of the registry. He did not take a wrapped fork; the drawer no longer contained one.

At the door he paused. "Miss Farnsworth, you have a good name. Doris earned hers in pie and stubbornness. Don't spend yours like pennies."

"Truth isn't a penny," she said. "It's a counterweight."

He nodded—more human than she preferred—and left.

The inn inhaled. Guests began to talk again about moon, pie, lake. Amelia and Clara retreated to the kitchen. Lady Grey leapt to the counter. Amelia set down the blue ribbon. It gleamed—an innocent at a crime scene.

"Ledger ribbon," Clara said at once.

"Under the linen cupboard," Amelia said. "Lady Grey found it."

"If someone bookmarked *kept safe* and carried the ribbon in a cuff..." Clara shaded behind it in her notebook. "It could have tugged free."

"Or been planted without meaning to," Amelia said. "Satin bread crumbs."

"Reiner asked for maker's marks yesterday," Clara said. "Humphries smells of tobacco and debt. The quiet woman listens more than she reads. Our universe is small and full of motives."

"And Harlow has an apron where it doesn't belong," Amelia said. "He'll call it evidence."

Lady Grey tapped the ribbon twice, then looked toward the back stairs—the narrow service stair for deliveries and secrets. She padded away without looking back. They followed.

The stair smelled of a century of polish. On the second landing a small window angled toward the café garden. Lady Grey rose and peered down like a harbor master. On the bricks below: a scuff where someone braced a foot; on the outside sill, a smear—recent enough. A climb or a quick descent.

"Someone used our back stair window," Amelia said.

Clara ran a finger along the interior sill. Gray dust came away. She sniffed. "Not garden dirt. Graphite—pencil. Ledger dust."

Sometimes the universe commits to a theme too hard not to laugh.

"Humphries's window faces the alley," Clara said. "He could have seen or come. Or anyone who knows these stairs."

"And Reiner," Amelia said. "He measures windows with his eyes."

Back in the kitchen, the kettle objected; Amelia made tea because sometimes you must. Clara drew a quick plan of the inn: parlor, desk, dining, front stairs, service stairs, back window, alley. Arrows from café wall to staff window; from Room Five to landing; from linen cupboard to the same spot. *Probable. Possible.* She underlined *humor me.*

Lady Grey set a paw on the service-stair arrow, full weight. *Here. A door.*

"Understood," Amelia said. "We'll have Haines dust it while Harlow practices a speech."

Laurel swept in with a municipal tote that could hide a bylaw. "Ten minutes," she said. "Give me something that stands up in a room full of paper."

They gave her the fork (noted as in Harlow's custody), the apron (bagged), the ribbon, the service-stair smear. Laurel wrote three bullets and a fourth—**CAT SAID SO**—and circled it, wry. "I'll steer Harlow toward 'planted' instead of 'smoking gun,' and remind the county there are two juries: the twelve, and everybody."

She left; the old house sighed the way buildings do when someone exits with a plan.

Evening grew like a moth's wing—soft, insistent. People gathered because they don't know how not to. The quiet woman read without turning pages, the young couple told questions in hats, Humphries asked for stronger tea and got weak coffee he didn't taste. Amelia stood behind the desk, hand on the closed reservation book; Clara leaned beside her, pencil waiting for the *oh* that always arrived.

Lady Grey hopped between them, facing out. She read faces, hands, pockets, shoes. At Humphries, whiskers stiffened; then she looked toward the back stairs. Her tail curled along the ledger like punctuation.

"Tonight?" Amelia breathed. The cat didn't answer. She didn't need to.

At nine-thirty the quiet woman went up, the book a tent in her lap. At ten, the young couple giggled to the landing and hushed, sobered by a shadow. Humphries lingered; at ten-fifteen he rose and climbed, weariness arranged to look ordinary.

They waited. At ten-twenty the service stair creaked—one quick step, weight on the ball—then the small squeak of a window latch that squeaks only when someone forgets the lift-and-slide trick.

Lady Grey's ears went forward.

"Shall we?" Clara whispered. Amelia nodded, as if agreeing to open a door in a dream.

They moved together—silent over wood that knew them—to the shadow by the service window. The latch sat one notch off. On the sill, in the dust, an oval of absence: the clean mark of a case corner set down and lifted again—same angle as Humphries's polished case. Beside it, a smaller rectangle with serrated edges—the imprint of a matchbook. Backward stencil: **K...Y**. A Duluth lounge whose matches crawl into drawers.

"We call Haines," Clara said. "Before anyone walks. Before the inn inhales and blows this away."

Amelia nodded, stroked the cat's back—something alive and sure under her hand. "You keep better watch than all our locks."

Lady Grey pressed her head into Amelia's palm with the gravity of a witness.

Back at the desk, the telephone found the deputy who can be led where he needs to go. Clara gave Haines the words his pen required, then the ones he'd want: "If you come now, you can lift a matchbook impression off a sill and maybe carry it to a courtroom."

He was on his way.

They hung up. Woman, woman, cat stood in the quiet that followed. Outside, the lake wrote its endless sentence. Inside, Lady Grey sat, stillness like motion: a watch turning, a tide, a second hand saying yes, yes, yes.

Chapter 20

A Suspicious Historian

The walk to the historian's cottage always took Amelia a little out of her way, and today she let it. The lakeshore path unspooled between birches shedding papery curls, sun scattering across the water in shifting coins. A breeze carried lakeweed, damp stone, and the metal tang of worry.

Clara kept pace, pencil tucked behind her ear, notebook hugged to her ribs. "If Colby knows that crest, it'll be indexed in his head—dates, donors, who married whom, who buried what."

"Or the law," Amelia murmured.

Lady Grey trotted ahead, tail a jaunty question mark, glancing back as if asking whether to interrogate the suspect alone.

"Do we tell him about the fork?" Clara asked.

"Only that a second piece turned up," Amelia said. "Not where, not how."

They rounded the last bend. Edwin Colby's ivy-draped cottage leaned toward the lake as if listening for a confession. The porch was scrubbed to silver; a lone rocker waited.

Colby stepped out before they reached the steps, cardigan tired, eyes the faded blue of a man who remembered too much of the town. "Miss Farnsworth. Miss Henderson. And Her Majesty."

"We're hoping you can help identify a crest," Amelia said.

Clara opened to a neat sketch: a crown above a small sailing ship.

Colby's face tightened, then smoothed. "Ah. The Gentlemen of the Shore."

"A social club?" Clara asked.

"Lakefront men," Colby said lightly. "Merchants, boat owners, a banker or two. They met, ate, congratulated one another, stamped silver to prove they existed."

"And commissioned a set," Amelia said.

"Men like that would stamp their initials on the wind." He gestured them to the porch.

"Who designed the crest?" Clara asked. "Any charter?"

"A local engraver," Colby said, eyes sliding lake-ward. "Clubs like that write minutes in toasts."

Lady Grey's fur rose along her spine, a low hum building in her chest.

"You know a lot for a club that left no charters," Clara said, mild as a pin.

Colby's sleeve rode up; for a heartbeat a sailor's tattoo—anchor, rope —ghosted his wrist. He yanked the cuff down. "I read," he said. "I listen when old men stop boasting and start dying. Why vivisect a crest?"

"A piece of silver was found," Amelia said. "Then another. Vernon is dead. Doris stands in the town's sights. We need what the crest means."

"You fancy yourselves archivists of the living," he said softly. "Archivists die when shelves fall."

"What were the Gentlemen beyond myth?" Clara pressed.

"Network. Protection. Convenience," he said at last. "Introductions arranged where no one had to ask in public."

"Liquor," Amelia said.

He didn't answer, which was an answer.

"The silver?" Clara asked. "Payment? Proof?"

"A thing you can hold is a thing you can say we to," he said. "Value binds men to the we."

"Who kept the pieces?" Amelia asked.

"Stories," Colby murmured. "A ladle that poured punch and messages. A sugar spoon that paid a debt. A service divided and cached when the wrong eyes grew curious—under a pier, a floorboard, a garden when the ground was soft."

Lady Grey hissed—no drama, just a cold line.

"I'm sorry for your friend," he said. "I am."

"Then help us," Amelia said.

He rocked once. "The Gentlemen had a motto," he said, almost to himself. "*Quid latet, valet*. What is hidden holds value." He stood. "Lesson and curse."

As he turned, his cardigan snagged; a small brass disk skittered to Lady Grey's paw. His face moved—surprise, calculation. "An old token," he said roughly. "Manufactured nostalgia."

Clara crouched. Half-dollar size: crown over a three-sailed ship; tiny letters around the edge—G.O.S.; softened wear; faint notches at the cardinal points.

"Gentlemen of the Shore," she murmured.

"Give it back," Colby said, heat at last.

Amelia put the token in his palm—trust and witness both. He pocketed it without thanks; that pocket sagged more than its mate.

"We'll go," Amelia said. "Thank you."

"Be careful," he said, and went inside. The door clicked—retreat more than dismissal.

On the porch, Lady Grey pawed at a split board where a knot had been painted over. Amelia eased it up. In the neat hollow: a frayed strip of pale-blue ribbon, a folded card, the brittle corner of a photo. The card bore crown and ship, *Gentlemen of the Shore: Summer Convocation*. Hand-lettered: *M. Colby—Guest*. Year: 1969.

"Guest," Clara said. "A witness with a seat."

Amelia slid the card back, replaced the board. "We didn't come to burglarize a historian," she said. Lady Grey sat, solemn. Not triumph—*noted*.

They took the shortcut home. Clara scribbled while walking: *Token verifies name; motto explains motive; silver as social currency; smuggling embraced rather than admitted. If tokens tracked admission, they may track debts—or who held which piece when.*

"Which makes the set dangerous," Amelia said. "Control the pieces, control the narrative."

"Tell Laurel?" Clara asked.

"Tell her the club's name and motto," Amelia said. "She'll subpoena without asking how we know the ribbon's exact blue."

The square had thinned to pastry-crumb debates. The empty counter where the glass dome had stood rang louder than any bell. A poster announced a council session; beneath it, Laurel's inked warning: *Keep to the point or I will gavel you into brevity.*

Back at the inn, the parlor turned strategy room. Amelia set the fork on the table; its tarnished crest caught lamplight like a sullen eye. Clara boxed **G.O.S.** and **Quid latet, valet**, linking them with an arrow like a fuse.

"Say the service was divided," Clara said. "Pieces cached—spoon and fork in Doris's garden, others along the shore. Who knew? Finches. Colby adjacent. Descendants. If Vernon arrived with debt and rumor, he'd dig—threaten wrong ears."

"And someone made sure he told none," Amelia said.

Lady Grey pressed her paw flat on the fork's crown—claws sheathed, weight saying *hold*.

A knock: three quick, one slow—Laurel's rhythm. "Haines lifted a partial from your service-stair sill," she said, entering. "Not enough to match, enough to make Harlow snarl. Also, our Duluth gentleman —Humphries—keeps a matchbook from Kestrel Bay."

"'K...Y,'" Clara said. "We saw the impression."

"Colby?" Laurel asked.

"Gentlemen of the Shore," Amelia said simply. "Motto, tokens, invites. He confirmed, then un-confirmed. He's terrified of the past's teeth."

"The past bites hardest when muzzled," Laurel said. "I found the name only in charitable donations—masked by a 'Lakeside Improvement Fund.' I can request minutes, bank ledgers, officer names. Give me a place to trade—a piece with a witness who doesn't live in a cardigan."

Amelia's mind skipped stones. "There's a place no one disturbs because everyone assumes someone else owns it."

Clara's eyes lit. "The old lighthouse keeper's shed."

"Shipwright's Point?" Laurel said. "County deed says belongs to nobody—bureaucrat for 'we don't want the maintenance.' It's padlocked."

"Padlocks and lakes," Amelia said. "A romance as old as mistakes."

"If it's county, I don't need a warrant," Laurel said, already turning. "I need bolt cutters and a helpful narrative."

Evening leaned in. They ate soup because soup keeps doubt busy, washed bowls because dishes obey rules. The phone rang after eleven. Laurel's voice came steady, holding two truths. "We have a ladle," she said. "Crown and ship. Tarnish that would make a bishop swear. Wrapped in oilcloth beneath the keeper's cot. Faint initials on the underside—D.F. Likely Doris's father or grandfather. It ties the set to custody, not crime. It buys me hours."

"Tell your cat she's earned her retainer," Laurel added.

"She accepts payment in cream," Amelia said, fragile and grateful.

Lady Grey received the news like a duchess expecting it. In the window's dark glass, a man with a sample case crossed the far edge of the square—Humphries? The silhouette paused, regarded the alley to the inn's service stair, then chose the longer, brighter way like a man trying to look harmless.

"Tomorrow Shipwright's Point with Laurel," Amelia said.

"Circle back to Colby. Keep Harlow from spending the town's patience faster than we can earn it."

"And tonight, sleep if we can," Clara said, sliding her pencil into the notebook's spine.

They dimmed the lamps. Lady Grey took her watch at the upstairs window, tail flicking in slow, satisfied punctuation. Outside, the lake whispered the motto without Latin: what's hidden matters. Inside, two women and a cat settled into a night that felt less like a trap and more like a map.

Chapter 21

Sabotage at the Inn

Morning arrived wrong.

Not loudly—no shattered panes, no shouts—just off, as if the inn had inhaled and forgotten to exhale. Early chatter hiccuped, the samovar rattled late, even the lake hesitated.

Balancing linens, Amelia hummed her route-marking tune—until Lady Grey streaked past, ears flat, tail exclamation.

"Darling?" The cat fired toward the back stair.

At the cellar door she reared and drummed the panel with both paws. The latch slid with a reluctant scrape; cold damp rose—old wood, disturbed earth. Amelia lit the lantern. Steps complained. Lady Grey went first, tight as a spring.

The cellar, usually soldier-neat—wine ranked, preserves squared—looked skewed. Muddy boot prints stitched a careless seam. The far rack sagged as if shoved. In the lantern's wobble: absence. A bottle-shaped gap.

"Château Margaux," Amelia breathed—her parents' anniversary bottle.

Clara arrived, hair awry, apron crooked. "The kettle wouldn't boil, then—oh." She studied the prints. "Too big for a dare. Too careless for anyone who knows your habits." Palm to bowed wood. "They dragged it. The bottle's camouflage."

"Camouflage that knows my heart," Amelia said.

Lady Grey pressed her shoulder to the rack and scratched the lowest strut—her open-sesame. Amelia and Clara unloaded bottle after bottle, glass lined like witnesses. The cat patrolled, tail ticking time.

"Why here?" Amelia whispered.

"Because the wall predates us," Clara said. "Clean spaces under dirty ones. Inns cover noise with noise."

They worked until the room remembered itself. Then Lady Grey sat at the wall right of the rack, paws tucked, stare fixed. Clara tapped with a wooden spoon.

Tap. Tap. Tap—hollow.

"This," Clara said. "Built to open."

They didn't pry. Clara sketched the seam, counted bricks, marked one with a faint X. "Tools later—Laurel and Haines."

They reset the illusion: bottles back, rack braced, dust coaxed over foreign footprints. The latch clicked—not enough, but something.

Upstairs, breakfast demanded hands. Guests brought rumor like luggage. At table three: the county board; by the window: courthouse narrators; Humphries, the bland salesman, ate slowly and smiled on the wrong side.

Laurel arrived on coffee steam, hair wind-snarled. One look at their faces erased hello. "What did the house say?"

"Hollow," Clara answered. "Behind the rack."

"Haines is coming back from the point," Laurel said. "He's charmed by the ladle; he'll learn to love your wall."

"When have we ever waited?" Clara muttered, making Laurel laugh—small relief.

After the plate tide receded, Laurel led them down; Haines followed with a dented tool bag and a patient face. Lady Grey descended at his feet like a furry chaperone.

Tap. Tap—hollow. "Panel," he said. A thin chisel worked the seam; dust sighed. "There's a hook." The section yielded and swung inward. Oilcloth and time.

Inside: a shallow niche lined with boat wood. Three parcels, twined and sealed with a near-flat crown.

Laurel nodded once. "One."

Haines lifted the first bundle, photographed, gloved, slit twine. Silver woke: a ladle, a serving fork, a sugar shell—each crested crown and ship. Tiny letters beneath: D.F.

"Doris's father," Amelia said—prayer and lever.

"Or grandfather," Haines said. "Finch hands, not recent theft." Custody—a bridge word.

Lady Grey tapped the ladle bowl, dainty benediction.

Two more bundles: paired spoons; an extravagant fish slice. Beneath, a scrap clung to the plank. Clara lifted it with tweezers: a sketched shoreline—Shipwright's Point, a dot near the keeper's shed, a second dot under a small rectangle, tiny numerals beside each.

"Two caches," Clara whispered. "Lake and four walls."

"Colby's cottage is a rectangle," Amelia said.

"So is half the town," Laurel answered, but she didn't deny it. The remnant sealed, the inn's underlying hum—icebox, stair light, phone line—went out. The lantern flame stood suddenly alone.

"Power," Clara said. "And phone."

Laurel moved. Haines took the stairs two at a time; Lady Grey streaked after him. At the breaker box: switches fine, wires quiet. "Cut," Haines said. "Clean slice in the alley."

"Who reaches our alley unseen?" Laurel asked.

"Anyone with a bag," Amelia said, Humphries' sample case flashing in memory. "Or a historian with pockets. Or a debt collector. Or—"

"—or someone who doesn't want phones to ring," Clara finished.

They staged calm. Generator on. Tea restored a sliver of order. Lady Grey glowered at the back door like a duchess facing poor manners. Guests cooed over lamplight; Mrs. Lennox called it "positively colonial." Humphries ate with the pace of a man who prefers being elsewhere when others are not.

In the alley, Haines showed Amelia the surgical cut—ends taped back like a warning to sparrows. "They listened for a brick," Amelia said. "When it didn't open, they cut our voice."

Back below, Laurel resealed the niche—canvas and conscience. "We'll document tonight," she said. "For now, undisturbed. If anyone checks, that's its own answer."

They climbed. "Colby first?" Clara asked.

"Laurel first," Laurel said. "Colby second. Humphries third. Harlow last—always last to anything not his idea." To Amelia: "Two locks on your cellar. Something heavy in front that doesn't look like a barricade. Make normal loud so spies must work."

Afternoon unrolled like gauze. Power returned; the phone decided it could reach Laurel. Guests arrived sun-flushed from the point; one announced the keeper's padlock looked "odd," as if he'd discovered a comet. Laurel wrote it down without writing it down.

Near dusk, Amelia noticed the cellar key wasn't where it should be. Not fallen. Gone.

"Clara," she said, face unchanged.

Clara understood. Laurel hadn't left; she came at once. "Assume they made a wax impression days ago," she said. "Today they wanted the real thing." She looked to Lady Grey on the mantel, staring at the empty hook like insult. "All right, Your Grace. Where?"

Lady Grey padded to the service stair and sat, eyes on the knob. The stair whispered if you pressed your ear.

"We watch," Amelia said. "Let them try—not to see the wall opened, but to learn their gait."

"Haines in the alley," Laurel said. "Weston out front in errand-boy disguise with a billy long enough to banish regret. You two do not go to the cellar without me."

"Promise," they said.

They set the stage: lamps low; a book open and unread in Amelia's lap; Clara at the escritoire copying nothing with great seriousness; Lady Grey on the hearth, eyes not closed. Outside, the square thinned; the lake turned pewter.

The first try slid along the alley, retreated when Weston coughed like a large man in a small coat. The second came an hour later, more confident; Haines offered a single polite "Evening," and the shadow remembered elsewhere.

Near midnight, cleverness tried the pantry window. It lifted an inch, then two. A slender hand slipped in, felt for a key that wasn't there, froze when a plan met its first fact. Lady Grey made no sound —only stood and stared. The weight of her regard traveled up the arm to the mind that sent it. After five counts, the hand withdrew. The window sighed shut, embarrassed.

Laurel's knock followed, gentle. "They're learning it won't be simple," she said. "People get dangerous when habits fail."

Amelia steadied her shaking hands on the unread book. "We're past simple," she said. "Past careful."

"Tomorrow we bring a crew and take the wall down clean," Laurel said. "Catalogue and move it to the county vault where Harlow's temper can't reach. Tonight"—she nodded to Lady Grey— "we let your cat keep doing her work."

"Watching," Amelia said.

"Guarding," Clara said.

The inn settled into soldier's sleep—light, alert. Toward morning, when lamps guttered to their last polite inch, Lady Grey padded to Amelia's chair, set both paws on her knee, and looked up.

"Thank you," Amelia whispered—not for the paws, but for a house unbroken, a wall that had given up its quiet, hours bought for Doris.

The cat blinked a slow benediction and returned to her post. A gull laughed once at the new light. The first kettle rattled toward boil. The house exhaled.

And in the cellar, behind canvas and cunning—and a small gray sentinel's attention—silver waited. Not as treasure, but as testimony, while a town prepared to learn which favorite stories would no longer hold.

Chapter 22

Lady Grey Leads the Way

Dawn scraped a pale edge along the lake, dusting roofs with silver. From the inn's back step, Amelia tried to notice the quiet—the late gulls, the birches whispering—yet her mind stayed in the cellar: the clean-sliced service line, Haines's breathing panel, and those oilcloth bundles—ladle, sugar shell, serving fork—each crowned-and-shipped and softly initialed D.F.

Laurel had resealed the niche museum-clean; Haines patched the wire and posted a man in the alley; Weston loitered out front. The house slept with one eye open. Amelia pretended to.

A velvet brush at her ankle: Lady Grey's two-note summons—purpose, not porridge.

"All right," Amelia said. "Show me."

Clara joined with her "unsuitable" ribbon and notebook. Lady Grey led them down the back stair to the cellar door, pressed the familiar spot with authority. Cool air rose—damp stone, vinegar ghost. The braced wine rack stood straighter, still complicit.

But the cat pawed not at Haines's seam—at the rack's back plank. The answering tap was wrong: hollow.

"You're insufferable when you're right," Amelia told the cat.

"We're insufferable," Clara said, sliding bottles with librarian care while Amelia chalked where each stood—order matters.

Clara mapped the sound, eased a paring knife into the seam. The board sighed free: a long, clean cavity between stud and brick. At its center, a blue-black lockbox—corners softened, clasp asleep under rust. Serious weight inside; not coins.

They set it down like a family Bible. Lady Grey sniffed iron and paper, then sat, paws tucked: proceed.

"Vernon wasn't wrong," Clara murmured.

"Someone knew enough to kill him for being right," Amelia said.

"Do we tell Laurel now?" Clara asked.

"Not yet. We read first," Amelia said. "We hand Laurel what Harlow can't twist."

Clara worked the clasp with warm water and patience, eyed the shallow barrel keyway. Hairpins, tension, listening. Click, click—one pin stubborn. Ten minutes later her hand cramped; plan B: borrow Mr. Larkin's smallest miracles.

"Breakfast first," Amelia said, as bacon and yeast climbed the stair.

They slid the box beneath folded linen; Lady Grey stretched along it like an extra lock. "Watch," Amelia said. The cat blinked: obviously.

Upstairs, the hob flamed obedient blue. Guests wanted feeding without admitting the second appetite. Humphries, rumor's chair, admired Prohibition myths and folded his napkin like regret. A newcomer with dealer's hands asked to "view" the café garden; Amelia refused pleasantly.

By ten, dishes quieted. Clara returned with Larkin's kit. In the cellar the cat approved: appropriate tools are moral. Picks like silver fish, a simple turning tool, a rake. Clara listened with metal; twice the core thought about turning and didn't; she went quieter. "Come on, darling. You've held a hundred hands. Hold mine." Consent arrived with a soft sigh; the lid yielded.

They paused—then, together, lifted.

Muslin first. Beneath: envelopes tied with twine; a roll of oilcloth with the flat promise of flatware; at the bottom, a ledger wrapped in leather.

Clara chose a letter marked For D. The seal gave. She read aloud:

Doris,

If this reaches you it means I lacked the courage to say out loud what I did in darkness. The men called it a club. It was a syndicate with table manners… We lied. When it began to turn, I hid what I could where honest hands might find it when law and shame were speaking again. If the law is just, give it the law. If the law is Harlow and his kind, give it to the women who kept the town warm while the men played brave. I am sorry… – A.F.

"Andrew Finch," Amelia said.

They untied the ledger. Columns, neat hand: dates, initials, roles (The Banker, The Shoreman), night deliveries, lake shipments, a tiny spoon-and-fork drawing; the crest sketched once, as if the future needed reminding.

Amelia unrolled the oilcloth: a fish slice patterned between waves and wheat, a heavy serving spoon, a modest pickle fork. On the fish slice's back: *Property of the Gentlemen of the Shore.* Someone had once scratched lightly at *Gentlemen*—as if to make the metal doubt itself.

"It's all here," Clara whispered.

They skimmed enough to see names that still echo, a note square labeled *Keeper's shed*—a twin to yesterday's map scrap—and a fat *V.* in a column that suggested Vernon's debts ran both directions.

They repacked the box precisely, added a dated note with Laurel's name, and—Amelia, half sacrilege, half insurance—slipped a fingernail-square of muslin into her pocket. Lady Grey tapped the plank to match its earlier thunk: restored. Approved.

"Lunch invitation," Amelia said. "We tell Laurel with tea, not telephone."

Laurel arrived at noon; Haines ten minutes later. After touch and meeting, they read A.F., turned the ledger, looked older. "Enough," Laurel said. "Not an ending, but enough to reroute Harlow. He'll try; I'll trip him."

Haines tapped *Keeper's shed.* "Someone goes tonight. I prefer us."

"Done," Laurel said. "Amelia, stay. Clara, write me the warrant I want."

Laurel pressed both palms to the box, then to Lady Grey's gaze. "Guarded here," she decided. "Two plain-clothes admirers of your evening menu posted inside."

The day performed ordinary for those who ignore undertows. A family arrived with too many suitcases. Mrs. Cranston preferred generator coffee. Humphries tipped the wrong amount, staring the jar down while doing it. Clara drafted; Laurel honed knives into scalpels.

Near dusk, Haines and Weston took the back road to the point with ropes and a lantern meant to be trouble. Laurel left by another path. Amelia breathed the prayer that's mostly breath. The lockbox slept under linen; Lady Grey divided her watch between hearth, sill, and service door.

Half past nine: the thin complaint of a service stair board with poor discretion. Lady Grey's ears cut forward. She flowed to the stair, set one paw on the first tread, looked at Amelia: now.

Amelia rang the small silver bell twice. Weston coughed like two large men; Haines's shadow slid along the alley. The knob did not turn. Minds change when they count unseen men.

Laurel slipped in later, lake breeze and old dust on her cuff. "The keeper's shed had a false floor," she said. "No body. A crate like your box, and a colder ledger—names you won't love, sums that explain Vernon. We have both. Harlow will have to come to me."

"And Colby?" Clara asked.

"Nine sharp," Laurel said. "Haines, a warrant, my best smile. We'll be polite, and we won't leave without his long memory."

"Doris?" Amelia whispered.

"Soon," Laurel said. "Soon enough Harlow will call it premature and I'll call it preventative medicine."

The inn finally exhaled. The kettle sighed. Lady Grey finished her circuit and curled atop the linen that hid the box—period and pledge.

Amelia set the pen where her aunt had always left it and looked at the house the way you look at someone you love while they're still in the room. It contained the day. It contained the hurt. It contained, for now, the proof.

"Tomorrow," Clara said, "we open the rest—with light, a camera, and a lawyer."

"Tonight," Amelia said, "we practice the smaller bravery of sleeping."

Lady Grey blinked—benediction—and tucked her head under her paw.

Outside, the lake lifted the moon with practiced grace. Inside, under linen and watch and will, the lockbox held still—its contents not treasure so much as testimony: names, numbers, and a letter that had finally reached its Doris. At the top of the stair, the little silver bell waited—ready to speak if the house needed a voice again.

Chapter 23

The Lockbox's Secrets

The cellar fogged at Amelia's lips and swallowed the lantern's uneven glow. Stone kept its counsel; preserves cast squat shadows; bottle shoulders offered a dull glint. Iron damp mixed with the bitter ghost of old ink. In the middle, the lockbox waited—steel matte with years, corners softened by patience.

They lifted the lid together. Linen, mildew, the mineral dry of ink exhaled. No coins; no glitter. Paper. Letters bound with thread-bare ribbon, swollen envelopes, a ledger strapped in leather. Underneath, an oilcloth roll—flatter, promising metal wrapped in muslin.

Gloves on, Clara moved the top bundle to a towel. Lady Grey leaned in, drew the scent, and sat back: at last.

The first sheets refused coyness—columns, dates, amounts: tidy math for wrong deeds. Across the top, Deliveries—night. Weeks down the side; numbers that didn't belong to fish on the right.

"Smuggling manifests," Clara murmured. "Late '31 into '33. Short runs in '34, '36." A cramped marginal note: weather held—fog assisted—watch bell muffled. "Minutes like a club; records like a syndicate."

Names tucked into columns, plain and coded: Finch in two

hands; Holloway; Denvers; a C. with a flourish; Keeper written as if title were disguise. A second hand—impatient, heavier—threaded through.

"Our own," Amelia said. Anger arrived like grief.

Lady Grey tapped barrels shifted, then fixed her gaze on the stack: continue.

IOUs slid loose—foxed edges, shabby urgency: to be settled next run; in kind if not coin; two bottles to J. for silence; for M.—favors later. Signatures muddied by haste and fear.

"These alone blot half the portraits," Clara said evenly. "It isn't just taking. It's owing."

Amelia found thicker paper, ink newer: V. Finch—knows. Demands share. No date. The jagged speed of a hand writing too fast for posterity.

"Vernon," she whispered. "Not just swagger. He had this—in his hand."

"Leverage," Clara said. "Or a gun he didn't know how to hold. Either way, anyone near these lines had reason to quiet him."

Amelia's hands shook. Lady Grey pressed her head to Amelia's wrist—an anchor, purr rising like a small motor.

Clara lifted the leather-tied ledger. Inside: same columns, fewer euphemisms. Along one margin: minutes kept separately—by the Master—burn on order, the last words scratched like an argument with itself.

"They called themselves gentlemen to make crime feel like a hobby," Clara said. She turned a page and stopped. "Oh."

"What?"

She angled it. A 1932 row—two raids in the paper, one missing— read: South wall behind racks—Tumblebrook House, triple-checked, beside a small rectangle. Another note: key by A.F.—if necessary, improvise.

"They wrote my cellar down," Amelia said, both loyal and livid.

They worked down through seasons; names recurred, some struck through as if erasure absolved. Folded small, oil-stained: a sketch map—lighthouse point, Keeper shed, floor penciled by a cut square. Clara tapped *we beat you there* and slid it into an envelope for Laurel.

They unrolled the oilcloth together. Muslin stitched and restitched; three pieces lay on decades of softness: a fish slice hammered between wave and sheaf; a shallow serving spoon; a small knife split at the tip—a pickle fork if you spoke the dialect. Each handle wore the crown-and-ship. On the slice's underside: *Property of the Gentlemen of the Shore.* Someone had once knifed gently at *Gentlemen*—as if to make the metal doubt them.

"Not just paying with silver," Clara said. "Paying with identity."

"And hiding it under a woman's wine," Amelia said. She rewrapped the pieces. "These stay here under watch until Laurel can move them where Harlow needs permission to breathe."

They copied—Clara precise, Amelia relentless. The cellar turned scriptorium; the lantern, a monkish sun. Lady Grey patrolled: table, stair, rack, back; listening between their breaths. They took rubbings of signatures, traced the map, transcribed IOUs without "improving" grammar. Two sets where possible—one for Laurel's vault, one hidden here. Originals into a fresh envelope: *Primary Evidence— Keep Sealed Unless Counsel Present.*

Halfway through, a board above betrayed a nightly conspirator's foot. Lady Grey froze. The room shrank; oil hissed softly. The sound didn't return. Only then did Amelia feel how hard she'd gripped the table.

Clara resumed. "We tell Laurel before midday. Haines enough to move bodies. No more."

Amelia nodded. "And we walk like two men with hats down are timing us."

More sums; a line that made Amelia hiss: *Payment held at inn until Keeper clears.* In the margin: *C. will object. Overrule.* Colby's porch face rose—too-casual lies, the faded blue-black under his cuff.

The lantern dimmed; Clara fed it. They sorted, copied, rewrapped. Originals back in exact order—linen, envelopes, ledger, oilcloth—with a fresh page atop: Catalog begun, and a list for the next honest opener.

Amelia drew linen over the box and set the plank with hinge-level care. Lady Grey pressed a paw to the board, listened for the right hollow, then hopped down with soft approval.

At the stairs, Clara paused—fatigue and ferocity sharing her face. "We can't keep the house safe by making it a museum," she said. "But we can make it safer by telling truth in the right order."

"That's you," Amelia said. "Right order."

"And you," Clara said frankly. "Right home."

Upstairs, the kitchen had the collapsed look of a room remembering itself. Amelia poured two teas because ritual counts. Lady Grey sat on the ledger page where Keeper—floor was penciled, stamping it filed. Her purr rose low and even, like a still lake—complete.

"In the morning," Amelia said, "Laurel first. Copies in hand. She opens it in the vault with Haines present, then calls Harlow after she's written the words he'll have to repeat."

"You make it sound like a service," Clara said.

"It will be."

They tried for sleep and achieved something adjacent. When a thin noise lifted, Lady Grey was already upright on the coverlet—eyes bright, ears forward—a hunter turned sentinel.

Morning arrived reluctantly. Mist lifted from the lake and snared in birches. Amelia lit lamps against the gray, slid scones into the oven—busy hands for memorizing minds. Cold air at the back door had opinions. Clara came with hair tied in her ribbon of intention and three envelopes: Laurel, Vault, Doris.

"Walk with me?" she asked.

"Through a town whose names are in our pockets?" Amelia said. "You're not leaving my reach."

Weston stood guard at the desk with a book he hadn't read and a look he'd been waiting to wear. Laurel's door opened before they knocked.

"Primary findings," Clara said, setting the first envelope down. "Rubbings. Not exhaustive. Sufficient."

Laurel read like a good mind accepting weight—narrowing, widening, a small exhale at A.F., leashed anger at Gentlemen, surprised grief at For D. Her jaw ticked at Payment held at inn.

"Harlow will howl," she said. "He'll call this gossip aged into delusion. He'll say the kettle is enough."

Clara slid over Vault. "Then lock the thing that can drown him."

"At ten I'll be in his office with your note to Doris and the ledger. He'll see she is innocent by noon or at five, depending on the distance between pride and sense. We'll accept either and forgive neither."

"Colby?" Amelia asked.

"Nine sharp," Laurel said. "Warrant and a piano teacher's patience."

Outside, the square was awake, not comfortable. People wanted to look without being seen looking. Humphries half-raised his hat and regretted it midair. Mrs. Cranston began a sentence and lost herself at the comma.

Back at the inn, breakfast learned itself. The world doesn't stop for revelation; it rearranges to hold it. Amelia poured steady coffee; Clara translated questions at table four into the language of none of your business. Lady Grey patrolled, then paused at the cellar, regarded the linen-swaddled silver, and set her paw on the fold like a signature.

"Tonight," Amelia whispered—confession and oath—"we finish copying. Tomorrow Laurel carries it into light so shadows have fewer places to hide."

Lady Grey blinked—consent—and moved to the stair. The house hummed. The lake glittered at noon and feigned innocence. And the lockbox—behind wood, behind brick, behind a cat—kept the soundless thrum of the town's heart, written at last in a hand that would not blur when it was needed most.

Chapter 24

Doris in Distress

The café smelled of warm bread and thyme, but cheer wouldn't stick. Festival bunting frayed outside; inside, careful voices oiled every stare. Doris had opened by seven —kettle on, scones in—insisting routine might steady her. It didn't.

Amelia and Clara slipped in during a lull, Lady Grey padding to her hearth post—curled neat, ears busy. Doris moved with a smile that had lost its anchor, wiping her apron more than flour required.

"Busy is a blessing," she told Amelia, voice thin. A glance toward a whispering table made her sway.

"Doris!" Amelia caught her as the coffeepot clinked down. Chairs scraped; water appeared; Clara slid a folded sweater under Doris's head. Lady Grey planted herself at Doris's feet, tail puffed, purr steady as a motor.

A minute lengthened; Doris exhaled and blinked back. "Too much of them," she whispered, eyes flicking to Mrs. Cranston's stare.

"Sip," Amelia said, cool cloth to temple. "All's well. Back to breakfasts."

The room resumed its performance of normal—forks tapping,

throats clearing—while whispers softened and sharpened: stress of guilt... family curse... Harlow already—

"Whispers make a rope," Clara murmured. "We need a knife."

"Truth," Amelia said. "Slower than rumor."

They settled Doris in the fireside chair. Lady Grey hopped up and kneaded her apron until Doris let out a watery laugh. Clara, all librarian steel, ushered lingerers to pay and leave.

"I can't hold steady," Doris breathed. "Like the whole world's leaning—waiting to say 'told you so.'"

"Let it lean," Amelia said. "It can fall on us for a change."

"Then find who did it," Doris said. "Before Harlow pins my apron to his board."

At the counter, Clara caught a new thread—Duluth debts around Vernon—then rejoined them. "We'll find them. New rules: you never open alone. Weston or I at dawn; Amelia afternoons; I'll pry a patrol from Haines."

"Bless Laurel," Doris said faintly.

"In your office," Amelia said. "Feet up. Tea."

They shepherded her into the squat office. Lady Grey sniffed the air, ears tall, then pawed the inbox: a square cream envelope, no return address, wax cracked.

"Open it," Doris said, flat with dread.

Clara lifted a card, letters blocky and ragged: **STAY SHUT.** On the back: crown over ship.

Dust motes stilled.

"Placed where you'd be alone," Clara said. "To frighten—or justify what comes next."

"I won't give them satisfaction," Doris whispered.

"You won't give them opportunity either," Amelia said.

Lady Grey carried the card to the counter and set it by the tip jar: show them.

"Room first," Doris said, steadier. "Let the town see it."

Amelia raised the card. "Someone left this for Doris—the same someone hiding behind notes and gossip. She'll open when she chooses and serve the kind. News goes to police; cruelty to the lake. Until then—eat your scones."

That pricked the room's conscience. The bell chimed; the café exhaled. Hattie arrived with lemon drops and command. "Sit. Drink. Chew. I'll guard the door and the manners."

Laurel met them briskly; Haines watched rumor like weather. Clara set copies on the desk. "Enough to wedge a door."

"We'll post an alley uniform," Haines said.

"Bring the STAY SHUT note," Laurel added. "Public threats change tolerance."

They handed over the card, rubbings, names—wide margins redacted. Laurel read, swore once. "Say 'Gentlemen of the Shore' again," she muttered, "and I'll rename the pier Hypocrites' Dock."

Before leaving, she caught Amelia's sleeve. "You're nowhere near Harlow at three. I'll be the mouth. Your job is to stay alive."

Back at the café, dignity reassembled around Hattie's glare and the note on display. People read, tipped awkwardly. Doris had enough color to scold Hattie for overfilling a custard tart. "You'll ruin shapes."

"I'll ruin decorum before hunger," Hattie said.

The back door chimed: Haines, hat in hand, then Laurel—seen, steadying the room by existing. "We've begun," she told Doris. "Two copies where Harlow can't reach."

It held until the roses. Brown-papered, courier "no one." Too-red blooms; inside, a crest-embossed card, ink heavy as a ledger smear.

"Photographs," Laurel said, voice a knell. "Then dry them. Not here where fear eats sugar."

Effect achieved: the room moved further to Doris's side.

On the walk back to the inn for sandwiches, Clara's indignation stretched. "They stamped threats, roses, silver—loved that crown more than the town."

"They captained a ship that never left shore," Amelia said.

On the desk lay another scrap in the same hand: **LEAVE THE PAST.**

"We're fond of digging," Clara said dryly.

"Let them buy more paper," Amelia said. "We'll use it to wrap scones when this is done."

They ate quick bread—chewing keeps hands busy while minds sharpen. Lady Grey stood sentry at the cellar door. Plans formed: finish copies tonight; Laurel makes it official tomorrow; then speak in the square—Haines up front, Laurel beside him, Doris with free coffee, Weston with a bell, Lady Grey judging from the fountain rim.

They returned with sandwiches and a plan disguised as chatter. Laurel kept promise—seen by Doris, laughed at something small, left with a folder and Haines—law and care walking together. The room softened. Teenagers left a note under the sugar jar: *We believe you, Ms. Finch.*

At three, Laurel phoned: the vault had the ledger; Harlow had not charged Doris today. "We bought time. Spend it like cash."

Evening pressed gold back into the windows. Those who came did it on purpose now. The threat card collected coins and resentment. The back door rattled—paused—moved on under Haines's shadow. The room relaxed.

"My grandmother's grandmother said secrets are muscles or tumors," Doris murmured near close. "Some keep you strong. Some grow until you're made of them."

"This one's a tumor," she added. "Cut it out."

"We're working on it," Clara said.

"Go home," Doris ordered, maternal again. "You look grey."

"Not you," she told Lady Grey, scratching behind her ear. "You're perfect."

They left with the last light. Haines took his alley post; Weston locked up with a conspirator's pride. On the inn porch, lake breath cooled Amelia's face. "Tomorrow," Clara said. "Copies, Colby, the square. Keep Doris upright until Laurel's paper works."

"Tonight," Amelia said, "we let Lady Grey do hers."

The cat had already taken station at the cellar door, tail neatly wound. They descended to cool iron and steady damp. The lockbox waited, patience made object. Amelia laid a hand on its lid and felt—irrationally, honestly—the same rhythm as the cat's purr, the lake's lap, and Doris's breath beginning to even.

"Tomorrow," she told the room. The cellar kept its temperature, listened, and did not tell.

Chapter 25

Hidden Enemies

Sun came up knife-bright, turning the lake to scales and making Tumblebrook squint. Carts rattled, tempers shortened, children ran until a parent's bark skimmed them to the curb. Vernon Finch's death sat like grit—chores possible, comfort not.

Amelia swept the inn steps in long, even arcs, trying to keep her thoughts in rhythm: Doris pretending not to flinch at the café bell; Laurel sharpening law; the lockbox in the cellar warming like a coal; Haines's alley patrol there because the mayor insisted. Clara leaned on the rail, muttering dates and initials over her notebook. Lady Grey lay like a silken scarf, eyes half-shut, ears working.

They didn't notice the shadow until it crossed Amelia's broom.

"Mrs. Farnsworth," the man said. Tall, tidy, dusted by travel, hat lifted with a flourish a little too pleased with itself. A thick folder rode his arm.

"I am," Amelia said. "And you are—?"

"Henry Wycliffe. Antiques dealer. Collector. Historian, when honesty allows. I'm calling about property. A spoon brazenly displayed at your recent festivities."

Lady Grey slid off the rail and sat at the porch edge, tail a question mark.

"And your business with our spoon?" Amelia asked.

He fanned papers like a croupier—browned letters, ledger leaves, an invoice stamped with a crown and ship. "This service was commissioned by my family in the 1890s. Our crest is on every piece. Your spoon bears it. The law calls that proof."

Clara skimmed without asking. " 'Twelve place settings... fish set... tea service.' No household name. A post office box. 'Bill second address on delivery.' Odd for respectability."

"Discretion," Wycliffe said. "A virtue of the prosperous."

"Or the smuggled," Clara returned. "These are copies."

His smile iced. Lady Grey rose and hissed—bone-deep, no drama. Wycliffe flinched; along the fence a boy whispered, "Cat knows."

"Your animal has poor manners," he said.

"She has an excellent sense for character," Amelia said.

He shut the folder with a crack. "If the spoon is not returned— expect restitution. Skeletons rattle when you open the wrong cupboard." A shallow bow, and he was gone, leaving whispers to trail him.

"He's here for leverage," Clara said, writing Skeletons—what cupboard? "Papers to terrify, not prove."

Lady Grey kneaded Amelia's lap until her breath remembered better work.

"Let's see if his crest matches ours," Clara said. "If not, he's hitching his name to someone else's stain."

Inside felt cooler—the way fear pulls heat from a room. Amelia poured coffee like a spell. By ten, Clara had an armful of heraldry from Mr. Larkin; by eleven, a note from Laurel via Haines: Do not let Harlow see Wycliffe's papers before I do. Haines had added: Please.

In the parlor's good light, Clara spread lockbox pages and the sketch of the crest; Lady Grey perched like a whiskered magistrate.

"Crown first," Clara said: five points, crosslet, pearl rim.

Wycliffe's showed four visible points, primmer lines. "Ship?" Ours has three etched planks; his two. Sails lean differently. "Not the same die."

"Maybe not the same maker," Amelia said.

"Or a reproduction," Clara murmured, studying the invoice stamp. "Edge too crisp for pressure. Convenient."

Lady Grey set a paw on the crest, then on the lockbox line V. Finch—knows. Demands share.

"Your cat annotates," Clara said.

They worked until light reached the windows. Piece by piece, Wycliffe's certainty frayed.

At noon Laurel welcomed Haines with a tin of sandwiches. "He came to me first," she said. "Announced he'd sue Doris, you, the festival committee, and—my favorite—my office for 'encouraging criminal culture with bunting.' I offered my vault or the bin; he chose huff."

"He won't be the last," she added. "Paper proves money sat where it shouldn't."

"Hidden enemies," Amelia said.

"The kind that introduce themselves," Laurel said, passing Haines a list. "Two more uniforms will drift. Quietly."

Lady Grey watched the square. Three people studied the fountain too hard. Haines read the street without moving.

"Can we release a town statement soon?" Amelia asked.

"Two days," Laurel said. "Midday in the square. Harlow will attend. And you won't be the ones talking."

Clara bristled; Laurel stayed kind but immovable. "Let me be the mouth. Be the bones."

Haines tucked a note in his pocket. "We'll watch Colby's house too. He's... active."

"Active?" Amelia asked.

"Produced minutes with opinions that needed a warning label," Haines said. "Then walked the pier twice speaking to no one."

Laurel stood. "Don't go anywhere alone. If Wycliffe returns, summon me. He respects the doors he thinks will resist him."

By late afternoon, the inn became a sieve for whispers again: a salesman swore Vernon met a man like Wycliffe in a Duluth lobby; a retired teacher remembered pouring drinks for "gentlemen" who toasted carefully; a young mother repeated a story of a crate lost and found in reeds by the boathouse. Each scrap entered into Clara's notebook.

After supper, Weston arrived with a twine-bound packet from Mr. Larkin. Inside: a thin ledger; a battered booklet—*Shoreline Gentlemen's Club*; three calling cards; a parchment crest with initials H.D., E.W., C.F.

"E.W.," Amelia said. "Edward Wycliffe?"

"Or Edwin-something," Clara said. Names pricked: Finch. Holloway. Denvers. Wycliffe. Two entries were just dashes. Lady Grey's tail flicked; she sat on the ledger like a paperweight with opinions.

They copied stains and opened the thin ledger: dinners, dues, then deliveries: night—2 crates; boathouse—late; payment: silver (crest). On a fragile page: *ware to Margaux.*

"Margaux," Amelia murmured—like the stolen bottle. "Or a code."

"Smugglers love a pun," Clara said. "If hiding spots wore wine names..."

Lady Grey trotted toward the cellar and meowed. "Lamp," Amelia said. "And the small hammer."

Cool iron air, lantern gold. The lockbox waited, lid closed, heavier for being known. "Bordeaux left, Burgundy right," Clara mapped. "Margaux... here." Tap, tap—solid; then an eager hollow behind a crate Amelia hadn't moved in years. Mortar teased, a brick surrendered, and behind it: oilskin tied with tired twine. Inside: tarnished silver—a fish fork with the crest, a ladle, two spoons.

"Not a full set," Clara said, throat tight. "Enough to prove the set and this hiding place."

Lady Grey sniffed each piece, chirped, then froze—ears pricked. Overhead: slick shoe on stone; the back-door latch failed to catch; then deliberate silence.

Amelia lowered the lantern. "Front stairs," she mouthed. Weston nodded and slipped off. Silver rewrapped, brick replaced—enough to slow, not stop. They climbed into amber parlor light.

A figure stood at the front desk, brim shadowing his face. Not Wycliffe—shorter, broader. The polished dealer who'd shadowed Vernon at the festival.

"Evening," Amelia said, only a woman in an apron. "The desk is closed. If you need a room, we're full."

He turned. A smile tried and failed. "Terribly sorry. Thought I left a parcel." The accent shifted. "Mr. Ash."

"First name?" Clara asked mildly.

"Edwin." His glance slid across ledger, cubbies, keys. "I admire your inn."

"Admiration pays best in daylight," Amelia said. "We open at seven."

"Then I'll return." He left carefully. Men trying to appear innocent are taught not to look back.

"E.W.," Clara repeated. "From the booklet."

"Wycliffe's cousin," Amelia said.

"Or a man willing to be mistaken for one," Clara said.

Lady Grey sniffed the bell and sneezed. "Agreed," Amelia said.

They slept poorly. Morning brought frosted-glass sky and a wind even the lake respected. Amelia proofed dough; Clara inked; Weston beat eggs; Lady Grey performed a census. Doris arrived with lemon bars and the STAY SHUT card like a dare. "If you can't fight a rumor," she said, "feed it until it slows."

Customers came on deliberate feet. Haines stood long enough to be noticed; Laurel swept through with a nod that could mean greeting or warning; Mrs. Cranston brought an unsolicited pie and cut slices big enough to make suspicion drowsy.

At ten, Wycliffe returned—hat heroically clean—and tried a

smile on Laurel. It slid off. "Submit documents," she said. "Or enjoy the coffee. Two days. Present your claim in daylight."

"Public trials are an American vice," he said.

"Transparency is a local virtue," Laurel replied.

He left, careful not huffy. From a far table, Ash watched and wrote in a little book neither ledger nor diary.

By noon, Mr. Larkin delivered a yellow telegram that made hearts jump by habit. Clara read and coughed. "Duluth. The silversmith's granddaughter—Nora G.—says the crown-and-ship die went missing in 1931. She has correspondence. Passing through tonight. Seven."

"Laurel will want to listen," Amelia said.

"Harlow will try," Clara said.

"We host here with witnesses," Amelia said. "And cookies."

The parlor became a set: chairs in a semicircle, tea tray ready, lockbox back in the cellar, freshly found silver photographed and rewrapped. Nora arrived—sensible shoes, brooch shaped like an anvil.

"My grandfather trained under Unterberg," she said, shaking hands like forging a pact. "Order for a crown-and-ship crest in 1893 —client named Wycliffe. In 1931 the die went missing. He suspected men with lake voices—smugglers. A stolen die lets anyone stamp a gentleman onto a thief."

"So Wycliffe's crest could be his, theirs, or no one's," Laurel said.

Nora nodded. Lady Grey sniffed the letters, approved, then pivoted to the window. Ash stood across the street watching the reflection, lighting a cigarette he didn't inhale. He flicked it away with a wrist that said, *See me.*

"Two days," Laurel said to the air. "Let them come."

After Nora left—to embarrassed applause—another knock. Colby. He hovered, bones remembering they could break.

"Don't make me sit," he said. "If I sit, I'll stay."

"Then stand," Laurel said. "And speak."

"The club was meant to 'promote the shoreline,' " he said. "Men don't like rooms named for their crimes. When I was young, I carried a box from a boathouse to a cellar and practiced not asking. I've held the town together with string. The string cut my hands." He fumbled out a key. "Small safe in my office, false back—originals I couldn't burn when my wife asked me to cleanse the house."

Laurel took it. "Go home. Leave the door unlocked for Haines."

"I'm tired of being suspicious," he said, and left before tea could shame him.

Tasks portioned: Laurel to Colby; Haines to shadow Ash without theatre; Amelia to tuck the new silver deeper; Clara to draft a statement with scalpels instead of adjectives. In the cellar, Lady Grey paused and looked up: question or promise. "Together," Amelia said.

They sealed the brick better, smoothed mortar with the back of a spoon, slid the lockbox under a crate too heavy for curiosity. Lady Grey paced, approved.

Back upstairs, Weston tried and failed to wear an ordinary face. He held a folded note—no envelope, smelling of tobacco and rain. The same blocky hand, ink pressed hard enough to dent:

TWO DAYS IS TOO LONG.
FINDERS KEEPERS.
LEAVE THE REST.

Below, a wax seal—cleaner, deeper, precise—the crest struck by a real die.

Clara looked to Laurel; Laurel to Haines; Haines to the door as if sight might pull the sender back.

Lady Grey rested her paw on the seal and met Amelia's eyes.

"Hidden enemies," Amelia said, voice leveled for everyone's fear. "Then we won't hide."

Laurel slid the note into a folder as if sheathing a knife. "Two days," she said, as if words could make time behave. "They don't choose the tempo."

Amelia moved to the window. The square had quieted; the fountain's lip shone like a coin. Near the boathouse, wind ran a hand through reeds. Upstairs, a guest turned; the house took the weight and did not complain.

"Two days," she said—to Laurel, to the night, to the cat. "We hold."

Lady Grey's purr rose—not a lullaby; a drum.

Chapter 26

The Threat Escalates

The wind off Tumblebrook Lake had teeth that evening. It threaded through streets with an out-of-season chill, snapped porch flags like reprimands, and pressed curtains tight as if the glass itself were breathing. Inside the inn, fire glowed and lamplight spread a fragile warmth—an eggshell over a drumbeat.

Clara's notes sprawled across the desk like constellations—names orbiting dates, arrows chasing rumors, the crest redrawn until the paper thinned. Lady Grey prowled in deliberate loops, tail flicking, eyes on corners that never quite stayed still. Amelia stood by the window, watching the lake hold its breath.

Clara noticed the envelope first.

It lay half-swallowed beneath the front door, parchment trembling with each draft—a paper heartbeat. She rose, pointed. Amelia crossed the room, crouched, and slid a nail beneath the flap.

You're stirring ghosts that don't forgive.

The handwriting bit into the paper, strokes gouged as if the pen were a knife. Amelia read twice, then handed it to Clara. The hearth's glow shrank.

"Different hand," Clara murmured, comparing it to the earlier warning—*Some treasures best remain buried.* "The first wanted theatre. This one wants to spit in our tea. See the 'g'? Angry. Scared."

"So not one ghost," Amelia said. "A chorus."

Lady Grey sprang to the desk, tapped the note twice, and—without hesitation—dropped it into the fire. Paper curled, blackened, and sighed into ash.

"Lady Grey!" Clara started forward.

"It's all right," Amelia said. "We only needed what we already saw." The cat's purr rose—not comfort, but cadence. "Let it burn."

"Two hands," Clara said. "At least two people scrambling to keep the past buried." She exhaled. "Smuggling gave them a private stage. We've pulled the curtain too soon."

Amelia poured tea that cooled before reaching the desk. "We divide the hunt. I'll take Vernon's orbit—debts, threats, Duluth shadows. You trace the money—who profited long after the barrels went dry."

Clara was already writing. "And we stop assuming the killer is singular. Vernon stood in a circle. Anyone could have stepped forward—or pushed."

Something thumped in the alley. Lady Grey's ears flicked toward the back door. She padded down the hall, pausing—coming?

They found the latch unnervingly straight, but unseated. "Haines checked this after supper," Amelia whispered.

"Fresh scuff," Clara said. "Someone eased it, then thought better."

Lady Grey stood on her hind legs, paw to the iron, indicating, not scratching. Amelia slid the bolt home. The sound felt good.

Back in the parlor, she lifted the telephone receiver. A bright hum answered—then died. She jiggled the cradle. Nothing.

"Lines are cut," Clara said, grabbing her coat. "We fetch."

"Weston!" Amelia called. The young man appeared like hope. "To the mayor's. Tell Haines our line's gone dumb and we're collecting notes like postage."

He nodded and vanished into the weather.

They waited, listening to the inn breathe—the difference between ordinary and wrong. Fire popped. Boards creaked—the right ones. Then a new sound: *tink*—glass, sugar scattering.

The pantry window had surrendered a triangle of glass to a rock wrapped in paper. The pebble landed in the sugar bowl, the pouch splitting open. Across the crystals, a smear of dark wax bore the crest: crown over ship.

"Too tidy," Clara said. "They wanted the seal seen. A breadcrumb for Harlow."

Amelia lifted the paper with a fork. The wax was still pliable, stamped by a clean die. "For Laurel," she said. "With sugar for her town they're salting."

Haines arrived with Weston and the storm on his coat. He took in the scene. "It's for show," he said. "A placard—'This way to the past.' Laurel's on her way."

"Is Doris safe?" Amelia asked.

"In her office, sandwich in hand," he said. "She's out of this one."

"Laurel?"

"Coming." He handed them a whistle. "Three blasts, and I'll wake the dead."

Lady Grey sniffed the sugar, sneezed, and pressed her paw onto the wax seal as if signing off.

Laurel entered crisp and cold. She examined the cut line, the sugar, the note. "Two hands, one staged rock," she said. "Someone frightened, someone theatrical. They're trying to crowd us. We won't hurry."

"Wycliffe?" Clara asked. "Or Ash?"

"Ash is a hired echo. Wycliffe's too proud to whisper." Laurel slipped the note into an envelope marked *EVIDENCE.* "We'll watch both."

Wind skittered in the alley again. Haines reappeared. "Half your carriage bolts loosened. You'd have spun off at the bridge."

"Then we walk," Laurel said. "Or borrow Mrs. Winthrop's pony cart."

The lineman fixed the cut wires. Laurel's call to her office was short, precise. "Call in Larkin," she said when she hung up. "If the bookshop's been a haven, it's now a ladder."

Mr. Larkin arrived, cardigan and indignation in tow. "Someone pried my back door," he announced. "Didn't get in—but the knob feels jellied."

"Glue," Haines said. "A quiet man's jam."

"You're safe here," Laurel said. "Weston, Room Two. Mr. Larkin, bring what you can carry in two arms and a stubborn heart."

The inn turned watchful. Clara photographed the crest and sugar scatter; Amelia brewed coffee strong enough to melt worry; Haines checked latches. Lady Grey patrolled the halls like a general inspecting her line.

At half past eleven, bells—three—from the far square. "Larkin's shop," Haines said. He and Laurel were moving before the sound died.

They found the back door cracked, the shop breathing fear and paper. A glass case's lock was snapped; contents gone.

"What was here?" Laurel asked.

"Calling cards," Larkin said. "The Shoreline booklet. A ledger—thin—and gone."

Haines scanned prints. "Two men. One careful, one not." He pointed at toppled books. "Came in back, out front."

The bell jangled. A shadow fled down the square. Haines caught a sleeve, took an elbow. The man—Ash—vanished between bakery and bank.

"Let him go," Laurel said. "He knows we know."

They listed what was stolen, swept the rest. "When they can't shake us," Clara said, "they erase the evidence."

"They forget truth isn't paper," Laurel said. "It's people."

Back at the inn, the threats multiplied—hinge oiled silent, alley lamp unscrewed, vase nudged wrong. None violent. All meant.

"Death by small cautions," Amelia said. "They want us tired."

"We won't," Clara said, yawning. "Shifts. Weston till one, me till three, Amelia till dawn. Laurel doesn't sleep."

"I sleep like a lion," Laurel said. "Briefly, with claws."

At two, paper rasped under a door—Doris's office. They crossed the square, entered quietly.

The room was neat—receipt books, tea jars, pencils lined like soldiers. On the floor, a white envelope. No seal.

Laurel opened it.

Return what isn't yours and you can keep what is.
We know where you sleep.

Inside: a photograph of Amelia's window, lamp on, a woman drawing curtains. On the back, the crest.

Lady Grey stepped in, sniffed, and the low growl that rose wasn't a hiss—it was a promise.

"Enough," Laurel said. "Morning we go public. Harlow stands with us or regrets it. We'll show what we can prove, name what we can't. Take the dark away from them."

"And if they escalate?" Amelia asked.

"We escalate back," Laurel said. "With light. With names."

Lady Grey jumped onto the counter where the spoon once gleamed and thumped her tail—a verdict.

Back at the inn they nailed the back latch, tied a bell thread at the cellar stairs, hid one wrapped piece of silver in flour—no thief searches a larder. They wrote letters to themselves explaining their choices—proof of courage in handwriting.

At four, Amelia stood by her window, watching fishermen cross the square under pewter sky. The wind had softened. Dawn arrived shy and certain.

Another envelope slid under the door—deep, unbroken seal. Laurel and Haines beside her, Clara perched nearby.

TWO DAYS IS TOO LONG.
We warned you.

Inside: a brass key, its bow shaped like a crown, and two kernels of wheat.

"Crown, key, wheat," Clara murmured. "The crates marked C/K/W—maybe not locations, but people."

"Or both," Laurel said. "They love riddles. We'll answer with truth."

Lady Grey leapt to the sill, tail flicking as dawn spilled across the room.

"They threatened with ghosts," Laurel said. "We'll answer with names."

Chapter 27

The Second Murder

Morning broke pale and unsettled, the sky a muddle of gray that refused to open. Tumblebrook moved in hushed currents; spoons tapped like timid birds. Doris Finch tied on her apron with a brave mouth and raw eyes, serving toast as if it might shatter.

Amelia tried to let breakfast steady her—napkin, plate, pour—but the room's weight rode her like an extra shawl. Clara tapped her pencil in the corner, names from the lockbox colonizing another page. Lady Grey had the windowsill, watching not sparrows but the ribbon of river at the street's end, a low growl caught in her throat.

The scream cut the town clean in two.

It came from the water—too raw to be anything but real. Doris dropped a tray; mugs burst into bright shards. "Down by the river!" someone cried.

Amelia and Clara were already moving, the bell clanging behind them. Lady Grey streaked ahead—sure paws, tail high. Townsfolk boiled from shops; whispers outran feet; the church bell chimed once by accident, then twice as if it had learned something.

By the reeds a clumsy ring had formed—fishermen hat-in-hand, boys on fence rails, Mrs. Cranston breathing through a handkerchief. At the center lay Henry Wycliffe, ruined in the way tidy men cannot bear: coat muddied, cuff dark, hat rocking in the shallows. One hand clutched his chest; the other gripped a torn ledger page.

Chief Harlow bent over him, jaw clamped. He lifted the page and read, voice made to be obeyed: "**The Silver Spoon Heist.**"

The words rang. Two bodies in a week dragged the story from rumor to blood.

"He had something," Clara said.

"And someone stopped him bringing it to us," Amelia answered, eyeing the fresh black letters.

Lady Grey slipped through knees to the body, sniffed the page once before Harlow tucked it away, then turned to the water. Ears sharpened; tail wrote slow punctuation. Reeds trembled with no wind.

"Something else is down there," Amelia whispered.

"Or someone," Clara said.

"Back," Harlow ordered, strain leaking through scold.

Laurel arrived coat unbuttoned, boots muddy without apology. Haines came with rope and two men better at boats than speeches. "Sweep the bank," he said. "Could be a fall. Could be a throw."

"Or a meet gone bad," Laurel added, reading the pressed story in grass. She touched a dew-softened crescent. "Knee. Someone knelt— before or after."

Clara pointed to Wycliffe's curled fingers. "Dirt under nails. Fresh ink. He wrote—or tore—from that page."

Harlow glanced up the street. Ash, the lanky hireling, stood half-hidden near the baker's cart, hat low. He vanished when Harlow's stare tried to stick.

The crowd decided on a story by majority. "The town is marked," Mrs. Cranston announced. "Smuggling debts come due," an old woman told the air.

Doris pushed through and saw too much. Amelia and Clara lowered her to gentler grass. "Two in a week," she whispered.

Lady Grey crept until dew touched her paws, then held. Haines followed her line and threw a hook. Rope rasped; the river tugged. They hauled up a slatted crate—bread-box size, wired shut, wood stained and swollen. The wire had been cut and twisted back wrong, like buttons done in the dark.

Laurel raised a palm. "Wait." To Harlow: "We open this together —and direct the theater."

They cut the wire. The lid sighed. Inside: oilcloth-wrapped paper and silver pressed like stones—no spoon or fork, but a long-handled ladle, bowl dull as ash, handle stamped with the insolent crown-and-ship.

A collective breath lifted the crowd. "Proof," someone said.

"Proof of what?" Laurel asked. "That silver sinks? That men with more money than sense lived here?"

"Proof Doris hoarded a trove," Mrs. Cranston declared, finding the worst sentence and using it.

Amelia's voice cut clean. "That crate's been under water longer than any of us. The wire's new." To Haines: "Someone's been opening old mouths and asking them to talk."

"There's paper," Clara murmured. "Ink not drowned." She kept hands off. "Harlow—eyes on you."

He lifted the sheets with care. On top, the crest in wax. Across the page: **C/K/W—Boathouse slot 3, dawn**, today's date, and **H.W.**

"Wycliffe," Clara said.

"And smugglers' shorthand," Laurel finished. "Not accident— appointment. He arrived with leverage and found a blade, or with nothing and found both."

"Anyone see the handoff?" Harlow asked. Heads slid aside.

Lady Grey arced around Harlow's boots and rested a paw on the ladle's crown, then looked up at Amelia and made a bell-clear sound.

"Another piece," Amelia told Laurel. "Another anchor to pull."

"Two murders, one river," Laurel said. "Plain words at noon in the square. We bring what can be brought, say what can be said, and stop letting strangers and shadows tell our story."

Harlow opened his mouth. Laurel's eyebrow rose. He shut it.

"Doris," Amelia murmured, "you don't have to be looked at."

"If I hide, they'll call it guilt," Doris said, small and stubborn. "I'll be there at noon."

"Then we'll hold your chin up," Amelia said.

They walked back through a town learning to make space for tragedy. In the café, careful tried for normal. Lady Grey took the hearth and watched the door like a lighthouse—steady, unblinking.

Clara spread a fresh sheet. "Map," she said—river bend, reeds, knee-print, crate, Ash's vanishing point.

"Laurel wants noon," Amelia said. "We'll give her noon—and something to carry through it."

They split the hours. Haines canvassed and found a boy who'd seen two men at dawn—one careful, one with a limp. Weston fetched the post: a late letter to Wycliffe stamped with a small crest. Mr. Larkin weaponized indignation into an index card of Shoreline names—asterisks for suspects, doubles for the disliked. Clara matched pantry wax to crate wax—same teeth.

Amelia brewed coffee and brewed again. She wrapped the ladle bowl in flannel and slid it into a flour tin—thieves look for diamonds; cooks for flour.

By half past eleven the square had edges. Laurel took the library steps; Harlow flanked; Haines roved. Mr. Larkin clutched a book like an oath. Mrs. Winthrop arrived with smelling salts—the practicality of a woman who knows communities need remedies. Weston held a slate—**NOON**—and glowed with duty.

Clara and Amelia arrived with Lady Grey, who sat squarely, tail curled to perfection. Doris walked between them—chin up, mouth a line.

Laurel raised a hand; murmurs dropped a gear. "At dawn, Henry

Wycliffe was found by the river," she said. "He is dead." Quiet wavered. "He carried a page referencing a theft by men who called themselves gentlemen. A crate was retrieved. It held silver and paper—today's date and Mr. Wycliffe's initials." She let it sit. "Some will call this a curse. Some will call it Mrs. Finch's guilt. Breathe. Then listen."

Harlow surprised them. "We are treating both deaths as homicides," he said. "Multiple persons of interest. We have not arrested Mrs. Finch and will not unless evidence points only and clearly to her. Some of you have decided truth's shape before you've let it arrive. Let it arrive."

Clara nudged Amelia, relief real. Laurel nodded to Mr. Larkin.

"There is a history here," he said, naming ledger names like rows in a garden someone else planted. "If you hear your grandfather's name, take it as information, not indictment. Towns carry echoes. We choose the ones we add."

Mrs. Cranston tried to interrupt. Laurel lifted a finger. Silence.

Haines spoke next. "Two notes, two hands," he said. "A pretty seal through a window. A latch set not-quite-true. A wheel loosened. A telephone cut. None of that is a curse. All of it is a person."

"Or persons," Clara breathed. Haines dipped his head.

Amelia held up the brass key with the crown bow and two kernels of wheat. "These were pushed under our door," she said. "Crown, key, wheat—C/K/W in ledgers—marking crates, places, maybe people. If you've seen this in attics or barns or memory, tell Laurel, Haines, me, or Clara. If you're shy, tell Lady Grey; she keeps counsel. But tell someone."

The square's laugh—small and grateful—proved a town can still smile. Lady Grey blinked a bow.

From the back, Ash cut sideways. "Words and trinkets," he sneered. "A man's dead. Another's dead. You count crumbs."

"Step forward if you have more than disdain," Laurel said. "Name?"

"Ash."

"An apt name," Laurel replied. "Everything you touch smells burned."

He half-stepped, then melted into people tired of being pressed into a scene.

Mr. Colby's voice came quiet. "The club wasn't meant for smuggling," he said. "It had a charter. Minutes." He heard himself and stopped. Lady Grey pinned him. He lowered his gaze; the faded sailor tattoo flashed and hid.

"History is not a plea," Larkin said, gentle enough not to slap.

Laurel finished plainly. "You'll hear stories before supper. Half will be wrong. Bring what you hear; we'll test the bones." She looked to Doris. "Mrs. Finch will run her café and sleep in her bed. Object with better than rumor."

Because tenderness keeps people human, Mrs. Winthrop stepped forward. "Lavender pastilles," she announced. "For nerves. Those with strongest opinions may take two."

Laughter bridged a flood. People came forward not to be pleased but to be part of something not fear. Gus Phelps patted Doris's shoulder; Mrs. Cranston sniffed and palmed three pastilles; boys thumb-wrestled seriously; the tension moved. Sometimes that's enough.

Amelia exhaled. Clara grazed her sleeve, quick and grateful. Lady Grey pressed her head to Doris's shin, and some portion of the day became survivable.

They hadn't found a murderer. They'd found a way to keep standing while looking for one.

Reverberations rang all day. Laurel kept Harlow and Haines at the river until light failed; they found drag marks by boathouse slot three and a notched boot print—distinct, maybe findable. Weston returned with a paper and three anonymous notes tucked inside scolding the square for meeting. Larkin found his door not glued and took it as taunt.

Amelia and Clara walked Doris home between them. The cat trotted ahead like a small gray magistrate. The parlor felt wary but warm—a room's sound when a hard thing has been done with decent form. Tea. Flour brushed from the ladle; hidden deeper (an empty sugar tin labeled **nutmeg**—even thieves respect a clear label). Silence until bodies remembered how.

Then cards on the table.

"Wycliffe had a rendezvous," Clara said. "He brought leverage—or thought so. Someone came better armed. *The Silver Spoon Heist* wasn't flourish—breadcrumb or boast."

"Two hands in the notes," Amelia said. "Two modes in the crimes: tidy and messy. The tidy hand—crest, wax, timing—wants us to see a story. The messy—cut lines, loosened wheel—wants us to make mistakes. Wycliffe got both."

Lady Grey, on the sofa back, made a small, satisfied sound.

"The river will keep giving," Clara said. "C/K/W suggests at least two more slots. If one is boathouse, one might be carriage house, one wheatfield. Or crown, key, wheat are chests for three people." She tapped the crown-bowed key. "If this fits anything, I'll find the lock if I have to try every door."

"Start with Colby's shed," Amelia said. "He flinched like lumber keeps his secrets."

"We'll ask nicely first," Clara said.

They drafted the morning's list: field behind the old granary (wheat), boathouse (key), Colby's outbuildings (crown, for pride), two farms where Shoreline names seeped into barns; Ash's lodgings; Wycliffe's room—Laurel's badge for the last two.

"And Doris," Amelia said, a small prayer. "We keep her in sight. We keep each other in sight." She reached for Lady Grey. The cat permitted the touch, then faced the door, watching for what all three knew would come.

Because it would. Murder doesn't happen twice in a week and then take a holiday. But the town had been asked to stand together long enough for truth to pass through. That mattered.

Outside, gray slid toward evening. Far downriver, a lantern bobbed where it should not. Haines would already be there—a quiet outline under trees. Laurel two steps behind, hatless, set for work. Weston running; that's how Weston spent courage.

Amelia banked the fire and dimmed the lamps. The inn changed key, like an instrument tuned safer. Lady Grey took first watch—ears a metronome, gaze a vow. Clara's pencil rested but did not sleep.

Two deaths had made a promise.

The living returned one.

Chapter 28

Community Panic

The second murder struck Tumblebrook like a stone into still water; ripples widened until no shoreline was untouched. Morning came bright, but the town wore a hush like mourning crepe. Children were walked to the schoolhouse and retrieved at the first rumor. The tavern sign creaked though the door stayed half-latched. The church vestibule filled with candles two days early, wax softening into nervous stalagmites.

At the inn, empty chairs said more than talk. The breakfast room had thinned to gauze. China still clinked, butter still broke warm crumb, but every glance slid toward the river.

Amelia stood at the desk with the ledger open and a charcoal pencil idle. Telegrams perched like nervous birds:

WE REGRET—CANCELING UNTIL FURTHER NOTICE.

UNABLE TO TRAVEL—FAMILY MATTERS.

PLEASE HOLD DEPOSIT—RETURN WHEN SAFE.

Polite lies for I'm frightened of your town.

Lady Grey stepped onto the ledger's blank margin, whiskers tickling Amelia's wrist.

"They're frightened," Amelia said. "Two deaths and only whispers to hold them together."

Clara came in with the dry air of worry on her coat. "The café's half-empty. Doris is working past the tremor. Two men from the granary stood in the doorway and didn't order. One said thyme smells like graves."

Tumblebrook had always tasted of story; now it acquired a palate for omen.

By noon, the inn had the quiet of a fort under siege. A delivery boy left bread and ran. The florist brought daisies: For courage. The grocer—generous for five winters—sent word new accounts must be paid in advance, "just for now." Guests ate alone upstairs. Pewter lids kept soup warm; silence kept rumors warmer.

In the parlor, Clara sighed into a chair. "If this continues, you'll be cooking for ghosts."

"My livelihood matters less than Doris's freedom," Amelia said, steadying herself on the words. "I won't let them condemn her by consensus."

"We pull the root," Clara said. "Rumor grows from misread fact, bent memory, an old wound."

Lady Grey paced, then froze at the door, staring at the dark triangle between jamb and sill as if it had spoken.

"Feels it too," Amelia murmured. "The town's changed temperature."

By late afternoon the shape of it showed. The bell tolled early. Doors along the square made their own weather—half-shut, curtains drawn. Laurel moved doorway to doorway with notices: Noon statement updated—details to follow. Harlow's deputy traced the perimeter with a lantern unlit.

In the café, Doris set plates with a courtesy she hadn't always mustered. Kindness keeps you human when unkindness would prove someone else's point. Her hands did their old dance, but fatigue draped her shoulders. "If I stop moving," she told Amelia, "I'll feel the floor."

Two men by the window snapped their talk shut. A leaflet vanished into a coat: CITIZENS FOR A SAFE TOWN, stamped with a shaky crown. "Someone's organizing distrust," Clara hissed.

"Someone always organized it," Doris said. "We simply hadn't been sent the minutes."

A chalk crown appeared on the back door; Doris scrubbed it off. "No one curses me on my wood."

Mr. Larkin found a handbill pasted over his hours: STOP DIGGING. LET THE DEAD LIE. He peeled it and catalogued the cheap purple wax. At the barber's, sentences braided to nonsense —"I heard—who knows—they say—go on"—until no one knew who'd spoken first. Three visitors paid with bank-wet notes and asked, too casually, for the boathouses, the granary, "the old crown place."

Harlow pushed where he could: Haines at the river with two lumberyard boys; "enough" in low rooms where enough had already happened. Laurel used names to pull the crowd back to itself. "Mr. Phelps, walk your daughter. Mrs. Cranston, bake your loaves." Names steadied more than warnings.

Back at the inn, Amelia lit the fire; the small cheer of flame pushed back the draft that had crept under everything. She warmed stones for guests who wouldn't ask. Clara sat cross-legged on the carpet, pages fanned like a white fort: HEIST in the center, V.F., H.W., C/K/W, barley heads for Granary Road, Boathouse 3, the morning's crown-key sketched and measured.

Lady Grey took the hearth like a director. When the kettle sighed, she looked at it and then at Amelia until tea was poured.

"We'll stand by Doris," Amelia said.

"And by you," Clara answered. "If the inn empties, we'll sit in every chair."

A knock: three short, then one. Haines, coat damp with river. "Keep to the inn after dark unless you're with one of us. There's talk of a vigil. Laurel's trying to turn it into a search party with a map." He tipped his hat. "If you hear singing—go upstairs."

The vigil tried to be a vigil. Men with lanterns gathered, hoping courage would follow. Laurel and Harlow routed them toward the river path with rope and a task: find a notched boot heel. It's easier to behave when behavior has a job. Still, a song started and died; a stone rattled a shutter; someone chalked a crown on the inn's sign and rubbed it away, ashamed of sudden bravery. Lady Grey watched from the stair and did not move—except once, when a figure without a lantern lingered half a step behind. She stared until the figure felt it and went.

Upstairs, Amelia made rounds with hot bricks and small, unnecessary kindnesses; the house answered with its familiar repertoire. Clara slept with her notebook open, a pencil line scored straight across the page where sleep had taken her. Lady Grey laid herself like a sash across Amelia's calves—heavy enough to be felt, light enough not to pin.

Morning returns without asking. Panic's first sharpness blurs at daylight and sharpens again by noon. New traces dotted the square: KEEP OUR TOWN CLEAN chalked near the pump, clean underlined until the chalk broke; a crooked reward notice in proud block letters; a wet mark from a bucket thrown across Mrs. Cranston's stoop because fear must do something.

At eight, the inn's telephone rattled back and brought one necessary thing: a Duluth voice willing to say aloud the debt Vernon owed and to whom. Clara underlined the name twice—pressure point. Mr. Larkin arrived with lake-route books and a parcel for Doris: a new door latch. "Harder to ply with glue."

Doris opened with her jaw set and hair pinned tight. She tied her apron, let anyone else tie the strings, and served eggs to the man with the SAFE TOWN leaflet. "Jam?" she asked. Mercy can be strategy.

Laurel posted an official notice beneath the reward handbill: NO CURFEW. NO VIGILANTE GROUPS. REPORT INFORMATION TO CHIEF HARLOW OR MAYOR LAUREL WESTON **—especially** women, she added aloud, and waited until chins came up.

Harlow sent Haines to the boathouse and a deputy to the

granary; he invited Mr. Colby to converse. The historian declined, then reconsidered when Lady Grey sat on his threshold like a visitation. Some doors unlock by keys; some by cats. He came that evening with a folder and the look of a man ready to carry one more thing he should have carried earlier.

The town didn't recover, not yet. But panic sopped itself up enough to keep its feet. People worked. Yeast returned to the noon air. A child laughed and wasn't shushed. In the parlor, Amelia set the brass key on a saucer as if it were a relic and wrote three travelers' names in the ledger with her cleanest hand. When she closed the book, it sounded less like resignation and more like a promise kept between breaths.

"Hold," she whispered—to the house, the town, herself.

Lady Grey blinked slow agreement and took up her watch.

Chapter 29

Clara's Cross-Reference

The morning after Wycliffe rose from the river wore a sky the color of tarnished pewter—like a spoon left too long in a damp drawer. Tumblebrook moved as if under a palm pressed to its crown: errands shortened, greetings clipped, every latch clack loud as a gavel. The baker lifted his shutters late; the smith struck with the carefulness of grief. Even the river kept its voice low where it curled beside the green.

Inside Gossamer Fables, the hush was the good kind—the one made by old paper and dust in a shaft of light, by the private negotiation between a researcher and a stubborn past. Mr. Larkin opened the door with a bell too bright for his face; his tie was awry, his spectacles smudged.

"I've pulled what I could," he said, stagehand to a set, leading Clara to the long oak table. "Town ledgers, harbor notices, Duluth papers on microfilm. Municipal minutes, though the index is a mischievous liar."

"Thank you." Clara set down her satchel and unbuttoned her cuffs as if for surgery. "If there's a pattern, it will forgive neither smudged ink nor bad indexing."

Lady Grey slipped in behind and sprang to a chair with the solemnity of an appointed judge. Paws tucked, tail looped, ears ticking to the rhythm of paper sliding and leather sighing.

Clara began with newspapers. *Duluth Daily Herald*, June 1932: **SILVER STOLEN FROM LAKESIDE ESTATE—WARE-HOUSEMAN QUESTIONED.** Names dotted the column like pebbles in shallow water. Dockworker O'Shea. Brewer Cartwright. A Finch—Malcolm, second cousin to the Tumblebrook branch—"on the premises during a routine delivery."

She underlined *Finch* and penciled to the margin: proximity, not accusation. A year later, different paper, same tune: tableware bound for Two Harbors vanished between Palma and Knife River. Interviewed: two teamsters, one watchman, another Finch "occasionally engaged as casual labor." One coincidence is a hiccup. Two is a cough. Three is a throat clearing before speech.

"Let's hear you," Clara murmured to the stack.

Lady Grey rose, padded across the oak, and planted one paw on a Silver Bay clipping. Clara smoothed it beneath whiskers. **WARE-HOUSE INTRUSION—VALUABLE UTENSILS MISS-ING.** And twining through the paragraph again, that ivy of a last name: Finch.

"Good girl," Clara said. "You've an archivist's nose."

Morning became a measured procession: page turn, breath held, a thin pencil line, a dot in the margin. Mrs. Winthrop's careful annotations from twenty years ago surfaced like life rings: *see also Harbor Board minutes, May '31; insurance claim filed, July '33.* Clara followed each arrow as if it were thread through dark trees.

By noon a shape emerged, like a rubbing revealing what lay beneath. The silver thefts strung from Duluth to Grand Marais—never consecutive, never blatant, always near the Finches enough to warm their coats and never enough to scorch them. Witness. Laborer. Cousin. The name brushed civic minutes, then slipped behind a ledger's curtain. Not pointing—hovering.

"History leaves fingerprints even when gloves were worn," Mr.

Larkin said from his ladder. He descended with a cracked-green volume. "Shoreline Association minutes. The 'gentlemen's club' Mr. Colby pretends was martini olives and monologues."

Clara opened to May 1931. The hand was thin and smug.

Motion carried to accept the Crest & Keel Navigation Company as a sustaining member. Mr. Denvers to liaise. Mr. Finch to serve as local 'quartermaster' for uplake shipments. Monthly dues settled in kind.

Crest & Keel. Her pencil stopped. Crown above ship—crest and keel—a company, not a family. Branding, not pedigree.

"Is your crest here?" she asked.

Larkin fetched a slim booklet: **LAKE MARKS AND MERCHANT SIGILS, 1895–1938.** Page sixteen held it: a simple crown, three points, above a stylized two-masted hull. *C&K NAVIGATION—DULUTH.* Caption: *Used on crate stencils, mooring documents, invoice seals. Consolidated small carriers; dissolved under litigation, 1934.*

Litigation. Clara flipped to the index. *Wycliffe, H. & Sons v. Crest & Keel,* 1899:

Plaintiff alleges loss of consigned goods; defendant alleges act of God. Settlement sealed.

"Wycliffe," she breathed. "He didn't come for gossip alone. His family's story and this crest climb the same staircase."

"If the staircase was rotten," Larkin said, "they all fell—but some landed on better carpets."

Clara copied the sigil—crisp crown points, shaded hull—into her notebook and ringed it with names and dates: C&K dues in minutes; storage in granary; crates stenciled *CROWN-12*; boat slips leased under aliases. She pulled the property ledger: the grain annex purchased 1930 by *North Shore Holdings*—a paper entity with no officers. In the margin, a faint later hand: *C&K?*—erased, then ghosted back when she held the page to the window.

"Grain," she whispered. "Wheat." Like the kernels left with the brass key. The granary had not been metaphor. It had been warehouse.

Lady Grey trilled and pressed her cheek to Clara's sleeve.

Microfilm next. Larkin threaded the Duluth reels with a practised touch. The whir and click became a heartbeat under focus. Harbormaster reports—quiet phrases with iron skeletons: *special consignment; moved at night tide; no inspection—club pass.* September 1932 listed crates departing C&K's yard: *Service set, banquet—CROWN-12–CROWN-16.* No consignee—just a dot.

"And the banquet service never arrived," Clara told the machine, "unless it arrived and re-arrived in other men's cupboards."

She printed the page. The warm strip slid out, the small line a thread inviting a pull. She pulled harder.

Municipal minutes, October '32, were dust-dry—invocation, road repair, new fire hoses—then, near the bottom, a quiet line:

Mayor raises concern re: misuse of private club seals for harbor clearance; urges discretion; matter referred to subcommittee.

Referred and forgotten—or remembered too well.

"Someone bought permission with dinner," she said.

Larkin made a noncommittal sound with agreement tucked inside.

Then the page that stumbled her heart: a photocopy in the archives folder, a single leaf torn ragged down one side. Crude title in thick pencil: **THE SILVER SPOON HEIST.** A few lines, then an abrupt stop mid-sentence. The tear's curve matched the piece Chief Harlow had lifted from Wycliffe's stiff fingers.

Clara laid them side by side—the shop copy and her memory of the edge—and matched the paper's ragged teeth. Perfect.

"Wycliffe had half," she whispered. "Someone else took the other."

"Where would a sheet like that come from?" Larkin asked.

"A draft," Clara said. "Not a newspaper. Not a legal notice. A narrative trying to become a record—or a record masquerading as a story so it could travel safer." No watermark. No printer's mark. Pencil on cheap paper—the kind kept in hall drawers for council notes.

Back to the Shoreline minutes. November '32 carried a vacant line beside *guest speaker*—and in the margin, a careless pencil **C** that half-decided to be a **K**. Clumsy. Impatient.

"Two hands," she murmured, remembering the notes slid under the inn door. The tidy hand that loved stamps and wax. The hurried hand that loved cheap chalk and worse glue. Two signatures in ink; two methods in the street.

Patterns wanted repetition. She let them have it.

She cross-referenced the Shoreline roll with lodge membership. Four names overlapped: Holloway, Denvers, Finch (Malcolm), and H. Wycliffe, Jr.—a courtesy member via C&K sponsorship in 1900, struck two years later when dues "went to litigation." She wrote the names in a column and drew lines to IOUs. Holloway owing Denvers. Denvers owing Finch. Finch owing C/K. All debt meeting in a circle called *leverage*.

Afternoon went on being afternoon. The bell chimed three times: once for a woman asking for a devotional "for courage," once for a fisherman returning *Moby-Dick* with the air of a man who'd tried to read his own blood pressure, once for no one at all. Lady Grey, having supervised hours of exhumation, dozed with one paw on **LAKE MARKS AND MERCHANT SIGILS** as if to keep it from wandering.

By three, Clara's notebook bristled—arrows, underlines, dates drawn like trellis. A clean timeline unfurled:

1899 — Wycliffe firm litigates Crest & Keel over lost consignments; case sealed.

1900–02 — Wycliffe Jr. entangled with Shoreline; removed.

1928–34 — Silver thefts spike along the North Shore in C&K's shadow.

1931 — C&K pays "dues" to Shoreline *in kind*; Finch named "quartermaster."

Sept 1932 — Banquet service CROWN-12–16 routed through Tumblebrook; records smudge.

Oct 1932 — Mayor warns of seal misuse; subcommittee never reports.

1933–34 — C&K dissolves under litigation; Shoreline minutes thin, then stop.

1970s–80s — Family ledger notes *crest pieces—kept safe.*

A web, and in the center—of course—the crown over the little ship.

"The silver isn't cursed," Clara said, closing the notebook with her palm. "It's evidence. A ledger that forgot it was a fork. A spoon that remembers better than men."

Larkin, pretending to reshelve so he could still listen, nodded. "Evidence is the only thing louder than gossip—if you speak it properly."

She gathered copies, slid originals into sleeves, tucked sketches between heavier boards so the pencil wouldn't smear. The satchel's weight tugged at her shoulder—and at a dozen threads in town.

"Careful," Larkin murmured—not to the papers, to the woman carrying them.

"I intend to be," Clara said. "Just not so careful we go quiet."

She paid for nothing—Larkin wouldn't allow it—and thanked him twice, which made him feel less accomplice and more librarian.

Lady Grey hopped down and walked beside her into the pewter day, tail high. The square had rearranged itself: a **CITIZENS FOR A SAFE TOWN** leaflet skew on a post; a crown chalked on the pump, then smudged; Laurel's precise hand beneath: **NO CURFEW. NO VIGILANCE WITHOUT LAW. REPORT.**

Clara lifted her chin and crossed. Whispers eddied behind; ahead, the river resumed its unhelpful, unconcerned work—moving on. She couldn't shake the image of Lady Grey on the bank, staring as if the answer wore waterweed for a veil.

"We're close," Clara told the cat, who didn't slow. "Closer than anyone wants us."

Lady Grey purred and flicked an ear toward the lake's steel

mirror. Her eyes fixed the horizon as though a name might heave out of it like a net.

Halfway to the inn, a man in a brown cap slipped from a doorway and matched her pace just behind her shoulder—too close for chance, too careful for friendliness. Flour dust on his boots. Silent. In the glass of a shop window she caught his reflection: brim low, jaw set, left hand in his pocket, right hand brushing his hip like a man accustomed to touching a tool not there now.

She slowed. He slowed. She stopped to admire a haberdasher's display that didn't interest her. He stopped to tie a shoe that didn't need tying. Lady Grey turned and regarded him with a flat, sovereign stare—the kind that suggests a cat would like to reconsider the arrangement of your bones. He peeled off at the next corner, as if he'd meant only to walk that far.

At the inn's steps, Amelia stood with a damp cloth and a calm stitched to her overnight. One look at Clara's face and she had them inside, bolt slid, kettle thinking for itself.

Clara spread her notes, slid **THE SILVER SPOON HEIST** to the center, and traced the torn edge.

"Crest & Keel," she said. "Not a family—a company. The crown and ship are corporate ink. Shoreline took dues in kind. The granary annex belongs to a shell. Crates CROWN-12 to -16 are our banquet service. Wycliffe's lawsuit knotted him to the same rope he tried to hang Doris with. He had half a page; someone else took the other—years ago or last week—and kept the habit of tearing right into their fingers."

Amelia's eyes brightened the way fear does when made to share a chair with clarity. "So if we find the rest of the service—here, the granary, the boathouse—"

"—we find the rest of the record," Clara finished. "Proof, not rumor. The kind Harlow can't sand into an easier shape."

Lady Grey leapt to the hearth and tapped the brass key with a paw. Again. Then a deliberate swipe so it rang against the saucer.

"The granary," Amelia said.

"The granary," Clara agreed. "And after that, C&K's last book-keeping. Somewhere there's a mirror of this—Duluth's insurance clerk's basement, Mr. Colby's desk, the bottom of a river trunk."

A knock—three short, one long—echoed like a familiar chapter ending. Haines stood with damp on his coat and patience in his mouth. "Laurel asks you're never alone on the river road," he said. "Errands with company and daylight."

"We're not errands," Clara said mildly.

Haines gave half a smile. "No, Miss Henderson. You're trouble. The good kind."

When the door shut, her satchel crackled with a sound paper makes when it is not your paper. Clara reached in and drew out a folded slip she had not folded.

Stop pulling threads. Some knots hold the town together.

She showed it to Amelia, then turned it for Lady Grey, who hissed—refusal, not fear—and set a paw on *knots* until the paper wrinkled.

"Too late," Clara said. She tucked the note beneath the saucer with the brass key and the two wheat kernels, as if to teach it its place.

Outside, the lake brightened in a brief lift of cloud; for one breath the horizon looked like a ruled line. Then the pewter returned, and the town resumed its patient unraveling.

Clara put pencil to a fresh page and wrote, steady: **GRANARY. BOATHOUSE. DULUTH RECORDS.** She underlined each and, as an afterthought that wasn't, added: **Wycliffe papers— 1899.**

Lady Grey's purr thrummed—low, insistent—as if to say: at last, you're hearing the whole song.

Chapter 30

Hidden Passages

The storm rinsed Tumblebrook clean and left its bones showing. Cobblestones shone pewter; gutters whispered; thyme and wet rosemary breathed up from Doris's garden like the town exhaling memory. From the street, the Finch Café looked itself—hand-lettered sign rocking, flower boxes bowed by rain, lamplight honeying the panes. Inside, the hush had weight. The kettle hissed; chair legs sounded like accusations.

Amelia and Clara lingered after closing, tea gone cold. Doris had folded into a blanket upstairs, humming on a thread that broke and reknotted. Lady Grey prowled lean circuits around flour sacks and the back hallway, tail high, whiskers testing drafts. Twice she circled the pantry. The third time she stopped, one paw lifted, ears pricked toward a strip of baseboard where paint had bubbled and split.

"Where's she off to now?" Amelia asked, brushing flour from her skirt.

"She doesn't do theater," Clara said, rising. "She does proof."

The cat slid into the narrow service corridor behind the kitchen, body pouring through shadow. Damp drew sweat from the stone;

yeast and wet burlap made a domestic fog that didn't quite cover a metallic smell beneath.

Lady Grey stopped at a crooked board, tapped—once, twice, again. When neither woman moved quickly enough, she wriggled toward a slot narrower than a letter box and vanished in a soft rasp of wood.

"Good heavens," Amelia whispered, kneeling with the lantern.

A faint meow answered from below, purposeful.

Clara pressed her palm to the plaster; paint lifted in papery curls. "Cold air," she said. "From underneath."

They worked the board up with a paring knife and a spoon handle—the café's crowbars. The wood fought, then sighed. Damp iron, mildew, old coins, and earth rose—air that hadn't tasted light in years. Lantern glow poured into a slot just wide enough to steal courage.

"This has been shut a long time," Amelia said.

"Or kept shut by people who knew why," Clara replied, knotting her satchel. "Forgetting can be a discipline."

They slid through. Timber grazed shawl and sleeve; grit sang under their soles—nail heads, sand, a sliver of glass pricking through Amelia's shoe. The passage bent and sloped down. The flame guttered, recovered. Lady Grey's voice came ahead—two short chirps, the sound she used when she had a mouse cornered and wanted it admired.

The passage opened into a low chamber.

Amelia lifted the lantern. Light climbed cobwebbed beams, changed color on damp stone, fell back heavy with dust. Ceiling timbers were stout—built for weight. The earthen floor bore shallow arcs and double tracks: barrel and handcart work, often and in haste.

Clara crouched by the nearest stack. Crates—old pine swollen with humidity, iron-strapped corners furred with rot—leaned like tired men. Her fingers brushed a ghost of paint, breathed on it. A faint stencil surfaced: a small crown above a two-masted hull. Below, paler hand: CROWN-14.

"Crest & Keel," she said, tight with the relief of a fact in its place. "Company mark, not family."

"So the crest's been under Doris's kitchen this whole time," Amelia said.

Lady Grey leapt to the top plank, planted a paw on CROWN-14, meowed once, and scrabbled at the rusted latch. The iron complained, then gave. The lid lifted with a wet rasp.

Inside, the past gleamed through tarnish: serving spoons with deep fluted bowls; two ladles; knife handles like bird bones; dented goblets. Each bore the crown-and-ship faint at the throat—struck by a die long since rotted.

Clara didn't touch. "Crate numbers match the harbormaster's list," she said. "CROWN-12 to -16. This one came to ground here."

Amelia let out a breath. "Then Vernon wasn't dream-chasing. He had a map—even if it was instinct and greed."

Under straw lay a flat oilcloth parcel—paper among metal. Inside: three pocket ledgers swollen by damp, the kind a man keeps under his coat when he wants to remember what to forget.

Clara set them on an upturned crate. Ink had bled, but some columns held: dates, initials, amounts not polite even then. H/Denvers—tally due in kind. M. Finch—qtrmstr—dock fee to Shoreline in crates. Seal used: C&K courtesy—see Mayor. Handwriting changed line to line—neat, then impatient, then neat again.

"Two hands," Amelia murmured. "Like the notes. Tidy and messy."

"A company's ink and a town's chalk," Clara said. An entry dated spring: CROWN-12, -13, -14—break bulk to Finch cellar, east corridor; margin arrow: storage fee paid—Shoreline dues in kind—speaker waived.

Lady Grey padded to the far wall where stone gave to timber. She braced, ears forward, and tapped. The wall answered—not just hollow, but echo, the interior kind a doctor listens for.

Clara pressed her cheek to the seam. Cool wood. A draft like a house's exhale. Beyond: river cold, silt, iron-green weed.

"There's more," she said, hunger slipping into her voice. "A run. A chute. Or a tunnel to the granary."

"The purple wax," Amelia said. "Laurel's envelope. If Shoreline used seals, residue might be on the other side."

"Or the hinge," Clara said, running a finger along the edge. It came away faint violet. She held it to the lantern and smiled without pleasure. "The exact shade."

They needed tools they didn't have. Even if a soup spoon could pry the boards, no one wants to be the women whose café collapses into a hole that empties toward a river.

"Tomorrow," Amelia said. "With Haines. And a pry bar that isn't a butter knife."

Lady Grey gave a single, unconvinced chirp.

Footsteps moved above—a tread across the kitchen, a pause, the hollow ring of a ladle set too hard. Doris? Or a house rehearsing how to be haunted.

The lantern wheezed. "We have proof," Amelia whispered, as if to the silver, the ink, the dusty air. "We can come back for the rest."

They closed what they could not lock. Clara rewound the oilcloth precisely and tucked it beneath straw, lowered the crate lid, pressed her palm to wood as if time might settle. Lady Grey led them up the slope, tail high like a taper.

Back in the kitchen, ordinary light looked indecent. The oak table wore its familiar knife marks. Upstairs, Doris's humming faltered, then resumed.

Amelia set the lantern down and gripped the counter until her hands stopped shaking. "We opened a door," she said. "Dues in kind. Shoreline stamps. C&K crates in our cellar. It isn't a story anymore— it's evidence."

"Evidence speaks louder than gossip," Clara said. "And it speaks names."

Lady Grey pattered once around the lantern, leaving four neat commas in dust. She sat, knees tidy, and looked at Amelia plainly: Do it properly or not at all.

They fetched a mop and warm water. It felt treasonous to mop flour when the underworld needed prying, but a café is a café. Work steadied their breath. When the board went back, Clara slid a teacup in front of it—camouflage that looks like nothing.

"Tomorrow morning," Clara said. "Haines. A crowbar. Laurel—if Harlow will sign a search order for a seam under a café."

"And if he won't?" Amelia asked.

"Then we take him the ledger leaf and ask whether he prefers headlines that read SHERIFF IGNORES EVIDENCE or CELLAR RAID EXPOSES SHORELINE DUES. He likes the law. We'll give him the law."

They slept badly and briefly. At dawn the kitchen looked exactly itself. The board hid the mouth. The lantern glass betrayed nothing. Doris poured coffee with the jerky care of someone who has slept on a cliff edge. "You two are up early," she said, not looking at the board because she didn't know she should. "The storm rattled my windows. I dreamed of—" She stopped. "I can't remember."

"Don't try," Amelia said, kissed her cheek, and filled her cup.

Haines arrived at nine with a toolbox and the particular politeness men wear when they expect to be yelled at later. "Laurel says I'm here unofficially," he said. "Which is to say, officially later, if we're lucky."

They showed him the board and the seam. He didn't ask if they were sure.

The crowbar went where the paring knife had been patient. Boards took their time, then gave with a bark of nails and a long sigh from beyond. Cold air climbed their ankles—river and beetle, wet rope.

Haines held his lamp up. The tunnel ran six paces, then shouldered left—low enough a man must go bent and a woman sideways. The floor was packed hard—boots had taught it. Under one turn, Clara's shoulder brushed a smear that glowed faintly: purple wax rubbed flat by coats and years. She touched it and tapped the brass key in her pocket, as if introducing cousins.

"Shoreline," she said.

"Crest & Keel's courtesy," Amelia added. The ledger had said it, and the ledger didn't lie.

The tunnel shouldered right and then fell—not steeply, the kind a barrow likes. Air moved. Silt sharpened. Ahead, a slatted screen shrugged weak daylight: a drainage vent facing the river under the granary's shadow. In front of it, a small shelf with a pulley above—an exact stage for a crate to pause before sliding into a boat hugging the bank.

"Trapdoor delivery," Haines murmured. "They brought the lake inside."

On the shelf: a broken slate and a nub of chalk, two bites taken to coax it sharp. Clara turned the slate. Tidy columns, then a scrawl: —no more nights— with the s bitten off, as if the writer had been interrupted in the act of becoming brave.

Lady Grey sat squarely on the shelf and tipped her head toward the screen. The river made private mouth noises inches beyond.

"Someone could still use this," Amelia said.

"Or someone did," Haines said, tapping a clean streak in the dust, fresh as a new part in hair.

They photographed with Clara's box camera; light from the screen did half the work. Haines measured shelf and pulley drop with his palm. Clara sketched brace and hinge, marking violet smears. Amelia held the lamp and tried not to weep for a café built with a crime under it like a second oven.

They didn't pry the screen. The town was jumpy enough without three people popping up like mushrooms on the bank.

Back in the kitchen, Haines sat on Doris's pie stool and looked at Amelia like a man handed a truth too big to carry alone. "This puts Laurel in the room," he said. "If Shoreline used this with C&K, and if we show the crates stopped here, Harlow will help—or he'll be pricing bait."

"Then let's set the table," Clara said, laying out photographs like plates: the CROWN-14 stencil, the ledger leaf, the fleck of purple wax she'd lifted, set on the saucer with the brass key and two wheat kernels. "He likes the law. We give him law—order, record, warrants."

"And we do ours," Amelia said. "Find the rest of the service. Tie it to the ledgers. Make the town hear the difference between inheritance and inventory."

Lady Grey lounged against the toolbox, one paw over its latch like a seal. Her eyes were half-closed; her ears tracked different kinds of trouble. The kitchen felt larger—not safer, exactly, but honest.

Doris came down at noon, hair pinned, apron tied. The lines around her mouth had softened. "We had custard in the icebox," she said, to have something she could say that wouldn't turn to ash. "We shouldn't waste it."

"We won't," Amelia said, and measured sugar in a way that looked ordinary.

They ate custard at the counter—eggs, nutmeg, and the kind of stubbornness that keeps boats upright. Haines left by the alley, promising to return with Laurel and a warrant. Clara packed and repacked her satchel because she couldn't stop counting copies. Amelia washed three spoons that didn't need washing.

A knock at the front: two short, two long. Laurel stood with Chief Harlow two steps behind, hands in his coat pockets as if the coat had asked him to carry them. His expression was the blank of a lake that refused to show its rocks.

"Miss Farnsworth," Laurel said. "Mr. Haines says there's a matter to see."

Amelia led them in. The board slid; the lantern breathed; the seam admitted. Harlow's jaw jumped once as he bent. His hat stayed in his hand.

Under the café, the river breathed through its lattice mouth and the crates didn't pretend. Laurel didn't speak for a long minute. When she did, her voice was even. "Photograph everything," she said. "Nothing moves until I say. Chief, fetch Deputy Norrin and the kit."

Harlow's hat turned, then his head, like two parts of a machine remembering their order. "You mean to tell me—"

"I mean to tell you to fetch the kit," Laurel said. "Then I'll tell you what it means."

He went. Not quickly. Not slowly. Like a man deciding whether a road is still a road if it turns out to be a bridge.

Laurel turned to Amelia and Clara. "You weren't wrong. And you weren't reckless. You were ahead." Gratitude flickered, then smoothed into professionalism. "Thank you."

Clara only nodded. In that kitchen, it felt like kneeling.

Amelia set a hand on Lady Grey and felt the purr through the thin skin between certainty and fear. The cat stared at Laurel, then blinked approval—more than most people get.

They worked until afternoon turned evening and the light changed its mind. The tunnel gave up small offerings: a crate slat with CROWN-13 intact; a broken seal—purple wax with crown and hull in reverse; a brass thumb-latch embossed C&K; and, lodged by the screen, a grandmother straight pin wrapped with a hair-thin thread of violet. Laurel folded each into paper as if tucking in a child.

No one spoke Vernon's name until they stood again in the kitchen and the world tried to be ordinary. Then Harlow said, roughly, as if the words had fought through old stubbornness, "If this is what I think, Mrs. Finch does not belong in a cell."

"She never did," Amelia said—more gently than he deserved.

Harlow nodded once, like a man lowering his chin to a blade of his own choosing. "Then it is time for me to clear her name."

When the door closed, the café exhaled. The storm's wash still glittered in the garden. People walked past the windows in twos and threes and pretended not to look in, which is how small towns watch. Far off, the church bell counted the hour as if hours were still the same size.

Amelia leaned into the counter and laughed once—odd, helpless —at nothing in particular. She looked at Clara; Clara looked at the floor; both felt the sting in their eyes as if the river had thrown up its light.

"We did something," Clara said.

"We opened a door," Amelia said.

Lady Grey sprang down, left a perfect print on Laurel's drying paper, then rubbed her cheek against the brass key. The key chimed; the wheat clicked. Small sounds. A chapter turning.

Outside, the lake put on evening steel. Inside, three women and a cat stood in a kitchen that now knew what had always been beneath it. The passage didn't just change the café's map. It changed what could be said about who Tumblebrook had been and what it was capable of becoming. Doors shut; doors opened; and the past—no longer rumor but a room—waited with boxes, numbers, and purple wax to be put on the record.

Clara uncapped her pen, wrote at the top of a clean page: GRANARY — BOATHOUSE — C&K LEDGER DUPLICATES, then, remembering to breathe.

Lady Grey's purr rolled on, steady as a sewing machine mending a rip.

Chapter 31

The Chamber's Contents

By the time the last cup was rinsed and Doris had climbed the stairs with a brave goodnight, the café felt like a stage after the curtain—props familiar, air unsettled, the next act waiting. Laurel had signed the paper Haines brought—Temporary Warrant of Entry: Subgrade Passage / Storage Chamber / Adjoining Run to River—and Harlow, jaw locked, had initialed beneath. Official ink didn't warm Amelia, but it steadied her spine.

They gathered at half past eight: Laurel with satchel and box camera; Haines with pry bar, line, and tools; Clara with notebook and a shallow tray; Amelia with two lanterns; and Lady Grey, who required none of the above. The cat brushed whiskers against the warrant like a feline notarization, then sat by the teacup disguising the lifted board.

"We work slow," Laurel said. "Touch only what must be touched."

Haines levered the board and went first. Lady Grey slipped after him; Clara and Amelia followed, flame flattening and recovering as the passage drank and returned their air. The chamber met them with mildew, iron, and straw—the smell of an old place remembering its job. Lantern light found beams that had held too much, grooves laid by barrels, and crates waiting like warnings.

Laurel stood still five beats, as if letting the room finish a sentence. "We begin with what names itself."

Flash powder whitened the chamber; then dimness again, the crates now more naked. Clara showed Laurel the stenciled plank—crown above hull, C&K nested in the negative space. "Crest & Keel Navigation," she said. "A firm, not a family."

"I'll want the slat," Laurel said. "Last."

Haines brushed rot from CROWN-14 until the latch recognized itself. The lid yielded to tarnished moons—spoon bowls, ladle lips, a fallen goblet—each with the shallow crown-and-ship. Laurel annotated, not touching. "Crate CROWN-14: mixed silver service. Photograph." Flash.

Lady Grey set a paw beside a ladle and stared at Laurel. "You get your own badge," Laurel murmured.

CROWN-12 held larger ware and, beneath straw, an oilcloth parcel. "Parcel 12-A," Laurel said, lifting it to Clara's tray. Inside: three pocket ledgers. Ink bleed had wintered some pages, but columns still ran: Date, Crate, Route, Dues, Silent—the last for Silent Partners. Initials—M.F., H.D., L.C., J.H., R.P.—accrued dots (cash), Xs (in kind), triangles (favor owed). In the margin by CROWN-9: Club dinner—set for twelve—ware from 9 & 10. Farther down: Speaker waived—Shoreline dues in bottles. No speeches. No names.

Haines breathed "H.D.," then shut his mouth. "No expansions aloud," Laurel said. "Copy first."

CROWN-13 yielded a tin of seals: purple wax, a brass press biting back crown and hull in reverse. Laurel warmed a scrap; the impression rose neat and sharp. "Purple," Amelia whispered—threading their week. "A company's way of saying ours," Laurel said.

They found a sailor's knife; a coil of chain; a tally slate with ghost numbers and the scrawl no more night—its s bitten off—the same hurried hand as at the river shelf. "Two hands," Clara said. "Steady clerk; harried local." "Keep hearing the duet," Laurel answered. "Who plans, who panics."

Lady Grey tapped the timber seam; the hollow reply coughed from the other side. "Hymn-pace," Haines said. "We pry later."

Clara opened a second ledger: tidy C&K schedules, then breaks—Drought year. Barrels spoiled. Mayor absent—dues carried. A page bore a fine brown spatter. "Duluth can tell wine or blood," Laurel said, already assigning.

Back at Silent Partners, a fresh line underlined V.F.—Vernon Finch—added later in the impatient hand: knows—demands share. The air tilted.

"Not the company's book," Clara said. "A score." "And now he's dead," Amelia blurted. Laurel penciled, neutral: V.F.—hand B—'knows—demands share'.

A collapsed corner exposed something bright: a great serving fork engraved not with the crest but Crown & Keel, dated 1899. "Commissioned," Clara said. "Made for them." "So the mark can be origin as well as ownership," Laurel said. Lady Grey batted a small object free: a glass button, purple, in cheap brass. Laurel enveloped it. "Luck's better than prints down here."

Laurel called stop after four crates: two cutlery, one serving, one paper and seals. The wall's seam remained a promise; the ledgers rode in Laurel's satchel, wrapped in oilcloth, then brown paper, then trust.

They crawled up like divers. The knife block and kettle looked indecently easy after the honest mess below. Clara laughed once—truth's straight line hurting as it lands. Lady Grey set a paw on Laurel's satchel. "Temporarily in my custody," Laurel told her. "Reports to you."

"We'll petition the granary tomorrow," Laurel said. "We have tunnel mouth, screen shelf, purple streak." Harlow, she added, "has shifted weight."

"And Doris?" Amelia asked.

"I've filed for her to be exonerated at dinner—tonight. The Chief brings her and apologizes, or he meets me at breakfast."

By midnight Harlow did just that. Doris cried like someone who preferred not to, then made tea, and something in the kitchen reset.

Morning brought better noises: saucers, pie gossip. People could smell that the gnawing thing finally had a shape. At Gossamer Fables, Laurel laid first prints across oak: CROWN-14, the crest, the purple seal, the slate. Clara spread her timeline; Amelia placed a clean copy of V.F.—knows—demands share where a headline might sit. "These initials are talk," Laurel said, tapping the list, "until the granary gives names. Tomorrow we fetch the book."

That evening they returned with warrant, braces, and Norrin's quiet hum. The seam remembered how to be a door. Behind: a book-keeper's closet and two strongboxes, a shelf of oilcloth bundles, and a tin like a cake tin that did not hold cake.

Laurel opened the tin first: purple wax sticks; a pinch of black temper; two spare seals—C&K and a simple crown; beneath, a note: If found, return to Shoreline office. Reward. C. The tidy hand.

Bundles shuffled like birds: accounting—Shoreline Dues, clean cousin to the ledger; minutes—Gentlemen of the Shore, bloodless arrangements, and in the impatient hand: talk too much—no names underlined twice; receipts—launderer, tailor, boatwright, and an invoice to C. Wycliffe & Sons—Buffalo, engraving: ship crest and crown, 40 impressions; press @ $2.10 (1901).

"Wycliffe's line," Clara said. "Merchants," Laurel replied. "Stamping a company that stamped its sins." "Not innocent," Amelia said, "but not the hand that—" She stopped.

At the back lay a thin book, plain card, dated 1932. Laurel opened it and exhaled, small: names, not initials; sums and notes; two crossed so hard the paper tore. One dead twenty years. One alive—the egg seller's father. A woman: kept books; went to Duluth. Beside M. Finch: qtrmstr—knows all routes. Beside V. Finch, the impatient hand again: no more nights.

"This," Laurel said softly, closing it with both hands, "is the book they'd kill for."

Haines sistered a brace beneath a sagging beam; the chamber accepted the help. They carried names upstairs as if bearing sleeping infants. Laurel locked the book in her satchel. "Daylight," she said. "No whispers in doorways. We ask, show, register—so rumor can't erase."

Clara wrote GRANARY — WARRANT — NAMES, then underlined: Silent Partners ≠ Silent Anymore.

Lady Grey, satisfied, sat with her back to the passage, purr stitching ordinary to extraordinary. They ate late—bread and butter tasting of grass and assurance. Doris came for water, saw lanterns and paper, and looked at the teacup guarding the board; her mouth trembled. Amelia put her arms around her. "We're bringing it up," she said. "Properly. You don't have to hold it alone under your feet."

"Then set another cup," Doris said, iron brightening her face. "If the past is coming to the table, it can have tea—and tell the truth."

Outside, the lake exhaled down the alley. Inside, women and a cat—and a few decent men—set shoulders to old work: lifting what was hidden, labeling without malice, placing it where the town could see. The chamber had given its first accounting; the closet, the book with names; the tunnel linked café to river, river to granary, granary to boats, boats to a company that stamped purple wax and crowns on commerce. Tomorrow, another paper; Harlow with it; doors that once opened only for secrets would open for the law.

Lady Grey's purr filled corners like a sewing machine repairing a town's tear.

Chapter 32

Old Crimes Resurface

Morning poured through lace like milk, softening corners that did not feel soft. Amelia opened the shutters early and laid the ledger on the corner table, its damp edges weighted under blue-willow saucers. Clara, pencils pared to dangerous points, titled a fresh page LINES OF INHERITANCE. Lady Grey held the window ledge like a dais, tail curled: sentence not finished.

"This column—Silent Partners—is the vein," Clara said, tapping with the pencil's wood. "Follow it to the heart. That's where a knife belongs."

"To lance it," Amelia said. "Draw out the rot."

Light slid across initials. "There," Clara whispered. "H.F.— keeper of the keys."

Doris's grandfather. The ledger made the old metaphor literal. Around it gathered quiet titles for unlawful roles: keeper of the keys, qtrmstr, dock-walk, scribe. They moved through names turned street signs—Sutter, Westcott, Denvers—and those that slept in the churchyard.

"L.S. could be Leland Sutter," Clara said, line to Sutter Hardware—current: Owen (grandson).

"E.W.—Elias Westcott," Amelia said. "His portrait still hangs in the school."

"And M.F.?"

"Matilda Finch," Amelia breathed. "Doris's great-aunt. She did figures."

Clara wrote: Matilda—bookkeeper. A woman's hand in "Gentlemen of the Shore" made hypocrisy tidy, not absent.

Lady Grey pressed a paw to a later amendment: V.G.—dues carried—says belongs.

"Not our Vernon," Clara said. "But someone else clutching 'inheritance.'"

"And our Vernon thought the same," Amelia murmured. "Someone cut the rope."

They matched letters to lineage—H.D. that might be Harlow's kin (Amelia refused that thought, for now), J.H. with a triangle (favor owed), R.P. with sums that sounded like handshakes. The page whispered complicity like a choir. Marginalia worsened the song: a crown marking "premium pieces," tidy notes on suppers, the harried hand slashing no speeches. no names. On a shipping slate: no more nights —the s bitten short. Clara's duet of hands had bones now.

By ten Laurel arrived, satchel in hand. "Magistrate at noon for the granary," she said, laying developed prints and turning the purple seal toward the light. "He dislikes agreeing with me; he'll like necessity."

"C&K—Crest & Keel," Clara said. "Invoice to C. Wycliffe & Sons—Buffalo—for the die."

"Henry's people cut the stamp," Laurel allowed. "Origin, not absolution."

She skimmed the ledger. "'Keeper of the keys'—Harold Finch." She didn't soften it. "Doris needn't carry that yet."

"She must soon," Amelia said.

"After the magistrate signs," Laurel replied. "Law first."

They worked like a small editorial board: Laurel sleeved brittle entries; Clara drew a family map that looked like rivers, then confession; Amelia sorted names by their willingness to live in a ledger, handing instruments like a scrub nurse.

By eleven they crossed to Gossamer Fables. Mr. Larkin cleared the back table, produced tea and the shop safe key. Lady Grey patrolled the aisles, staring books back into place. Clara slid out a 1931–34 clipping: SHORELINE DINNER HONORS—forks gleaming, goblets catching flash. Names matched initials. A younger Sutter posed with a carving knife; Elias Westcott leaned civic; a woman—likely Matilda Finch—rested a thin ledger under her palm.

"The fork handle's engraved," Clara said. "We have its twin."

"Proof of use," Laurel said. "Not just possession."

They copied names with powder-near-flame caution. At a quarter to noon Laurel left. "If his lunch is trout, he'll sign. If not, I borrow Duluth's sternness." Mr. Larkin locked the safe at her nod.

The square felt a fraction warmer. Laurel returned with a second warrant—Granary: Lower Storage / Drainage Screen / Ropeway— tidy and sufficient. Harlow would meet them at one; Haines would bring braces and that quiet authority that looks like nothing until boards need coaxing.

Doris, carefully dressed, came to the inn. "We've errands," Amelia said. "Your name is coming off the first line." Doris steadied. "Drag the past into my kitchen," she said. "I'll put a kettle on it." Lady Grey approved with a circuit.

They reached the granary by the river path. Harlow waited hat in hand; Haines's hammer spoke gently to joists. Light seeped through a grating; the ropeway sagged; the screen wore weeds and a bright smear of purple wax.

"Photograph," Laurel said. Flash pressed purple into memory.

"The shelf will hold if you step where I chalk," Haines said, drawing two Xs. "Only one at a time."

"Then one," Laurel decided. "Clara."

Clara braced, reached through slats; the river licked her knuckles.

Her fingers found wrapped paper. She tugged; it came free with a wet slurp. Two glass ampoules—stopped with purple wax—bobbled; she caught them, handed them back.

"Enough," Laurel said. "We don't tempt the river twice."

The parcel opened under a bone folder: a water-damaged broadsheet—THE SILVER SPOON HEIST—in the same block hand Wycliffe had clutched; beneath, a tidy list of crate "diversions," and, shorter and angrier, the hurried man's ledger: H.F.—keys; M.F.—books; L.S.—rope; E.W.—cart; at the bottom: V.F.—knows—demands share. no more nights. Laurel sleeved that page: hand B—confession by distribution.

The ampoules clouded faintly violet. "Brandy, not poison," Laurel judged. "Gifts for club nights." Into a padded box they went.

Under silt: a small strongbox, twin to those under the café. The lock relented; inside, receipts tied in purple ribbon and IOUs with familiar tremble. The top bore Elias Westcott's signature; amount crossed out and replaced: dues met—in kind; in the tidy hand, someone had added: river stone. Clara disliked the poetry.

"Routes, nights, names," Laurel said, placing paper beside ledger. "We won't need to raise our voices."

"You'll call in the names," Harlow said, lines easing.

"You will," Laurel corrected gently. "I'll sit. You'll speak. Chair on the aisle for Doris; not the front row."

"What of living men with dead fathers' initials?" Amelia asked.

"We show the page, not the noose," Laurel said. "Old crimes are crimes. Guilt isn't lamp oil. If living hands are clean, they help repair. If not"—she tapped the hurried page—"we'll know. This is a map, not a net."

Word outran them: a meeting at the hall. On the way, Owen Sutter planted himself, ledger like a shield. "You're dragging old bills into the street," he said. "My grandfather isn't here to answer."

"Neither is mine," Amelia replied. "The living can help truth speak—or pile new lies."

"You like a performance," he told Laurel.

"I like a record," she said. "Stand beside your name if it's clean."

He weighed his ledger, stared at the cat; Lady Grey didn't blink. He stepped aside. "Don't expect harmony."

"At least honesty," Clara said.

They ate proper stew because Laurel insisted. Doris set plates without spill; Lady Grey lioned the hearth.

At the hall, neighbors had washed their faces twice. Harlow spoke road-plain. "We recovered records of an old crime. Those men are dead. The crime is not. Two men have died this week. These papers bear on why."

Laurel held up the ladle crest. "Not a family mark. Crest & Keel. It ruled the river by night and fed tables by day." Purple seal; press; invoice to C. Wycliffe & Sons. "Draw your moral lines if you like; the facts draw practical ones."

Clara slid out the Silent Partners page. "An index," she said. "We won't read initials aloud yet. We'll say names when that is true."

Harlow lifted a hand; bristles lowered. "I will call those I need," he said. "Daylight. With the mayor. No midnight."

Laurel set the hurried page where all could see: V.F.—knows—demands share. no more nights. The room heard it.

"We'll bring the rest to light," Harlow said. "You'll let us. And you'll go home without pounding doors."

"Why not burn the books and be done?" Reid Parnell called.

"Because books tell truth when mouths are gone," Laurel said gently. "And because crimes didn't die with the men who taught them. We'll find the living hands."

The town shifted posture. Not relief; readiness. Mrs. Cranston squeezed Doris's hand. The Westcotts walked shoulder-level. Sutter detoured around Clara; Clara let him.

Back at the inn, tea large enough to float courage. Doris sipped without asking conversation to do more than it could. Clara set the program down like a weight. Laurel loosened her satchel strap. Lady Grey turned twice in Amelia's lap and settled: we are still here.

"Old crimes are walking again," Amelia said.

"They always were," Clara answered. "We turned on the lamplight."

"Tomorrow I speak with the names in the 1932 book," Laurel said. "Harlow sits. You do not. No cat. Low temperature."

"Is the hurried hand still in town?" Clara asked.

"He can't be far," Laurel said to the window. "Men who write no more nights want the ending to look like someone else's punctuation. He'll come for books, tunnel, or the easy target. The cat is smarter."

Lady Grey purred, deep and slow, thickening the air like honey. Amelia looked at the ledger, now dry enough to hold its own weight; at Doris, whose hands had quieted; at Clara's chart—now a map; at Laurel, who'd sharpened her pencil for the next act.

The crimes weren't finished. They had placed their feet in the room. But the room, at last, had a floor.

Chapter 33

A False Ally

By late afternoon the inn had settled into the deliberate quiet Amelia cultivated when nerves ran thin. She straightened the lace runner, nudged chairs a finger-width nearer the hearth, and smoothed the vase of sweet peas. At the escritoire Clara copied from the ledger with clerk's patience; Lady Grey kept the windowsill like a small gargoyle.

Three brisk taps broke the hush. Mr. Colby stood on the threshold—coat buttoned to the throat, hat brim trimming his spectacles into hard moons. He moved through the room with the air of a man who sees ledgers where others see parlor.

"Miss Farnsworth," he said. "Might I come in?"

"Of course," Amelia answered.

Colby spoke with calm certainty. "I have been told you've made discoveries concerning the town's past. Such documents belong to the historical society. It is my duty to preserve them. Private hands risk loss or misuse."

Lady Grey crossed to him; a small growl puffed from her chest. Amelia asked what made him certain such documents existed. He did not ask who else knew; he asked only to hold them. The cat batted his coat; fabric cracked. A metallic clink skittered on the boards and stopped: a small coin stamped with a crown over a narrow-bellied hull.

Amelia lifted the coin. "How did this come to be in your pocket, Mr. Colby?"

"Collectors' pieces," he said too quickly. "Old tokens."

"Curios with the exact crest stamped into goods hidden under Doris Finch's floor," Clara said. "Curios with the same purple wax in their creases."

Colby stiffened, finding hauteur. "You do not understand the danger you court. Let me do what I am trained to do."

"Or tell us why you carry proof you've already been where you insist we must not go," Amelia replied.

He left with a finality that felt like a missing tooth. Clara wrote three words: Colby—coin, urgent, avoids. Lady Grey settled into Amelia's lap like a paperweight.

Laurel arrived and turned the coin under the window light. "Not common," she said. "He did not expect to drop it."

Mr. Larkin had reported Colby called at the bookshop earlier to ask if the society might store "sensitive papers." Larkin had refused. Colby was making a sweep—door to door. Laurel suggested a counter: copies marked to betray handling. No originals. Identical packets for Harlow, the magistrate, Mr. Larkin—sealed, logged. One decoy would stay in the escritoire as bait.

They prepared three packets: club dinner photograph, purple seal impression, Silent Partners page (initials only), and the hurried slate—no more nights—on plain and thin paper variants. Clara pricked minute cipher marks; Amelia sealed with linen ties and plain wax; Laurel added a pale violet ink dot on each fold. The decoy went into the drawer; Lady Grey sat atop it like a guardian.

Dusk found the inn dim. A figure moved along the fence; Lady Grey's spine rippled. They did not pursue. Mr. Larkin arrived: Colby had gone from the archives to his cottage, carrying a leather folio "like a priest on the way to a last confession." He walked the lake path at odd hours and had keys to the society. Laurel stretched and announced they would stroll.

They walked the birch-shaded path to Colby's neat cottage. Laurel knocked once; Colby opened with spectacles adjusted and a practiced voice. Laurel set the purple seal on his desk. "Have you received any artifacts bearing this impression?" she asked. "Interfering with chain of custody in an active investigation is an error that lengthens a middle-aged summer."

Colby bristled. Lady Grey explored his cases, sniffed a moth-eaten velvet bag with tiny silver anchors, and found coins displayed in rows—crowns, ships, and a combined crest. Colby claimed tides and private conversations as his business. Laurel warned: "Not if you're fishing; very much if you're disposing."

He would not be pushed. They left; Clara exhaled. "He has done more than read minutes," she said.

At half past nine a young delivery boy arrived with a note: Bring the ledger copies to the society at once. Key matters must be secured before morning.—L. The loop on the k suggested Duluth stationery; the L suggested someone pretending to be Laurel. Two hands again—tidy copying tidy.

Laurel answered on their terms. They dressed another packet—empty but appearing weighty—pinned it with a different cipher and sent a reply: On our way.—A. They would meet him on their terms, two doors away, in the dark.

Shortly after, Colby returned. He entered with a key careful enough to avoid wear, lifted the top packet from the escritoire, and tucked it under his coat. Lady Grey's tail brushed from sill to desk; Colby froze. Laurel stepped from shadow.

"Mr. Colby," she said. "The society keeps unfortunate hours."

"A misunderstanding," he stammered, setting the packet down.

"You had the coin," Amelia said simply. "You prefer to hold the rope and call it a safety line. Do not come into my house after dusk again."

He nodded—an apology with no words—and left. Laurel locked

the door. Clara opened the packet to find the blank leaf inside, proof he would have tied and shelved it to feel the town safer by hiding truth.

Larkin later reported Colby had visited his shop and touched nothing. Clara wrote: Colby—curator of silence. Laurel made a schedule: morning interviews with Elias Westcott's grandson and Owen Sutter; an afternoon appointment with Colby—bring nothing; answer everything.

Doris asked whether to lay the tea cart for three or four. "Three," Laurel said. "And a fourth cup clean, on the side." Lady Grey curled in the sun, eyes half-closed but alert.

That morning Colby came for his interview. The inn passed the bowl of truth without spilling. Laurel spoke quietly; men who kept their chins high were not always those with nothing to hide. Colby's willingness to borrow thresholds was dangerous—different from evil, no safer.

At dusk a second note arrived: Bridge, dusk. Bring nothing. Come alone.—L. Clara sharpened. "He will try again."

"No," Laurel said, folding the note away. "We will." She set a plan: draw him where they chose and bring their own lamp.

Lady Grey answered with a small decisive mew. The inn, which had held its breath all day, exhaled.

They would not be lured to a bridge. They would set their own.

Chapter 34

Inn Guest Betrayal

Evening settled on Tumblebrook like lace—soft and deceptive. Lamps hummed, tabletops glowed, the hearth ticked. By look alone the inn was sanctuary; Amelia knew it was costume. She carried a tray—tea for Room Four's quiet lodger, shortbread for Mrs. Cranston, ice for Mr. Humphries's wrist. The escritoire's hidden coin weighed on her like a stitched secret.

Lady Grey patrolled: hearth to window to desk, tail flicking small cipher marks—street clear; do not relax.

Room Four's guest—Elliot—took his tea with practiced mildness, saucer centered, spectacles neutral, a face made to be forgotten.

"Miss Farnsworth," he said. "A private word?"

Clara set her linens down and took a chair opposite. Lady Grey settled against Amelia's shoes like a sandbag.

"I'm not an ordinary guest," he began. "I'm an investigator. Unofficial, effective. Heirloom thefts—silver, crests, corporate marks. The trail brought me here. I hear a spoon draws a crowd."

"And we are to applaud?" Clara asked.

"You're to let me help. Ledger, chamber—knowledge burns holes in pockets. It needs a safe."

"Yours?" Amelia asked. "Safekeeping—or safekeeping away?"

"I expose networks," he said. "Coins, dies, clubs that are not. Men like Colby muzzle history; men like Wycliffe monetize it. I map it."

Lady Grey stepped to his knee and pressed a paw to his coat pocket. Something faintly jingled.

"Change," he smiled.

"For coffee—or coins?" Clara said.

"We'll think on it," Amelia answered. He bowed and climbed, footsteps marking risers like a counted escape.

"Uninvited help," Clara wrote. Lady Grey took the foot of the stairs and held it.

The parlor thinned to the small noises of evening. Amelia bolted the porch door and checked the escritoire a third time; Clara made rounds like any innkeeper—also counting boots. Lady Grey chose the escritoire for a bed.

Betrayal arrived small: at half past nine the telephone went flat; at a quarter to ten the back-stair lamp was tamped low; a draft licked the hall. "He's testing," Clara said. "Let him think we aren't watching," Amelia answered.

Elliot returned, spectacles pocketed, hat in hand—calculated informality. "Telephone's out," he offered lightly. A narrow nick crossed his wrist. He drifted toward the back stair, humming, then disappeared.

They followed Elliot from the inn to Doris' garden.

"The chamber," Amelia whispered. The backdoor glass was warm. Inside, the board sat askew. The passage breathed.

Lady Grey's eyes flashed from the crack. She slipped ahead. Elliot's shadow moved first, shoes in his hand, scarf over his mouth, lamp low as a trapped firefly. He wasn't here to look. He was here to take.

Laurel's voice came from the stair. "Don't be heroic. Not until he's turned his pockets out."

They let him lead. In the chamber he set his lamp on a crate, laid out a cloth bag and twine with the care of a man who reuses packaging.

"Hello, Mr. Elliot," Laurel said.

He stilled. "How long have you known?"

"Since you recited a biography to a woman who measures people by how they stir tea," Laurel said. "You couldn't have known Colby's visit concerned us unless you watched him and waited."

"You cut the line," Clara added.

"I noticed it was out," he said.

"You observed it into silence," Amelia replied.

"You can't stop this," he said. "Let me take the metal—scatter it. Make it vanish; keep your book and virtue."

"If we let you, we help erase it," Laurel said.

He reached for the bag; Lady Grey pinned it with one paw. He yanked; the bag tore. Coins—crowns over ships—spilled and chimed. "Collecting relics?" Amelia asked. "Or seeding a market?"

"You'll be blamed for the silver," he pressed. "Paper can be challenged; metal will be tied to you by proximity. The fastest fix is water."

"Where you can fish it later," Laurel said.

"To say we're done living in that room," Amelia answered when he spoke of old sins feeding families.

He feinted toward Amelia, tore up a crate lid; goblets blushed into view. Laurel set her palm to his chest and denied direction. He bared his teeth, then backed for the passage. "See you on the bridge," he said—and slid away.

"Let him go," Laurel said. "He isn't the one with a ledger."

They replaced what he'd hoped to steal. Clara tallied and noted: Elliot—attempted extract; fresh scratch (left wrist). Lady Grey nosed the last coin into Clara's palm.

They arrived back at the inn. Amelia relit the back-stair lamp and tied a white strip to its chain. The escritoire was locked; the decoy packet sat intact beneath the cat.

"He cut it near the lane," Laurel said. "I'll have Harlow send a man."

Amelia set her hands on the escritoire. "Fear is cheaper than repairs," she said.

Laurel turned the coin once and set it on a saucer. "Fear is loud; records are durable. We'll pick durable."

A knock—neither shy nor official. Colby. Dark coat, leather folio, spectacles on. "I've had a letter," he said, showing an anonymous note urging him to move items "under my pillow." He let the nonsense show and looked at the escritoire. "I didn't write it. I came because someone stirs both pots."

"Elliot," Clara said.

"He came to the archives," Colby admitted, pride dented by accuracy. "Asked coin-provenance like a schoolboy with a locksmith's hands."

"Sit," Laurel said. "We'll show you something you can catalog better than rumor." They gave him three coins. He produced a loupe despite himself. "Two lots," he said. "The second copied the first."

"And who taught them?" Laurel asked.

"The society has a die," he said quietly. "It predates me."

"You intend to collect and control," Laurel said.

"I keep facts from becoming theater," he snapped, then steadied. "Latch your doors. He isn't the only guest who can take apart a lock without chipping the paint."

They set the watch: Clara on the settee, Laurel by the window, Amelia on a pallet, Lady Grey draped over the nearest chair. After two, someone tried the back door; the latch held. Rain began near three; dawn paled at four; Doris peeked in at six and withdrew as if from a ceremony.

Amelia closed her hand over the coin. "Inn guest betrayal," she said—sour and bracing.

Clara wrote the words, then underlined water.

Lady Grey sprang to the escritoire and settled like a statue on a tomb. Morning arrived and demanded its work—coffee, bread, small, honest clinks.

It would be easy to pretend nothing had changed.

The coin in Amelia's palm politely disagreed.

Chapter 35

Clara Connects the Dots

Rain stitched the town shut the next night, a quieting needle threading every eave and awning. Inside Gossamer Fables, the air smelled of paste and old ink—a comfort Clara felt in her bones. She had the back office to herself—the door bolted, the bell muted with velvet so the wind couldn't betray her. A brass lamp poured honeyed light across the oak table. Within its circle: the Finch ledger, three gray archival boxes marked *Bills of Lading, 1930–1935*, a fan of receipts, two warehouse permits, and a chipped teacup holding sharpened pencils.

Lady Grey had followed her through the downpour and now perched in a damask chair, tail neatly twined, amber eyes gleaming like two coins. A magistrate in fur.

Clara cracked the ledger's spine and turned to the ribboned page: *Silent Partners.* Initials marched down the column—H.F., L.S., E.W., D.K., J.T.—each with a sum and, in a second hand, a tiny crown above a ship. That crest had nagged at her for days.

She slid the top box closer. The manifests were onion-skin thin. On the corner of one: *Crown Shipping Line, Thunder Bay, Ontario.* A crown. A ship. Another manifest: *Crown.* A third: *Crown.* Her pulse ticked higher.

"Do you see?" she whispered to Lady Grey. "It's not ornamental —it's corporate."

The cat crossed the table and planted a paw on the Crown emblem, stamping approval. Clara laughed softly.

"Excellent. Co-counsel agrees."

Ledger to her left, manifests to her right, she began the work she loved: cross-reference.

— *Ledger, 12 May 1932:* crown mark, "club dinner," initials H.F. and L.S.

— *Manifest, SS Lark,* arrived 13 May 1932: freight listed as "assorted table service," consignee *Sutter & Finch Brokerage.*

She drew an arrow so deep the paper puckered. The rain found rhythm and kept time.

— *Ledger, 17 Oct 1933:* crown; "barrels shifted"; initials E.W.

— *Manifest, SS Gannet,* Duluth terminal 18 Oct: grain + "assorted valuables"; customs note initialed by a local name.

"They used the lake as a road," she murmured. "Everything honest on top, everything else wedged between crates."

Lady Grey nudged a receipt toward her: *O'Shaughnessy & Sons —packing rope, crown.* Back in the ledger, crown-and-ship meant a faint penciled star. No crown, no star. A code to itself—priority or contraband.

"They left their key in the door," she breathed.

She traced Crown routes on onionskin overlays: Thunder Bay to Duluth, east to Silver Bay, sometimes to a private dock unnamed. She taped each to the table edge so she could flip years like wings. Along the margins she wrote: *Sutter, Westcott, Denvers, Keene... Finch— keeper of the keys.* Keys to storerooms, to codes, to the map.

At the back of the ledger, shorthand entries yielded a legend: crown = Crown ship; ship alone = local barge; two crowns = double value; triangle = dry run.

"Good," she whispered. "He wasn't greedy—he was right."

Vernon Finch had believed the silver belonged by blood. The ledger showed what blood chose instead—to live by concealment.

Her pencil moved again. Three columns: Finch, Local Partners, External. H.F. and D.F. under the first; L.S. (Leland Sutter) and E.W. (Elias Westcott) the second. The third: A.R., C.G., W.P.—each tagged with crowns and extravagant sums. In the manifests, one name recurred: *W. Pierce, Crown Shipping Agent.*

"W.P.," she said, underlining thrice. "A man with a desk who knew which crates could bear extra weight."

Lady Grey's ears flicked toward the shop, then stilled. No footsteps. Clara bent to the last box: *Customs & Tariff Notations.* One 1934 declaration halted her—a shipment of "household wares" waved through. A note: *Same club lot; keys with H.F.* Meaningless before, now confession.

Crown Shipping wasn't a Finch invention—it was the machine they joined. The Gentlemen of the Shore bought standing with stolen metal, dined with evidence, and hid the rest beneath Doris Finch's kitchen.

"This is why they're panicked," Clara told the cat. "It isn't the silver. It's the ledger that gives the silver a voice."

Lady Grey stepped across papers and pressed her nose to an invoice: *Terrace & Cole, Thunder Bay—two crates, crown die blanks.*

"They cut their own coin," Clara whispered. The die existed on both sides of the water. Elliot's promise to "scatter the metal" had a second edge—anyone holding the die could flood the market with false relics. She wrote: *Locate die. Who has it now?*

Rain tested the glass. She sipped cold tea and steadied the lamp's flame. Next came *Tumblebrook Council Minutes, 1930–1936.*

Motion to approve wharf repairs, funded by private subscription (*H.F., L.S., E.W.*).

Keys, repairs, private money. The quay underwrote the scheme that used it. She jotted: *north quay = gate.* Watchman paid in petty cash—the town paid itself to look aside.

A soft scratch at the office door made the lamp tremble. Clara froze, listening. Wind, maybe. Lady Grey nosed the crack, then returned, calm. "Thank you," Clara murmured. "Sensible as always."

Back to the ledger. Two letters had puzzled her: V.G. On a Crown manifest—*V. Greer, dock foreman.* She circled hard. A Greer handled Crown's boxes before they crossed the lake. Not the same Vernon now dead in Doris's thyme.

Facts chose sides. She stacked her findings and wrote, with satisfying drama:

HOW THEY DID IT:

Source: Crown Shipping moves Canadian silver—estate pilfer, scrap.

Marking: Crown die blanks stamp crest as camouflage.

Transit: Honest cargo atop, silver beneath.

Gate: North quay repaired privately; Finch controls code.

Mask: "Club dinners" spend a token fraction; surplus buried under café.

Profit: Silent partners take cuts; reputations guarded still.

Present: Outsiders want leverage; Elliot wants metal; Colby wants control.

Then one more line: *Doris = heir to suspicion, not crime.*

Lady Grey washed her paw in ceremony. Clara stretched, pinned a fresh sheet to the wall, and sketched the lake's crescent, river's bite, and Tumblebrook's square. Between Thunder Bay and home, she plotted ship routes in pencil: *Lark. Gannet. Petrel. Crown Victor.* Water, made legible.

Morning: make copies—never originals. Colby's loupe would find honest work. She sorted what to carry and what to hide: ledger swaddled in brown paper, manifests copied and tied, council minutes left behind. The Terrace & Cole invoice went into a blue folder marked *Ship Chandlers—Misc.*

Lady Grey hopped onto the ledger like a wax seal. Clara smiled, lifted her, and earned a mild protest. "Guard the atlas, then," she said.

A gust rattled the windows; the office door eased open an inch, then stilled. Someone had the handle—then let go. Clara set her ear to the wood. Nothing. Chosen silence. She slipped the bolt with a decisive click.

"If you're the wind," she said softly, "you may knock again in poetry."

One more list, this time of calls: Amelia—now; Laurel—first light; Magistrate—bring Colby; Harlow—Crown tie thins motive.

At 8 pm, she gathered the blue folder and satchel, snuffed the lamp, and left the office dark but not empty—the way a theater remembers its set.

Rain hit like benediction. Lamps were smudges, most asleep. Above the apothecary, a shade lifted and fell. Clara didn't look longer. When you carry truth, you learn not to feed suspicion with your gaze.

Lady Grey trotted ahead, a slip of silver shadow. They went home the long way—for lighted streets and time to let thought settle.

Amelia opened the door before Clara could knock twice. One look at Clara's face and the satchel, and she reached for both. Lady Grey flowed to the escritoire.

"In the office," Clara whispered. "Crown Shipping—it's not a crest. It's a company. They threaded the lake with us as the needle."

Amelia's shoulders eased, the relief of shape revealed. "Come. Tea will keep the words from breaking."

On the parlor rug, rain whispering against the panes, Clara unfolded her map and pinned it to the escritoire lid. She spoke quickly, then slower as Amelia's shock turned to strategy. The table filled with proof—ledger, invoices, manifests—an altar to the god of paper.

"It's not a family sin," Clara said, "but a profession nested in the town's blindness. The Finches were keyholders. Crown was the artery. Doris is—"

"Standing in for their guilt," Amelia finished, touching the name gently. "We call Laurel now to let her know what you uncovered, she will decide how to proceed."

"And Elliot?"

"He tried the office door—or his shadow did. He'll try water next, to muddy the trail."

"Then we'll meet him upstream," Amelia said. "With copies, witnesses, and a cat who writes ethics lessons."

Lady Grey purred like a small engine.

Chapter 36

The Historian's Confession

Morning came brittle and thin, as if the light itself hesitated to touch Tumblebrook. Amelia rose from fractured sleep with the glint of metal still in her eyes and the memory of Clara's hand yanking her out of harm's arc. She moved through the inn on quiet habit—laying spoons, warming the pot—but her mind was already elsewhere.

By the time Clara came down—pale, notebook clutched like a compact shield—Amelia had decided. "We need to speak to Colby," she said, steady now. "He's tied too neatly into this. He came for our papers, called the crest a club's, and carried coins he had no right to. We've let him sidestep long enough."

Clara's fatigue sharpened into purpose. "Agreed. After last night, no more benefit of the doubt."

Lady Grey leapt to the windowsill and twitched her tail once, a small consent. That settled it.

Colby's cottage sat near the library, a squat mix of stone and timber half-hidden by ivy. The front plot had gone to lapses—roses unpruned, weeds ambitious, a birdbath chalk-dry. Amelia had always pictured Colby as part of the scenery, weathered into place; today the quaintness felt like a mask.

He opened before they could knock, resignation already arranged on his face. "Miss Farnsworth. Miss Henderson." A thin nod. "I suppose I should have expected you."

"We'd like a proper conversation," Amelia said. "May we?"

He stepped aside. The air inside had the layered smell of paper and damp smoke. Shelves bowed under books and binders; folders crowded every surface in his small, crabbed hand. The fire in the grate sputtered without warming anything.

Clara's glance skimmed the room and found what wasn't there: gaps on the shelves, lids pressed back too quickly. Colby caught the look and let his mouth curl. "Wondering what's missing?" he said. "What I burned. What I hid."

"We know you've been less than honest," Amelia said. "You called the crest a club emblem. We've matched it to Crown Shipping. The ledgers tie Finches and others to smuggling. You've known for years. Why bury it?"

He sank into a worn armchair and gestured them to sit. His hands trembled once and steadied. "Because truth destroys as surely as lies," he said hoarsely. "In the '50s Harold Finch asked me to help catalog town papers. He was... a mentor to me. That's when I found the ledgers, manifests, letters—what you've begun to find now. Smuggling. Preference. Respectable theft. I was young enough to want to shout it. Harold begged me not to."

"Begged," Clara said. "Or threatened?"

"Begged." His eyes watered and didn't spill. "He said the town was still mending after Prohibition. Exposing it would ruin families, graft shame to children who hadn't earned it. I believed him. I burned some, locked some away. I told myself I was protecting Tumblebrook."

Amelia measured him, listening for performance and finding something rawer. "You were shielding Harold," she said. "Not just a town."

"You're not wrong," he said quietly. "He was flawed and persuasive, and I mistook secrecy for care."

Clara flipped to a page of careful sketches—the crown above the hull. "You said nothing when Vernon came asking. Nothing when Doris was accused. Two men are dead. Did you think silence would keep the peace?"

Colby flinched. "I never wished for blood. When Vernon arrived I feared the past had found a new mouth. He was greedy, yes, but ignorant of how deep the pilings run. I thought if I minimized the crest he'd let it go."

"And instead he ended in Doris's thyme," Amelia said, voice gone thin. "That's what your silence bought."

His knuckles went white on the chair arms. "You think I don't know?" The confession cracked out of him. "Every whisper feels addressed to me. I tried to shield the town. I fed the hunger of those who live on shadows."

The fire hissed. Lady Grey slipped in unnoticed, sprang to the arm of Amelia's chair, and stared at Colby with her back just beginning to rise.

"You've admitted part of it," Amelia said, hand on the cat's spine. "But you're still holding something. You knew about Crown's partners. About the convenience of certain offices. What aren't you saying?"

He shut his mouth and let the clock tick three long beats. When he spoke again the word was careful. "Some truths carry more danger than shame. If I unlatch all of it, you may join Vernon and Wycliffe by the water. I won't be the one to hand you that."

"And if you don't," Clara said, softer and firmer, "more will die. Including us. Including Doris. Silence isn't protection now. It's complicity."

His jaw worked; pain passed over his face like cloud. "There are names that still buy favors," he said. "Men—and a few women— whose grandparents bought their seats with stolen silver. I thought if

I kept the record dull, we could live in the present. I made the shadows larger."

Amelia stood, Lady Grey a small sentinel at her elbow. "You've hidden enough. If you won't tell it, we'll find it and put our names to it. And when we do, it won't just be your conscience on trial. It will be the way this town tells its own story."

He lifted his eyes, weariness edged with fear. "Be careful, Miss Farnsworth," he said. "The roots go deeper than you think."

Clara gathered her notes. Lady Grey jumped down and led the way to air that didn't taste like old glue.

Outside, the sun had climbed but looked pale for the effort. Amelia drew a breath that reached the bottom of her lungs. "He gave us a piece," she said. "Not the hinge."

Clara wrote a single line as they walked. "The historian's confession is a map with blanks," she murmured. "We fill them."

At the gate, Lady Grey sat and watched the cottage with narrowed eyes, fur still lifted along the spine. She, too, had heard truth—and the secret that had slipped its leash behind it.

Chapter 37

Doris's Guilt

The café felt like a sealed box of memory. The familiar aroma of roasted beans and baked sugar had thinned beneath a heavier scent of dust and shuttered air. Yesterday's specials—*hazelnut shortbread, lemon-balm tea*—still ghosted across the chalkboard, handwriting pale as though etched on a tomb. Amelia closed the door with a careful push. The bell above gave only a faint, tired chime.

Doris sat alone at a corner table, her apron folded beside her like a lowered flag. Her fingers laced tightly in her lap; her shoulders sloped forward in a posture Amelia had never seen. The woman who once marshaled Harvest Festival booths with sharp wit and clapping hands now looked as though a single breath might scatter her. Stray wisps of hair clung damply to her temples; her eyes were swollen and raw.

Clara lingered near the counter, instinctively giving Amelia space. Lady Grey slipped from Amelia's arms to the tiled floor and trotted across the café with the silent authority of a small grey sentinel. She leapt onto Doris's lap without hesitation, curling into a warm, purring anchor. Doris's fingers clutched the cat immediately, trembling against the soft fur.

"I can't keep it in any longer," Doris whispered, voice cracking like thin ice. "It's crushing me."

Amelia slid into the chair opposite, folding her hands on the table. "Then tell me. You're not alone."

Doris stroked Lady Grey with frantic repetition, as though the cat's steady rhythm could lend her courage. "It's my family," she said. "The Finches. I've always known—deep down—that we weren't... clean. My grandfather Harold ruled our house like a fortress. My father never dared cross him. But at night..." Her voice wavered, eyes unfocused. "At night I'd lie awake and hear them arguing through the floorboards. My father whispering about debts, about shipments. My grandfather shouting about honor and keeping *the pact*."

She dragged a sleeve across her cheek. "They called it *the silver debt*. I didn't understand. I still don't. But I knew it wasn't about a bank account. It was something hidden. Something shameful. I prayed I'd never find out."

Clara stepped closer, notebook in hand but forgotten. "You never asked? Not even when you were older?"

A bitter laugh. "In our family, you didn't ask. You smiled. You baked. You poured tea and stayed out of the men's way. By the time I was old enough to demand answers, they were both dead. All I had left were whispers—and heavy looks from people who seemed to know more than I did. Sometimes I thought the whole town was in on a joke I wasn't allowed to hear."

Amelia reached across and covered Doris's hand. "The sins of the past don't define you. You built this café yourself. Whatever your grandfather hid, it's not yours to carry."

Doris shook her head. "That's exactly what people think. They see the Finch name. They whisper we always got away with too much. And now, with Vernon dead in my garden, they'll say it proves the curse. Sometimes I almost believe them."

Her fingers tightened on Lady Grey's fur until the cat flicked her tail. "When I see people whispering at the market, when children glance at me and then quickly away, I can almost hear my grandfather's voice in their stares: *We must pay the silver debt.* But I don't even know what we're paying for."

Lady Grey pressed her head firmly into Doris's palm, purr deepening as if to reject the thought outright. Doris's shoulders sagged a fraction. "She doesn't judge me," she whispered. "She just... stays."

Clara's voice was quiet but certain. "Staying is what matters. Amelia and I believe you. Lady Grey does too. That's stronger than whispers or curses."

Amelia squeezed her hand. "What's surfacing now isn't your doing. The ledger, the chamber, the smuggling—it's history rising. The guilty would love to let you bear the blame. Don't give them that power."

For a long moment, only Lady Grey's purr filled the café. Dust motes floated through the thin light leaking past the shutters, making everything look underwater.

Then Doris spoke again, more raggedly. "There's something I never told anyone. The night Vernon came to my garden—the night before he died—he wasn't alone." Her eyes flicked to Clara, then Amelia. "I heard another voice at the fence. Low, urgent. I thought it was a delivery boy. Then Vernon hissed something about *the ledger* and *the dock*. I couldn't make out the rest. When I went out, they'd gone. Next morning... you know what I found."

Amelia's breath caught. "Why didn't you tell Harlow?"

"Because I'm a Finch," Doris said simply. "Because I knew how it would sound. Because I was afraid the whisper of *another voice* would become *Doris hired a man.* I thought silence might protect me."

Clara crouched beside her chair, voice level. "Not telling nearly got you killed, Doris. Do you remember anything else—height, shape, accent?"

Doris shook her head, tears streaking. "Just the smell—metal and cloves. Like old pennies and spice."

Amelia and Clara exchanged a glance. The same metallic-clove scent they'd caught near the ledger chamber.

Amelia gentled her tone. "This matters. It helps prove you're not part of this. It gives us a thread to pull."

Lady Grey shifted, curling deeper into Doris's lap, eyes closing as though to say: enough for now.

For several minutes they sat like that—Clara crouched, Amelia leaning forward, Doris bent over the cat. The café felt less like a confessional than a triage ward for a wounded spirit.

Finally Doris straightened, eyes rimmed but steadier. "You truly think I can stand apart from it? That I'm not bound by their shadows?"

"I know it," Amelia said firmly. "And if the town has forgotten, we'll remind them. But you have to stand with us. No more hiding things that could clear you."

Clara nodded. "You aren't the one who hid ledgers in false walls or moved silver across the lake. You've been the one keeping this town fed. That's the truth people forget."

A watery smile flickered across Doris's face as she stroked Lady Grey's ears. "I don't know what I'd do without you."

"You'll find out," Amelia said, voice acquiring a new steel. "Because we're going to drag the truth into daylight. And when we do, they'll have to look at you differently."

For the first time since entering, Amelia felt the café shift. The silence no longer suffocated; it wrapped around them like a fragile cocoon. The motes in the beams of sunlight looked like ash lifting from a fire that had burned long enough.

Clara rose, resting a hand on Doris's shoulder. "We'll start with what you just told us—the other voice. The smell. The ledger at the dock. If you think of anything else, no matter how small, tell us. The smallest details might keep you alive."

Doris nodded, clinging to Lady Grey a final moment before letting her jump down. "All right. I'm frightened. But with you beside me, perhaps I can breathe again. Perhaps I can believe I'm not cursed after all."

Amelia squeezed her hand one last time. "Hold to that."

They left together, stepping back into the mid-afternoon sun. Behind them, the café door closed with its faint chime, but something had shifted: Doris Finch had handed them a new thread and, in doing so, had taken the first breath of her own freedom. Lady Grey trotted ahead on the cobblestones, tail high, as if to say: the hunt continues.

Chapter 38

The True Mastermind

By the time gulls began their racket over Tumblebrook Lake, Clara had already spread half the town's paper bones across the inn's breakfast table. Ink smudged her fingers; a few pins had lost their grip; fatigue rimmed her eyes, but the clarity there chilled Amelia more than coffee could steady.

"It isn't a feud," Clara said. "It's a business plan."

Lady Grey hopped to a chair, then onto a manifest, placing one paw like a stamp.

"Tell me," Amelia said.

"Harold Benton," Clara tapped. "A 'heritage revitalization' developer. His money snakes through shell companies—Toronto, Montreal, Rotterdam. He arrives when a town wobbles and offers a hand; while it leans, he picks the pockets. Antiques, silver, rare books, hardware—anything he can launder as 'historic salvage.' He didn't stumble on Finch silver; he hunted it. His investigators billed for a 'Finch line historical map' two months before Vernon came home."

"The map of everywhere the Finches touched water," Amelia murmured.

"Vernon gave Benton cover. I can't yet prove Benton bought his ticket, but here—" a bank stub—"H.B., with a countersignature from a woman on three Benton fronts. He paid the first boarding-house bill and retained a Duluth attorney 'in anticipation of an inheritance matter.'"

"Vernon was bait."

"Bait. And when bait wriggles, you cut it loose."

Mist lay on the lake like milk on a saucer. Somewhere in that brightness crouched all their dark finds: the chamber, the ledger, old debts that never stopped collecting.

"Benton's been to the café twice," Amelia said. "Left his card under the sugar bowl like he wanted it in Doris's pocket."

"He's a collector," Clara said. "Of things and people."

"There's more. Wycliffe—the spoon man—appears in a Montreal dealer's letter from a smuggling case. His job: muddy ownership with 'documents,' then vanish. Expendable."

Amelia saw his body by the river, the page clenched like a last prayer.

"And the man in Doris's garden," Clara added. "Clove cigarettes, winch grease—dock foreman from Duluth, paid on two Benton shipments. Short, heavy shoulders, favors his right leg, rope-burn scar."

The veil on the lake felt less romantic, more like a curtain before the worst act.

"How do we bring this to Harlow?" Amelia asked. "Say 'Rotterdam' and he'll throw us out on the syllables."

"Not if we bring this," Clara said, sliding a land registry copy over. A quitclaim deed for parcels by the boathouses: Harold Benton's LLC, and beneath it **Town of Tumblebrook—Provisional Trust** by Chief Inspector D. Harlow, signed a month after Benton announced his fund. Fine print: if land is "abandoned, contaminated, or encumbered by unclaimed chattel," the town may assign a **qualified restoration agent** for ninety days.

"Harlow," Amelia breathed.

"Not bribed—used," Clara said. "Benton sold him a safety play. Now he has a legal foot on the shoreline. In three weeks he can convert provisional to permanent and keep anything 'discovered' as salvage."

Lady Grey went very still, amber eyes steady: pick up your courage; the runway shortens.

"Then today," Amelia said. "Council—and something messier."

"Both," Clara agreed. "We need daylight and witnesses, and proof Harlow can't file away. We make Benton reach."

News outran the weather. By ten the clerk had an agenda; by eleven Harold Benton swept in wearing an excellent blue suit and a tie like sunlit water. He smiled like an uncle. Lady Grey slid from Amelia's shawl, wove around Benton's shoes, sniffed, flicked her tail, withdrew.

Inside, boiled coffee and polish. The council looked relieved to hand decisions to a man with a suit. Harlow stood at the back, hat in hand, looking like he'd slept badly.

"Public comment," the chairwoman said.

Amelia stood. "You know my inn. The porch squeaks, the lake never finishes cooling in summer. We live with small inconveniences because we love where we live. I'm told we've been offered tidy docks and plaques. Lovely—unless 'restoration' means moving artifacts to a warehouse before anyone else can see them. We ask for a temporary hold on shoreline assignments until a transparent inventory is made— with the historical society and librarian present. Anything found stays here until we all agree where it goes."

Benton's voice stayed velvet. "While we worry about stories, docks rot. We can't let sentiment stop safety and progress."

"Safety and progress are the coats fraud wears," Clara said. "Do you deny your holding company retained counsel for Vernon Finch the week before he arrived?"

Benton smiled. "I give to many such cases."

"Including a Montreal dealer arrested for smuggling silver," Clara said.

"Objection," Benton said pleasantly. "This is not a court."

"No," Amelia said. "It's a town."

The chairwoman set down her gavel. "Chief Harlow?"

"We can seek an injunction on new permits," he said. "Existing provisional assignments would need cause."

"Cause like conflict of interest?" Clara asked. "A developer paying a potential heir to stir a claim, then filing to steward the very shoreline where that claim might surface?"

Benton finally faced her fully. "You play with matches, Miss Henderson," he said softly. "Paper burns well."

"If there's evidence," Harlow began.

"Bring your papers," Benton said, letting the word expand. "I'll bring the facts."

"That's all," Amelia said. "We've made our ask."

Outside, the pier boards looked pale and damp. "He's too good to corner in a room," Clara said. "He argues with contracts."

"We won something," Amelia said. "A slip. Doubt slows permits."

"You think Harlow checks the retainer?"

"He's not a fool," Amelia said. "He's proud. Different problem."

"Then give him something pride can't unsee," Clara said. "The thing Benton wants most."

"The ledger behind the timber wall," Amelia whispered. "We never opened it."

"We lacked tools," Clara said. "We don't now."

"All right. Tonight."

They told no one. After closing, they lit a lantern, wrapped tools in a dish towel, and pried the crooked floorboard Lady Grey had once singled out. The cat led, tail like a small standard.

The chamber breathed its damp welcome. At the far timber wall, Clara set her ear to the grain. "Hollow." The pry bar worried the seam; wood gave in a breath and a splinter.

Cold air sighed—metal and cloves.

They froze; the smell lay down in the wood like a coat taken off.

Behind the boards: a shallow cavity, a metal chest just long enough for ledgers. Two rusted latches. They lifted the lid; paper exhaled. Inside: two ledgers tied with string, a stack of envelopes, and a maroon notebook with an elastic strap.

Clara opened the small book first. A neat hand, a date: **1951**.

Upon my honor and on behalf of the Gentlemen of the Shore, I commit inventory of vault B and hold keys until directed by the Chair. — H.F.

"Harold Finch," Clara breathed. She turned a page—items, then initials and disbursements. Sutter. Westcott. And at the bottom:

H.B. — Chair pro tem, to assume upon my decline.

They said it together. "Harold Benton."

"Not a newcomer," Clara said. "An inheritor. The office waited for him."

A clatter above. Not the passage—**the kitchen**.

They snapped the notebook shut, shoved the chest back, pulled the boards in. Lantern low. Elbows, knees, breath—until the first pane of kitchen light showed through the floorboards.

Two voices, muffled. One smooth. One with the grunt the garden had taught their bodies to hate.

"...down there?" the smooth voice asked. "Or did I flatter Miss Farnsworth by thinking she'd look?"

"Been disturbed," the other said. Clove drifted. "Board's scuffed."

"Then we confirm and tidy," said Harold Benton, unhurried. "Light."

A cone lanced through a gap. Wood slid and thudded back. "Nothing," the heavy man said. "Maybe they came and left."

"Perhaps the cat," Benton sighed. "She enjoys an entrance."

Lady Grey lay between them, tail touching Amelia's wrist, a silk thread of calm.

"Search the pantry," Benton said lightly. "If there's a ledger, it's up here."

Drawers whispered; a jar lid tapped. The cone shifted. "And Miss Finch?" the heavy man asked.

"Leave her," Benton said warmly. "She'll convulse herself in public and the town will do our work. With luck, her friends will spend their breath defending her, not asking about me."

The door opened, cool air slid in, closed. Silence returned like a cloth laid down.

They counted to one hundred by throat and cat-heart. In the kitchen at last, they turned the lantern up until walls were walls again.

"He's the Chair," Clara said, staring at the maroon cover. "The continuity our ledgers couldn't explain."

"And he was in Doris' kitchen while we were under his feet," Amelia said.

Lady Grey planted a paw on the notebook. Now?

"Now," Amelia said. "We go to Harlow with what he can't tuck away. Tonight. Before Benton finds the rest and rewrites us out."

Clara wrapped the book in a tea towel and slid it into her satchel as tenderly as a first edition. "We need a witness."

"Mr. Larkin," Amelia said. "Fussy and honest."

"And Doris?"

"Tomorrow," Amelia said. "One more night without his voice."

They closed like caretakers—dousing the lantern, settling the plank, wiping a ring no cup had left. Fog blew in from the lake. At the corner, an expensive engine idled, then turned down Maple with the confidence of a man never followed.

Lady Grey hopped a puddle that reflected the inn the way a bad man tells a good story—recognizable, skewed. She paused, tail erect, to be sure her humans hadn't lost their nerve.

They hadn't. They moved under the lamps toward a chief who disliked being wrong and a librarian who didn't mind being right, carrying a small notebook that named a Chair and ended a myth— proof that the man in the blue suit wasn't a savior but steward of the poison that had slicked Tumblebrook's water for decades.

The lake hissed softly. A gull laughed like gossip. The town held its breath.

The innkeeper, the archivist, and the cat did not. They went.

Chapter 39

Lady Grey's Find

The inn wore night like a shawl—soft over lamps, heavy on the banister. Amelia sat with a cold cup and a heart that wouldn't cool. The fire had fallen to a low red eye. Across from her, Clara dozed in an armchair—if dozing counted—papers fanned across her lap. Outside, the town kept its wary quiet.

A scrape. A soft thud.

Amelia set down the cup and looked to the doorway.

Lady Grey slid in with comet gravity, hall moonlight catching silver on silver—her fur, and the thing in her mouth. She trotted to Amelia, tail high, eyes bright: I have solved a problem you hadn't named.

"What have you found, darling?" Amelia kept her voice a thread.

The cat set a silk handkerchief on Amelia's slipper. It unfurled with expensive weight and a clean scent—cedar, spice, a peppery cologne she'd smelled in rooms where men wore authority like a coat.

Clara stirred. "What time—?"

Amelia smoothed the silk. Gold thread snared the firelight: a crown above a three-masted ship. Not a family crest—Crown Shipping's sign.

"I've seen this square in Harold Benton's pocket," she said.

They watched the stitched corner breathe in the lamplight. The room tilted, like a bridge when you realize how much river runs under it.

Clara touched the thread, then drew back. "Not heirloom. Current."

"On his person. In our town hall."

Lady Grey stepped into Amelia's lap, circled the silk once, and sat. Her purr rose, steady.

"Where did you pick it up, clever girl?" Clara asked.

Lady Grey hopped down, padded to the back stair, and flicked her tail toward the rear door in the narrow service hall. At the bottom corner, a silk snag clung to a brad.

"Same weave," Clara said, inhaling. "Cedar. Spice."

Amelia laid a palm to the wood. The lock felt warm. She pictured Benton's discreet band, his habit of handling things he meant to own.

"Not a stray find," she said. "He came here tonight."

"He follows papers," Clara said. "Of course he followed these." She straightened. "He'll miss this. Let's use what he never counts."

"Which is?"

"He thinks we're sentimental. We'll turn the other way."

They woke Mr. Larkin with a knock and coffee "strong enough to convince a ledger to stand upright." He appeared in a robe older than Tumblebrook, spectacles sliding, hair combed by habit.

"My word," he said, peering from faces to silk to cat—now installed on his hall table like an examiner. "Either a child is born, someone has died, or you've brought me a rare book."

"Chain of custody," Clara said. "Please."

He laid clean muslin, then the handkerchief, fetched cotton gloves, loupe, and softened with appreciation. "Hand work. Crown generous on the left—an artisan's flourish. Couching on the rigging. Late '40s to mid-'60s." He winced when told about the snag. "Breaking and entering with silk is a crime against craft."

He wrote a statement—found, date, hour, witnesses—had them

sign, sleeved the handkerchief, sealed it with red wax from his library fob, and set the packet like a small planet in the lamp's circle.

"What would you have me do?"

"Stand beside us with Harlow," Clara said. "And swear, if he balks."

"I am very good at balked men," Mr. Larkin said. "They are soothed by nouns."

Lady Grey bunted his wrist. Something in Amelia's ribs lifted. Witnesses, paper, process—Benton's money disliked those more than hard work.

Morning did not sweeten waiting. Shutters unlatched, sweepers banged bristles, ovens woke. After a thin breakfast service, Amelia hung a placard: Back at 10:15. Ring if urgent. Lady Grey sat on the ledger daring the town to define urgent.

They walked to the station with Mr. Larkin between them, the sealed envelope borne like a communion plate. Harlow met them at the door, bristling toward dignity.

"If this is about the council—"

"This is about your signature," Clara said, offering the packet.

He hesitated. "If you've come to make me a spectacle—"

"You managed that," Amelia said—not unkindly. "By trusting a man who talks like a promise."

Harlow looked to Mr. Larkin, who tipped his head like a chessman. "I'm here to witness one town mechanism inspecting another. The cat will provide moral clarity."

Harlow's mouth twitched despite himself. He broke the seal and slid the silk free. Words can be argued; silk has heft.

"You're certain it's his?" he asked.

"I saw it in his pocket," Amelia said. "The snag appeared last night."

Harlow sniffed and grimaced. "Who wears cloves in July?"

"Men who sign their rooms," Clara said.

He set the silk down, looked at all three, duty struggling with pride. Duty won a half-step. "I'll speak to Mr. Benton. Privately."

"No," Amelia said, surprising herself. "That's his best ground."

Clara placed a copy of the maroon page naming **H.B.—Chair pro tem**. "We want an evidentiary hold on the shoreline. No work. No 'safety inspections' without two non-police witnesses. Not to humiliate you, Chief—so the story doesn't leave town."

Harlow stared at copy and silk, then exhaled. "Fine," he said, angry at the concession. "Bring the original notebook when we're all in the room. If he starts with names, I'll end with them."

"It stays in Mr. Larkin's safe until then," Clara said. She told him about the scuffed board and voices over their heads. She left out how close the lantern had come to blowing out with fear.

"My men will sit your alley," Harlow said. "If I see Benton's car at your corner, I'll consider my morning vindicated."

They went to the café. Doris needed faces that weren't suspicious. The kitchen had become a sanctuary—dangers named, spaces read like a second book. The bell made its brave noise. Doris braced, then sagged and stood taller.

"Tea," she said. "Then—whatever it is."

They told her simply: the notebook, the handkerchief, the snag, the chief who'd said fine and meant—for once—I was wrong. At **Chair pro tem**, Doris gripped crockery until it made a small sound.

"So it was a club," she said—grief braided with bitterness. "Just not the kind that eats lamb under chandeliers." She wiped her cheek like a girl. "I hate him for finding the exact shape of our shame and trying to sell it back to us."

"You won't buy it," Amelia said. "We're taking it off the market."

"I'll bake a pie the day you do," Doris said. "No currants. All sugar."

By noon Harlow's boy found them. One word: "Now."

They reached the council chamber to find Harlow, the chairwoman and two members, Mr. Larkin with his safe-face envelope, and Harold Benton in a blue suit and a smile that wasn't.

"Chief," Benton said, all courtesy. "Happy to answer questions."

"There is a reason the historical society is represented," Harlow said, and set the silk on the table.

For the first time, Benton's face couldn't sell itself. A fractional tightening, a flare at the nose. Not fear—insult.

"Nice handkerchief," Harlow said, farmer-mild.

"Thousands bear crests," Benton replied, thinner. "Men of means enjoy ornament."

"And you left yours at Miss Farnsworth's back door," Harlow said. "Your cologne matches the snag."

"If one's missing, I'll buy another," Benton said. "If you've found one, return it."

"We'll keep this one," Harlow said, sliding over the copy naming **H.B.** "Tell me what *Chair pro tem* means."

"It means young women have made fiction a hobby," Benton said.

"Try again," Clara said, quiet.

He turned, the room cooling a degree. "I don't explain philanthropy to those who treat it like contraband."

"Philanthropy rarely requires breaking into inns," Amelia said.

He returned to Harlow. "You wanted a clean shoreline. I offered a plan and budget. If secret societies are today's subject, ask the council about the one they sit in. Or is female vigilante work part of governance now?"

"We're pausing your provisional assignments," Harlow said. "Effective now."

"Then we'll test it in court," Benton said easily. "Half this town's comforts bear my name. They'll enjoy, when the time comes, a repaired dock and the esteem of being respectable." He looked at Amelia, not kindly. "Inns do better in tidy towns."

"Mine does better in honest ones," she said.

"Mr. Benton," the chairwoman said, "until we sort this, you will restrict your activities to—"

"Waiting for your letters?" he offered.

"Waiting," she said.

He inclined his head to the room—and not to the women—and

left with the unhurried gait of a man who believes the ground will always hold him. The building exhaled.

"He won't run," Harlow said. "He'll reroute. If you have anything else that becomes a nail in his shoe, bring it now. Don't keep it for flourish."

"We'll try," Clara said.

Outside, noon looked borrowed from elsewhere—kids chasing gulls, fishermen mending nets. It felt obscene that the day had the nerve to be pleasant.

"One more step," Clara said.

"More than one," Amelia said. "But yes—what's next?"

"Everything we showed Harlow, we show Tumblebrook," Clara said. "Clean. No rumor. Ledger excerpts printed. The handkerchief described and witnessed. Mr. Larkin at the podium. In the library, in front of county maps. Invite everyone who's told Doris Finch with their eyes that she's cursed."

"An exhibition," Amelia said.

"A reckoning," Clara said. "With labels and a coat rack."

Lady Grey had found shade where shade found her. She leapt to the newel post and yawned—a delicate flash of fangs: a benediction.

"Tonight," Amelia said. "We set tables for the truth. Tomorrow, the town eats."

"Doris will bake something ruinous," Clara said.

"Let her. Let there be sugar. Anything that isn't rot."

They went inside. The inn received them with small dignities: soap-clean air, the second stair's familiar creak, the rectangle of light on the rug at this hour. The silk sat in Mr. Larkin's keeping and would sit under glass by evening, under eyes.

Amelia paused in the parlor, laid her hand on the mantel, and told the room—not loudly, just enough for wood to register, "We are nearly there."

Lady Grey pressed her face into Amelia's fingers and purred. It sounded like a motor finally catching—quiet, certain, made to go forward.

Chapter 40

Showdown at the Inn

The storm rolled in like a verdict. By night the sky split; rain strafed the windows; wind shouldered the inn until its beams groaned. Lamps outside guttered—shaken halos in the gale.

Amelia stood in the parlor, shawl tight, the silk handkerchief folded on the mantel—moon-pale, accusatory. Lightning flashed the lake to sheeted silver and was gone. Clara, near the hearth, sorted notes with storm-hardened focus. Lady Grey patrolled, whiskers forward, as if the weather hid something with feet.

The knock overrode thunder—two blows, notice not request.

"Open up, Miss Farnsworth. I've come for what belongs to me."

Harold Benton filled the doorway, rain slicking his fine coat, entitlement worn like a second spine. He stepped in without asking. "Where is it? You have something of mine. Misplaced."

"If you mean this," Amelia said, nodding to the silk, "it's evidence."

His gaze hawked to it—heat, then the practiced smooth. "You've learned a big word."

"We have ledgers," Clara said, rising—manifests, shell companies, the crest recurring for decades. "You funded Vernon to justify 'stewardship'—your word for taking."

"Margins," he said mildly. "Small people love paper when rooms get large."

He lunged for the mantel. His hand caught Amelia's forearm, spun her hard into marble. Pages scattered. "Do you know what happens to people who mistake leverage for truth?" he hissed.

"Let her go," Clara said, poker steady.

Lady Grey launched—claws through wool and into skin, teeth a whisper from his ear. He shouted; his grip broke; the cat corkscrewed free and puffed to twice her size.

"Vermin," he spat, touching blood, affronted to see it. "You'll regret this."

"Leave," Amelia said, voice steady. "Before the chief arrives."

"You think Harlow frightens me?"

"Witnesses do," Clara said. "We've filled our pockets with them."

Pride wrestled calculation and lost. He turned; wind tried to shove him back for a better exit. Clara latched the door, forehead to wood for two breaths. Lady Grey climbed into Amelia's lap and purred like a motor that wouldn't stall.

A second knock—thinner. Harlow, rain-drowned, swept the room with three looks: Amelia's arm, Benton's water on the boards, the silk. "He was here."

"Looking for what he left," Clara said.

"My men lost him at the mill bend." Harlow eyed the square. "He wants that more than pride wants apology." He set a car outside and another at the café. "Doors shut. Lamps lit."

They made tea because kettles steady hands. "Will he stop?" Amelia asked.

"No," Clara said. "He'll change shape—law, hires, gifts until doubters look unkind. So we write the captions first."

"Tomorrow—cases. The town," Amelia said.

"Doris," Clara added. "She'll come. Lady Grey nailed the courage in."

They slept in shifts. The cat watched the street because someone had to.

Morning decided to stop being night. Mr. Larkin had turned the library lobby into a small museum: two cases—left, the sealed envelope and silk; right, chosen ledger pages with tidy labels—plus the 1931 county map strung with red thread from docks to café to inn. Harlow stood like punctuation; the chairwoman ironed with wrath. Doris arrived in her best dress, no apron; at the silk she laughed, soft and unkind to the air. "He thought he could carry the town in his pocket and not lose a thread."

The room filled: dockmen, mill women, baker dusted with flour, smith in his good shirt, children shushed and wide-eyed. Elliot lingered by atlases; Colby came like a man who'd forgotten the hymns. Benton did not—yet.

Mr. Larkin welcomed, calm as a ledger. Clara spoke first—crest, dates, routes; Amelia followed—Vernon used, Doris heir to a kitchen, not a crime; Benton—thread at a door, threads to this room. Questions came; answers were nouns and proof, not theater. Lady Grey stretched across the silk's case like a living seal; a child giggled; awe won.

Then Benton entered—dry suit, fresh square, a smile calibrated to clinics and votes. "My neighbors," he began. "Misunderstanding."

Harlow set his palm on the nearest case: a line on a map. "You've reached the listening portion."

"You know me," Benton told the room. "I show up when things need doing—"

"You show up when there's a photographer," Doris said, even. "You didn't show up when my cousin died."

Respect recalculated. Benton adjusted his smile by an eighth of an inch, reached toward the case—toward the cat.

"Don't," Amelia said. He stopped. "What is this—your cat on the bench?" he tried.

"It's a reference desk," Mr. Larkin said cheerfully. "She files better than most men."

Laughter broke the tension's back. Benton pivoted—reputations, economies, calm tones—never saying crest, handkerchief, storm, door.

Clara read a line: "H.B.—Chair pro tem." Flour-dry words; they dried his mouth.

"Harry," the chairwoman said, kindness threaded with warning, "sit down."

He didn't. "You and I want the same thing," he told Amelia. "A future loosed from the past. Don't mistake me for an enemy when I've been this place's best friend."

"Friends don't break into houses," she said. "They knock in daylight. They bring bread."

"Mr. Benton," Harlow said, voice official, "you'll come with me now."

"To where?"

"A room with less echo. And remember how many eyes you've enjoyed." He held the silence. "Enjoy them."

Not cuffs, not victory—movement. Benton chose bemused obedience, let himself be flanked. As he passed, Lady Grey made a small sound like a clock finding its hour. He glanced, and for the first time showed something trustworthy: he disliked being watched by what he couldn't buy.

The door closed on him, the deputies, and rain admitting it wasn't thunder. People stayed—eyes softer for Doris, nods for Amelia and Clara. Mr. Larkin dusted imaginary crumbs with his plain handkerchief—starch, not spice.

"Tea," he said to all. "There's the business of it, and the mercy. Let's have both."

Doris laughed her battered laugh and went to the pot. Hot water over leaves isn't a cure, but it keeps a town upright.

Amelia studied the silk under glass—the crown and ship like a pin on a map. Clara joined her, shoulder to shoulder. The line held between them.

"We didn't win," Amelia said.

"No," Clara said. "We made losing hard."

"We'll keep making it hard."

"With paper, cats, and unbeautiful truth."

Lady Grey stepped along the case's edge, tail a banner, then dropped and trotted toward the back stacks, as if a new scent braided the corridors—cedar, something mechanical, the lake's old promise. Amelia followed. So did Clara. For once the town seemed to walk with them. The storm had wasted itself on the glass; inside, rooms finally remembered aloud.

Chapter 41

Final Clues Revealed

Morning rinsed Tumblebrook clean. Sun glazed wet shingles like fish scales; puddles kept scraps of sky. Neighbors reset signs and brooms; mist breathed off the lake—cedar, silt, coffee.

Inside, the storm lingered: a black scuff where Benton's ring struck, muddy commas from the door, a hairline crack catching light. Clara's pages lay fanned to dry. On the mantel, the silk handkerchief sat under a tumbler, the crown-and-ship gleaming like a trapped star.

Amelia stood at the window with a mug for heat more than hope. Sleep had come in scraps. Two boys sailed a stick-boat; calm unknotted—and tightened again.

Clara arrived quietly, a new stack hugged like a child, pins losing the vote, soot marking one cheekbone. She laid the papers down and exhaled. "We have him. By paper."

"Show me."

Ledgers from the chamber; Crown manifests Mr. Larkin had risked; telegrams, property offers, Benton Holdings notices. Ink too black to fade.

"Begin here." Silent Partners had reawakened months before Vernon's return: "H.B." threaded beside sums and tiny crowned ships. In another hand: adv. ret., disb., retainer.

"Harold Benton," Amelia said.

"Or a proxy. But—this is the hinge." An IOU in Vernon's tidy scrawl on boardinghouse paper: Received from H.B.—a sum that stunned—for services in pursuit of rightful Finch inheritance. Beside it, a bank draft stub from Benton three days prior.

"He bankrolled Vernon," Clara said. "Gave him shape in the story. And when the shape started talking—"

"He broke it," Amelia finished.

Lady Grey materialized, set a neat paw on the IOU: this, please.

"Pressure cheapens land," Clara went on. "He needed Doris in scandal. Vernon was the bellows." She slid out a brittle envelope: a Duluth clipping—Silver Heirloom Emerges?—circled and annotated: Wycliffe. Below: reliable shill; send letters—two tones.

"He fed appetite with one voice and fear with another," Amelia said.

"And then paid for silence," Clara added. A cheap Thunder Bay telegram to Chicago: deliverables accelerated; witness flustered; tertiary route required.

"And Elliot?" Amelia asked.

"A string on Benton's hand," Clara said. "Old Wisconsin charge —'facilitating heritage goods.' He turns up where silver whispers."

"Tell Harlow?"

"In five minutes. Also—this." From a ledger's back: a typed note to H. Finch from Crown Line, Thunder Bay.

RE: CLUB DINNERS. SHIPMENTS COINCIDENT. FEES WAIVED IF KEYS REMAIN LOCAL. SEE REPRESENTATIVE H.B. FOR SIGNATURES.

"H.B.—Henry Barrett," Clara said. "Crown's fixer in the thirties. And—SEND APPRENTICE COLBY FOR RECEIPTS WHEN SAFE." She sighed. "Our historian told the truth, just not enough. A boy sent to fetch paper and told not to read."

"So Benton didn't invent the network. He inherited the path," Amelia said.

They stitched the weave: the crest on a 1932 receipt; the same crest stitched into Benton's modern silk; a note—keeper of the keys—beside Harold Finch's initials and, later, keys restored to town—trailing off mid-line.

A soft thump at the back door. An envelope sat on the mat, damp at the edges. Inside: a key, the color of pennies, and six lines in a careful hand:

Miss Farnsworth—

The door in the chamber—timber over stone—was sealed the winter Harold died. This key turns the hasp behind the third board from the right. I did not turn it. If I am not where you can ask me why, know my debts are mine.

There is a list inside. It is the list I burned, except I did not. Some fires should be slow. —C.

Lady Grey looked pleased. "Not yet," Clara said, reading Amelia's intent. "Harlow first."

He arrived as if wired to their table—hat in hand, relief loosening his shoulders. "More?"

They gave him the IOU, the draft stub, the Crown letter, the telegram; Henry Barrett for the old H.B.; Colby's note without the word *coward*. The key rested in his palm.

"Third board from the right," he read. "Which wall?"

"The timber over stone," Amelia said. "Lady Grey's wall."

At her name, the cat made a dignified *hm*.

They went in daylight with tools and calm. Doris met them at the cellar door, hands folded like a nurse choosing bravery. "If it's the past, it's mine. If it's the truth, it's ours. Go on."

Lantern light spangled nail heads. The chamber received them like a theater waiting its last act. Lady Grey tapped the third board: hollow. Harlow found the hidden hasp; the key turned with a long sigh. Behind the board lay a shallow cavity, oilcloth and beeswax within, stamped with a crowned ship.

Harlow warmed, eased, unfolded. Not one document but many: full names, not initials; roles—porter, broker, police, captain—and, in later years, *desc.* adding sons, grandsons, daughters. Finches, Westcotts, Sutters—two names that thinned Harlow's mouth—and near the bottom of later pages: *Harold Benton* in a neat hand overcompensating for tremor. At the end, in pencil pressed hard: *Keys returned to community, not to a family. Do not make me a liar.* Signed *H.F.*

Silence held. "We'll photograph, then move," Harlow said gently. "Miss Finch?"

"No," Doris said—plain and steady. "Thank you. He tried to fix what he broke. It isn't enough. It is... not nothing."

They carried the parcel up in a tray. A crowd gathered despite *Closed for Repairs.* Tumblebrook had acquired a taste for public truth.

Mr. Larkin, exact as ever, stood ready with sleeves and labels. The chairwoman had knitting and patience. Harlow lifted a palm. "We've recovered a ledger of names. Some dead. Some perplexingly alive. We'll do this like a town that likes its reflection."

Elliot slid in, surprise rented by the hour. "Oh—bad time?"

"You came to take the list," Clara said, conversational. "You'll leave without it—and with a statement, your alias, and your employer's favorite restaurant."

Elliot paled. "I—I don't—"

"Your boots," Amelia said. Faces turned. "Square notch heels. We saw those prints by the river. Not fishermen: city cobbler, new, bought in a hurry." Harlow unfolded a slip. "The Duluth cobbler remembers his only sale. He'll point at you."

Elliot twitched; Lady Grey flowed into his path and sat. He stopped. Mr. Larkin suggested "Sit," in his *Treasure Island* voice. Elliot sat.

By late afternoon the parlor held a new order: IOU and stub sleeved; the Crown letter under glass; Colby's key on velvet; and, under a fresh tumbler, the silk square—pride stitched to proof.

Harlow's satchel tugged with virtuous weight. He promised Doris—quietly—that no one would make her a punchline while he had breath. She nodded and saved the crying for later, when Kay brought a molasses-dark loaf because consolation needs heft.

Toward evening Harlow returned before the warrants. Hat off, he looked properly at the women who'd turned deduction domestic and bravery habitual. "We'll serve him papers at dawn."

"Dawn?" Amelia said.

"Men like Benton think of themselves as morning creatures," Harlow said. "The knock with the coffee unsettles them."

"Poetry," Clara said.

"Paperwork," he replied, but his mouth almost remembered a smile. He nodded to Lady Grey. "Good work, madam."

She accepted like a general, then stretched on the sill into the last warmth, joints clicking, precise and satisfied.

When he'd gone and the inn resumed its pre-supper hum, Amelia let her hands be empty. Fear shrank a shade, leaving room for a fiercer taste—iron and oranges: hope, with work to do.

Clara warmed her palms at the fender, used in the best way. "We'll sleep when he's charged," she said, and yawned.

Amelia laughed, unpretty and liberating. "We'll sleep when Lady Grey permits."

The cat purred; the sound filled the room like bread scent—promise in air.

Outside, the lake lay down; on the far shore a single lamp winked in the old boathouse and died—a firefly rethinking itself. The town—stubborn, generous—had looked at its face and kept looking. Final clues stood in a line. Morning would knock on a door that had opened too easily for money. There would be fuss, press, lawyers; days when history tried a last denial.

But in a parlor with a cracked frame and a silk square under glass, what would not be denied had become legible. Paper had teeth. Friendship had a spine. A cat had grown, impossibly, more certain.

"Tomorrow," Amelia said into the low light.

"Tomorrow," Clara agreed.

Lady Grey stretched one inch further into the warmth, and the inn, at last, exhaled.

Chapter 42

Justice for Doris

By breakfast, Tumblebrook wore relief like a loose shawl—slipping now and then, but warm. Sun caught in puddles; brooms rasped stone; a wren scolded the storm for poor manners. People spoke softly, careful hands around a healing thing.

Amelia watched from the inn porch, brewing a second pot she didn't remember starting. Lady Grey lay long on the rail, tail punctuating the street's small restorations. Across the way, Clara turned the porch table into a desk, weighting the paper with mugs. The headline was blessedly plain: **DORIS FINCH CLEARED; INVESTIGATION FOCUSES ON DEVELOPER.**

"He names Benton without hedging," Clara said. "No room for gossip."

"What she deserved the first day," Amelia breathed. "Let's get her open."

The café's bell gave a tentative trill. Inside, glass shone, chairs were squared, chalk dusted the board: blueberry–lemon scones, rosemary shortbread, Wednesday Courage stew (on a Friday). In the herb bed, green insisted on itself.

Doris stood behind the counter, apron new-tight, hairpins resolute, hands worrying the hem. "I thought I'd open to silence."

"You never have," Amelia said, covering Doris's hands. "Not today."

Clara stacked plates, set cups, tuned spoons. "Rule of reopening: point; we'll do."

Doris laughed—startled, real. "You'll frighten the cinnamon right out of the rolls."

"Good," Clara said. "Fright blooms flavor."

Coffee burbled; the room filled with its hush. Mrs. Penrose arrived in a Sunday hat, Tommy Ellison with a coin and two-mallow permit, Mr. Larkin with a basket of 1919 journals "for proof people have weathered worse and still needed pastry."

By ten, the bell had found its voice. Conversations rose and fell: fences, school repairs, whether lightning danced or eyes did. Passing Doris, people touched a wrist, squeezed a shoulder. Trust returned like moss—slow but sure.

Glances hovered at the garden window. A few loud whisperers performed penance by ordering thirds. Clara's eyebrow: repentance-by-scone. Lady Grey inspected from the sill, then circulated, brushing Doris's calves and riding the kitchen door hinge like a judge. Her purr turned tight throats steady.

Near noon, Chief Harlow ducked under the lintel, uniform pressed, voice carrying to the corners. "On and off the record—Mrs. Finch is cleared." The room held still, then applauded tide-like. Doris bowed her head and made the sound of frost leaving a body.

"I expect the same confidence from her neighbors," Harlow added. The sentence made space. Caps came off; cuttings were offered; a fisherman declared the stew best in a year.

"That helps," Clara murmured. "Public consequence for public harm."

It didn't scrub everything. Two women gossiped hard enough to dent the air. Someone who owed Elliot lingered in the lane, ears pointed at the door. Change was genuine and in progress—both true.

By late afternoon, with cups ringed and crumbs constellated, Doris slid the bolt and finally cried. Amelia and Clara caught her before gravity did.

"I don't know how to trust the good to stay," she said.

"You don't have to tonight," Amelia answered. "Eat stew. Sleep. Let your hands stop tying knots."

"We'll do dawn coffee," Clara added. "You'll lie and call it rest."

"Tyrants," Doris sniffed, smiling.

"Democratic," Clara said. "Recallable."

Lady Grey vaulted up, butted Doris's chin, and was rocked like a ridiculous, rightful infant.

They banked the till under the flour, made small future lists—nutmeg, mending, repaint the sign Clara had loathed since 2011. Café windows threw light like knee-high stars.

On the walk back, Clara summarized the day. "Harlow'll serve Benton at dawn. Warrants written; judge ready. Benton expects hats-off courtesy."

"He'll get a constable with cold hands," Amelia said.

"Tonight we keep the inn quiet," Clara added. "Wounded men hire fools."

They checked latches, banked the fire. Amelia left a note: *Breakfast thirty minutes late; croissants to compensate.* Lady Grey tested the night at each window, then relaxed: frogs, not men.

Sleep found Amelia in fits and then held. Morning placed them on the porch with hot mugs. The lake lay smoothed; gulls strategized at the bakery. At 6:03 Harlow crossed the square, deputies like commas. He lifted two fingers; Amelia returned the salute. Lady Grey became a gargoyle.

Benton answered as a man who believes mornings belong to him. Robe that pretended to be a dressing gown; smile that pretended not to be a snarl. Paper passed. Understanding arrived, and his face emptied. He gestured; Harlow didn't blink. The deputies remained.

Some towns would cheer. Tumblebrook went still enough to hear wire sing. The baker stood in his door with croissants and didn't gloat. In a back window, a child stood on a stool, palms flat—learning law when it isn't a cudgel. The door closed without drama. The town exhaled on pitch.

"Now breakfast," Clara said.

They fed the inn with cheerful competence. A guest asked whether excitement would affect the jam. "On the contrary," Amelia said. "The jam has been waiting for justice to set."

By nine, they drifted back to the café as if the morning required pilgrimage. The bell rang with confidence; cinnamon and restitution scented the room. Doris tied her apron with less ferocity and poured Harlow coffee, black as a verdict.

"On the house," she said.

"On the record," he replied.

Apologies arrived—tender, clumsy, some collapsing under their own weight. Doris accepted what she could without becoming a receptacle. A Sutter nephew brought sunflowers; Doris kept two stems and deputized teens to plant the rest. "Come back in August and sit under what you made."

The chairwoman convened a public session—secrecy having proved unfit. Town hall smelled of polish and socks; windows open to honest air. Benton's seat sat empty. Harlow presented what he could; Mr. Larkin read 1919 journals; Clara diagrammed names into sense. Amelia didn't speak. She stayed shoulder-to-shoulder with Doris. Sometimes solidarity is a sentence.

There was ugliness. A Westcott wanted privacy for old sins; an Elder asked why the past should be used against the present. Clara, not unkind: "Because the present uses the past whenever it suits. Fair's fair." A mother in the back said, "We don't have to be descendants of what shamed us. We can be descendants of what we do now." The room shifted on new bricks.

A motion underwrote garden repairs from a general fund—acknowledgment, not charity. Another formed an archive committee—three elders, two young people, and Mr. Larkin—to house the ledgers with a placard almost comically plain: *We did this. We will do better.* The vote wasn't unanimous, which made it adult.

Toward dusk, people wandered to the café garden with trowels and twine. No orders given. Rosemary set straighter, thyme tied honest, soil loosened, Sutter sunflowers planted to cast August shade. Amelia fetched a pitcher; Clara found stakes; Lady Grey supervised from the fencepost, whiskers bright.

"You don't have to—" Doris began.

"Of course we do," Mrs. Penrose said. "It's our garden. We ate it for years and let it be slandered. We'll pay in the only currency that holds value: labor and water."

Doris cried again; no one made a spectacle of it. The sound rose and the evening took it like steam.

Harlow, ostensibly returning Clara's pencil, cleared his throat. "For what it's worth—arraignment Monday. He'll plead like men like him plead. It will get worse briefly. Then better properly."

"We know how to be steady," Amelia said, surprised by the truth of it.

"Good," Harlow said, leaving the pencil on the fencepost like a marked page.

Night drew in gently. The inn's lamps made gold squares; the café's windows made twins. On the porch, three small bouquets waited with a note: *We're sorry we were loud when we should have been kind.* Amelia left them where they were; people bloom at different hours.

Inside, the parlor held faint ghosts of muddy prints; the mantel its scratch; the silk glinted under glass—thesis, not trophy. Lady Grey sprawled across all three laps with boneless authority, certain she belonged on every table in town.

"To justice," Clara said, too tired to be clever.

"To Doris," Amelia said.

"To both," Doris answered. "And to the cat who held the town by the scruff until it remembered its manners."

Lady Grey purred so loudly the panes took an interest.

Plans budded at the edges: how to word the library plaque—no flinching, no preening; whether rosemary shortbread at the archive's opening counted as a joke or a rite. For once, urgency wasn't the loudest thing. Gratitude was.

When Amelia rose, it was the ache of work done, not dread. She banked the fire. Clara angled the chairs companionably. Doris kissed Lady Grey between the eyes and didn't look foolish. The town would still endure varnished lawyers and headlines trying theater out of bookkeeping. There would be more apologies and a few recantations. Rain would fall at the wrong hour; the herbs would drink anyway.

But this day belonged to justice spoken aloud and a café door that opened and stayed open—to Harlow's serious face, a child's palms on glass, a town hall discovering it liked the sound of truth. To the cat with a mouth full of silk and the women who decided loving a place means refusing to let it drown in its myths.

When lamps went out, the lake breathed. A loon called—a clean line. Lady Grey placed her paw in Amelia's palm and curled her toes one by one, as if counting. Amelia laughed, unguarded, and let herself be counted.

Chapter 43

Community Heals

The weeks after Chief Harlow's declaration didn't trumpet redemption; they drifted in like a mild breeze. The market opened, the lake stitched silver, the baker blessed croissants with sugar. Yet the tempo changed. People lingered; neighbors finished whole sentences; laughter started deeper, passing over a bruise that had begun to knit.

Amelia felt it first in innkeeper ways: teaspoons returned with saucers; thank-you notes tucked under napkin rings; the bell rang with requests instead of complaints. She took coffee on the porch while Lady Grey stretched along the rail, watching the square remember itself—chalk kingdoms, fishermen's calluses, Mrs. Penrose correcting posture without malice. The sign creaked its old creak. Home again.

Relief didn't erase decades. Under talk, Amelia heard the seam ripper of honesty. It began at Doris's café.

The confessions and the key

Sun pooled on the coffeepots; people arrived with appetite and left lighter, as if the telling were a tithe.

"My grandfather heard carts at midnight," Mrs. Penrose said, setting down her cup like a truth.

"Metal at night meant smith or smugglers," Mr. Larkin offered. "And the smith slept like a saint." He looked toward Doris. "We all edited."

Clara didn't hurry anyone. She recorded names and dates like scripture, leaving space where memory faltered. "Silence isn't storage," she told a doubtful table guarding a cigar box of receipts. "It's erasure. We're doing the opposite."

Artifacts arrived like relics: a ledger with ink like veins, a letter that never said silver yet meant nothing else. Mrs. Talbot brought a rusted key in linen. "My father called it the debt." The key lay cold in Clara's palm. Lady Grey sniffed, then tapped it—gentle, ceremonial —and the room exhaled in an unembarrassed laugh.

"It isn't weakness," Amelia said into the lull. "It's proof of surviving. We stop only if we keep quiet now."

A room for the truth

Gossamer Fables surrendered a front window for a small, serious room: two salvaged cases, a broad oak table, a lake map pricked with bright pins. Clara lettered the sign, tidy and unfashionable:
> **Tumblebrook Archive**
> **What We Did.**
> **What We Learned.**
> **What We Keep.**
> **Open shelves; open eyes.**

Colby came the first afternoon, contrition like a necessary coat. He set down the coin Lady Grey had once knocked free. "I called it collecting," he said. "It was not knowing and doing nothing. Which is a choice." Clara recorded it without flourish. "Accepted," she said—acknowledgment, not absolution.

Elliot filed an affidavit casting himself at a heroic angle; the committee—Clara, Mr. Larkin, Rose the schoolteacher, and two teens allergic to flattery—placed it under **Contested Accounts** with a note: *Practice discernment.* Elliot left on the early coach.

Repair as liturgy

On Saturdays they mended without spectacle. The apologetic Sutter nephew brought lumber; children crawled under tables with damp cloths and solemn joy. Someone put a fiddle in Mrs. Penrose's hands; music ran like clean water past the work.

The herb beds became conversation: thyme where heat makes it speak; rosemary where winter will test it. A path widened for wheelchairs without announcing itself; Doris simply pushed a chair through and hummed. Sunflowers turned blunt faces toward anything offering light.

Children asked without hypocrisy. "Why hide pretty things?" "Why didn't anyone tell?" "What happens to Mr. Benton?" Adults answered with new muscle. "Because pretty paid for ugly power." "Because silence can feel like safety." "He'll have a lawyer; we'll have to listen. We will too."

The square and the saying of it

When clarity deserved a breath, Harlow brought chairs into the square. No dais, no microphones—just a table draped in unbleached linen with the papers they were ready to show. Doris stood beside Amelia and Clara; the town stood around them.

"We aren't here to punish the dead or humiliate the living," Harlow said. "We're here to straighten the hallways in our heads."

"The archive is open," Clara said, notebook ballast in her hands. "We'll take your papers and give copies. Read everything. Correct us. Add what paper misses. This is a memory with doors."

Rose announced student interviews. "Extra credit for cookies. That's pedagogy."

People placed what they had: a boot-polish receipt from a busy dock night, a photograph of too-good silver in a too-small house, a recipe card noting when to dim lights during back-room sorting. A little girl set a smooth stone on the table; no one moved it. Meaning often arrives later.

Apologies and right-sized amends

Apologies arrived—clean and ivy-draped alike. Tumblebrook learned to love the first and nod at the second. The council, in plain language, committed festival proceeds to the archive and a fund for repairs and a scholarship. *We will not starve the part of ourselves that remembers.*

Colby volunteered boring hours—labeling, cross-referencing, papercuts. Penance works best when it uses a person's actual gifts. Sometimes Lady Grey allowed him as a perch.

Private reckonings

Harlow came before opening, set his hat under the counter. "I should have... sooner."

"You should have," Doris agreed, not unkind. "But you did. And you came to say it here."

He glanced at the staked green. "It's better," he said, meaning more than soil.

"Because we did it together," she answered.

Small good moments

A boy slipped from the dock. Half the quay moved; Lady Grey streaked along the edge yowling like a siren. He came up sputtering; the town laughed with love. The cat took two victory laps and cleaned her shoulder—unconcerned.

Teenagers, deputized as oral historians, wrote a ballad—part truth, part joke, entirely catchy. They performed at dusk. Clara hid behind a pillar, blushing; Amelia clapped until her hands stung.

The plaque that did not preen

On a Wednesday smelling of apples and chalk, the archive received a plaque at kid's-eye height. Mr. Larkin read Clara's sanded lines:

This town hid things. This town found things.
Now we place them where the light is.
If you are part of this place, so are you.

The circle at the garden

On a soft evening, people drifted to the café garden to put some things down and choose others up. Sprigs of thyme, a letter folded to softness, a photo with a thumbprint. Amelia set rosemary in a shallow bowl. "We're not closing a story," she said. "We're making sure it has a spine."

"I don't forgive the harm," Doris said, laying an old Finch page. "I don't condemn the fear. I will bake and pay taxes and open the door. That's the Finch I'm keeping."

Colby added his coin. "Let someone in fifty years mock our hair and thank our work."

Harlow cleared his throat. "My office will try to deserve your trust. If we don't, tell us."

A child placed the smooth stone beside the key. "It's a skipstone," she decided. "For when someone wants to throw something and it should be beautiful when it goes."

Lady Grey walked the artifacts like beats in a poem and curled around the bowl, warming the water. Laughter loosened what remained tight. They carried the herbs to the lake and let them float—no pageant, just thyme and rosemary riding toward wide water.

After

Life layered back on: work, school, fair rehearsals, pumpkin gossip. Benton's arraignment came with due process; the paper tried for theater; the town stayed sober. The archive was a place to put things; Harlow stopped by Tuesdays and read a page standing with his hat in hand. That mattered more than speeches.

The café thrummed; the inn filled with travelers who didn't know they were sleeping inside a story, and Amelia learned not to envy their ignorance. Clara taught **How to Argue Kindly About Facts** to teens, retirees, and a couple who rediscovered affection for footnotes. Mr. Larkin presided like a proud uncle.

On a Tuesday like clean paper, the first sunflower turned fully toward the lane. Doris pinned a card—**HELLO**—to the stake. Strangers smiled.

That night the three women ate stew on the inn porch while the square exhaled. Lady Grey hooked one paw over the rail like a pirate at ease. They watched warm rectangles of café and archive, the town hall honorable in its dark.

"We did something," Doris said—satisfaction's quieter cousin.

"We did many somethings," Clara said; precision comforts.

Amelia found Lady Grey's paw. The cat curled her toes into Amelia's palm—one, two, three, four—their new ritual. "We'll have to do more," Amelia said. "The kind you only see after you've cleaned the first window."

"Good," Doris said, surprising herself. "I've never liked staring through just one."

A breeze ran its hand over the rosemary. A single star pried a pocket in the blue. The town lay quiet—not from emptiness, but from learning the comfort of pauses.

Lady Grey purred, the sound stitching edges together—not to hide the seam, but to honor it. The women let themselves be mended. The lake breathed. The archive glowed low. Somewhere in a tidy notebook, Clara had written a line that read like a promise:

Healing isn't a ceremony. It's a schedule we keep together.

There would be testimonies and headlines and stubborn tenderness. But for now, the work held. Holding felt, finally, like rest.

Chapter 44

Festival Finale

By midmorning the square wore its courage openly. Banners lifted and settled in the lake breeze; bunting flashed; paper pennants tapped along twine like coins that had decided to stop hiding. Honeyed sun made even patched shutters look quaint. The Arts & Antiques Festival—halted, doubted, remade—had come to its final day.

Amelia stood still at the edge of the square. Roasted almonds, lilac soap, kettle corn, cedar shavings, and the mineral breath of the lake braided the air. Tourists returned with decent curiosity; locals moved like people who'd done hard things and could do more. The square hummed, not to drown memory, but to make a sweeter sound.

Clara bustled up with pamphlets tied in lavender string. She'd printed and lettered them herself:

The Lost Silver of Tumblebrook: What Happened, What We Kept, What We Learned

Inside: a river-timeline; a sketch of the crown-and-ship; a brief, firm paragraph on smuggling and complicity; two on repair; a map to the archive. People took them like recipes from a truthful neighbor.

"Distribution," she said, handing Amelia a stack.

Lady Grey trotted ahead, tail metronomic. She'd inspected the exhibit tent, patrolled the quilt booth, and pinned a loose ribbon like a silvery fish. She leapt to a lamppost base and sat, queenly.

Under white canvas with scalloped edges, two glass cases anchored the square. The first held the spoon and fork—tarnish softened, not erased—on cream linen, crest catching diffused light. The second held the rusted lockbox, lid open to show letters, IOUs, ledger pages in sleeves. Between them, a brass plaque:

Not a tale of shame, but of resilience. May we carry forward the lesson that truth, once unearthed, is brighter than silver kept hidden.

Doris greeted visitors in a blue dress and apron, cheeks pinked by sun and attention. Hands found hers; apologies stumbled; she took each with grace, though her fingers trembled on the glass. Once she leaned to the fork and whispered; Lady Grey flicked an ear, as if she heard.

At eleven, Chief Harlow kept the stage brief. "We named what needed naming. We'll handle what needs handling. The rest is yours —the keeping, the telling, the ordinary decency." He looked older in a good way. Grateful applause followed.

A dulcimer played something like walking home. Stalls opened: carved loons, rag rugs, tender lake horizons. Children hammered initials into copper disks and wore them like pilgrim badges. Couples swayed in the heat. Joy threaded everything with a mender's hand.

Clara managed the line with patient authority. "Short lines. Hands behind glass. Yes, the cat is permitted. No, you may not pick her up unless she picks you first." Lady Grey chose a strawberry-scented toddler and an elderly man who cried before the IOUs, anchoring his lap until he steadied. People began calling her—half teasing, wholly sincere—the Archivist.

"Miss Amelia!" Henry Penrose barreled up with Elsie Miller and co-conspirators carrying a tissue-wrapped box. Parents supervised from a decent distance.

"We have something for Lady Grey," Elsie announced.

"You do?" Amelia crouched. "Has she passed inspection?"

"She's the bravest cat in town," Henry beamed.

They opened the box: a tiny crown of folded silver paper and paste jewels, lavender sprigs tucked so it smelled like June.

"With the authority vested in us by the Festival Committee of Children, we crown you the Silver Queen," Elsie declared.

Lady Grey received the crown without flinch or vanity, dipped her head for placement, stepped onto the case edge, and sat. The crown slipped, caught on one ear, stayed. Approval rolled through the square.

"She now outranks the council," Clara murmured.

"At last—a leader who bites the right ankles," Amelia said.

Commerce followed affection. An artist sketched crowned Lady Grey above a spoon and printed bookmarks; an embroiderer stitched lavender coronets on handkerchiefs; a teen offered a poster and, at Clara's nudge, sent proceeds to the archive. By noon the donation jar brimmed with crumpled singles and careful children's change. History had a price; they chose how to pay.

A Duluth reporter asked before shooting. "You didn't sanitize," she told Clara after reading the pamphlet. "People trust that."

"We learned it from silver," Clara said, and stopped there.

The afternoon kept piling good on good—choir harmonies, warm bread shared, Mr. Larkin's fog-outwitting lighthouse keeper. Doris moved through it all wearing the town like a shawl instead of armor.

Amelia, lately practiced at vigilance, let herself relax in increments. She checked tent corners—no shadows, just teens taking selfies in the lens reflection. She refilled Clara's water with a lemon slice because Clara forgets luxury. She returned a paper crown to a toddler determined to sleep in it.

Two small crises offered themselves and failed to sour the day. A gust snapped a knot; a tent scallop flew; bottles chattered. Lady Grey streaked across cobbles, pinned the flapping edge with both paws, and three teenagers reached the line two seconds later, tying with exaggerated care. "She's union now," one said. "We owe breaks."

Later, a man in expensive shoes lingered at the IOUs with the wrong smile. "Valuable ephemera," he said. "Consider a private sale?"

Clara arrived like mist—everywhere, decisive. "We considered accession, provenance, and public access," she said, buttering toast from forty paces. "We chose a library over a ledger."

"Libraries cost money."

"Which we are raising," she said, nodding toward the jar and crowned-cat posters. "You may contribute—without ownership."

He began, *You don't understand,* but the square did. Colby, carrying acid-free folders, took position at Clara's shoulder; Mr. Larkin set a box of pamphlets between the man and the cases; Harlow's gaze traveled over. The man read the tableau—the past, standing—and left without stamping.

"Thank you," Clara told Colby. "Thank you," he said back, naming more than one moment.

As shadows lengthened into painter's ochre, the Community Dedication served as punctuation. Harlow spoke two sentences. Doris spoke three. Mr. Larkin read the plaque like a consecration. Amelia surprised herself: "Not every story ends in light," she said. "But this one stands in it. We'll still disagree and disappoint. Good. It means we're not finished."

Henry tugged her sleeve. "Say the cat part."

"We had help," Amelia said. "She has four feet and no patience." Laughter lifted; the day's last tension left like a candle's puff.

Music rose—fiddle, guitar, a high-schooler's astonishing whistle. Neighbors spun; children in paper crowns made a train that turned until it found itself. Lanterns lifted their gold; the lake sent a wind that smelled like tomorrow.

At the tent flap, Amelia joined Doris and Clara. They watched the fork and spoon—no longer prizes or proof, simply theirs—and Lady Grey, crown rakish, posted like a hatch guard.

"For years I thought it would end me," Doris said. "Today it put me back."

"You put you back," Clara said. "With assistance."

"We'll keep polishing," Amelia said. "Not the silver. The story."

They stayed to the last lantern. People stacked chairs with the hush that follows delight. Vendors zipped flaps with that small, satisfying sound. Colby packed the cases with respectful economy. Mr. Larkin gathered paper crowns for the archive—ephemera halfway to myth. The choir sang one last verse everyone somehow knew.

Fireworks offered a coda—earnest, well-timed: gold chrysanthemums, a blue peony, three white comets that stitched the black and doubled in the lake. Lady Grey watched with alert calm and chirruped at one pert burst—an approving review.

They walked home in the untidy procession of contentment. Amelia checked locks with a hand that no longer shook and turned toward the inn under a sky knitting back its stars.

On the porch she opened the guestbook. Names crowded the page. A Chicago couple wrote, *We came for antiques and stayed for honesty.* A child drew Lady Grey with six whiskers on one side and four on the other—imperfection as affection. Doris's rounder hand: *We did it.* Clara's initials corrected the date—joy likes accuracy.

Lady Grey leapt to the railing, crown tilted like a wink. Amelia rubbed her chin and felt the deep purr—a metronome, a motor, a benediction. "Her Majesty has done well," she said.

"Her Majesty expects sardines," Clara replied, bringing two mugs of tea, the look of a woman who'd carried a town's footnotes all day and would again tomorrow.

They drank in companionable quiet while lanterns dozed and the lake exhaled. Down the lane, Doris flipped her sign to **SEE YOU IN THE MORNING**—a new kind of promise.

"Tomorrow we pack the cases for the archive," Clara said. "I'll reorder sleeves. Rewrite the placard—Mr. Talbot asked what *provenance* means."

"I'll marinate peaches," Amelia said. "Truth-tellers deserve cobbler."

"Scholarly," Clara said.

"Nutmeg-forward," Amelia countered.

Lady Grey butted their wrists until they stroked in sync. The last lantern went out with the soft pop of a closing book. The festival ended not with a dropped curtain but a door propped open.

Tumblebrook would face courts, headlines, loud newcomers, winters that test cedar ribs. But tonight the town danced around its center and put the hard thing in a glass case instead of a wall. It crowned the right creature. It laughed without cruelty. It told its children the story plainly enough that the children made it a song.

Amelia gathered the guestbook. "Bed?"

"Footnotes," Clara said—which meant *five minutes, I promise.*

Lady Grey padded ahead and looked back at the threshold, checking their lesson had taken. It had—for tonight: truth kept is better than silver kept; a town is a room you clean together; a crown of paper and lavender can weigh exactly enough.

The door swung shut on a square at peace, and the festival—weathered, remade, triumphant—took its last breath like a lullaby.

Chapter 45

A Quiet Evening

The summer evening folded gently around Tumblebrook, as if the town were tucking in after a long season. Crickets took up their steady chorus; on the lake a loon called and was answered, sound slipping over water like silk. Festival bunting sagged in soft loops; a few paper crowns—lavender brittle now—clung to a bench as if reluctant to abdicate. Windows stood open; curtains breathed.

On the inn's porch, Amelia and Clara let their chairs creak into shared comfort. Teacups steamed; between them sat Doris's shortbread—"payment," Doris had said, "for holding this town together with ribbon, cinnamon, and sense."

Lady Grey dozed between them, crown retired to the windowsill like a well-earned medal. She slept as only a creature can who has outwaited two storms: paws twitching, whiskers tasting dream-currents, a purr ticking like a content metronome. Every so often her tail tapped Clara's knee; Clara, without looking, shaped it into a neater curve.

"I'll never get used to how quickly life changes here," Amelia said softly. "One week we're counting scones for the early ferry. The next we're prying up floorboards and naming killers."

"Small things and their disproportionate consequences," Clara said. "A spoon, a ledger, a cat. Aristotle would ache."

"It wasn't the spoon alone," Amelia said. "It was everything clinging to it—pride, fear, an old promise kept too long."

"Greed, too. The silver by weight was nothing. The story made people reckless."

"Stories spend dearer than money," Amelia said. "Unless you write them down and shelve them properly."

"An innkeeper's argument for libraries," Clara approved.

They let quiet settle. Fireflies stitched the garden; porch boards returned the day's warmth; up the lane a screen door thudded and a child laughed. Peace didn't erase the past; it laid a hand over it.

"Do you think they learned?" Clara asked. "About telling hard truths before they curdle."

"Some did," Amelia said. "Some aren't ready, and that's all right —until it isn't. But the record exists now." She nudged Clara. "Your record."

"Our record," Clara corrected, eyes on Lady Grey. "If we're precise. The archivist with whiskers gets first billing."

Lady Grey's ear twitched, satisfied.

"I thought we might lose the inn," Amelia admitted, lighter for saying it. "When rumor swelled. When Benton stood here dripping rain and menace."

"You kept the light in the window," Clara said simply. "That's work. People think light happens." She tipped her chin at the cat. "Also, a gray-furred sovereign guards the house."

Amelia bent to whisper, because dignity requires whispering. "You heard, Majesty. Your subjects are at rest." The purr deepened.

They ate shortbread the way women do after long danger— without apology. The night set itself in order.

"Tomorrow?" Clara asked—practical, hopeful.

"Ordinary, I hope," Amelia said. "Sticky buns. Someone misplacing a fountain pen and being sure it's stolen. A thunderhead that only threatens. A request for an extra blanket so I can remind someone it's July."

"Ordinary is out of circulation," Clara said, "but we're reprinting."

The hall clock chimed ten. Amelia fetched the mail. One envelope wore Colby's narrow script.

Linens, a Chicago couple's recipes—"Nonna's lemon knots, for your peaches"—and Colby's letter: *I've finished sorting the boxes. Enclosed, items accessioned at Gossamer Fables and duplicates lodged with the county. I would like the town to belong to more than one drawer. A pause in ink. I have also found a key. It opened nothing here. If it belongs to the Finches' old ledger cabinet, it belongs with you —with the town. Forgive an old man for choosing who forgets. I'd rather help you remember.*

Taped beneath: a small key, plain but for a tiny crown near the teeth. Both women laughed softly at fate's insistence on motifs.

"Doris will have opinions," Amelia said.

"And feed the key," Clara said. "Shortbread and opinions."

A line on Colby's list: *Copies placed with Lark County Records at 3:12 p.m.; receipt in triplicate.* Administrative poetry, sunlight diffused instead of spotlighted. Mr. Larkin's neat bill for sleeves and gloves followed. Clara set it aside, satisfied. "I'll see to this tomorrow. After I explain—again—that provenance isn't a vitamin."

"Tell Mr. Talbot it is," Amelia said. "Good for bones."

They gathered cups, shook crumbs to the dusk for grateful ants, and rose. Lady Grey flowed to the threshold, pausing to audit: garden, square, lamp, moon. All in order. She hopped to the windowsill with a foreman's air.

Inside, lemon oil and ember made domestic weather. The inn exhaled welcome. Amelia paused, hands in cool dishwater, to notice an ordinary happiness: washing two cups used by two people she loved, in a house that still felt like hers.

"Before bed," Clara said from the doorway—never between

Amelia and the room—"we should set a tray. Room Three likes chamomile and the clock turned to face the wall because it ticks too bravely."

"Mrs. Denby," Amelia said. "She asked to point the pillows north. I told her I collect superstitions; she said they aren't superstitions if they work."

They moved through small rites. A tray: two cups, a pot in a knit cozy the color of the lake on good days, two slices of shortbread under a dome in case the queen stopped by. Amelia added a sprig of thyme; Clara turned the clock and smiled at the tiny rebellion. Found kindness is a particular sweetness.

Back in the parlor, embers winked. "You were right," Clara said. "About tomorrow. I'd like to be bored."

"Bored and full," Amelia said. "I'm slicing the last peaches for morning tarts, and if anyone says peaches aren't breakfast I'll point them to the archive under Errors of Judgment."

"We'll need a drawer for culinary jurisprudence."

They tidied without hurry. The soft chime of a spoon finding its place braided into a rope sturdy enough to hold against storm-memory.

"Bed," Amelia said.

"Footnotes," Clara answered—reflex and joke. They went anyway.

Upstairs smelled faintly of paper and lavender. Doors stood like patient faces. Passing Room Two, Amelia squared the newspaper; the crossword was half-finished—*gannet* penciled lightly, as if the writer weren't sure the bird belonged here. Outside Room Six, someone had left a small shell with no note—private gratitude's grammar.

At the landing window Clara paused. The lake lay black-mirror under the moon. "Look," she whispered. A fish rose, wrote a circle, vanished. Ripples widened and became the lake's skin.

"Proof of life," she said.

"Plenty of it," Amelia answered.

They parted for their rooms with the ease of people who could find each other in the dark. Amelia's room had resumed its conspiracies: chair angled for morning light; bedside book open to the page she pretended not to have read ahead; her mother's stitched sampler: *Do your work. Be kind. Put the kettle on.*

Lady Grey arrived, leapt to the bed, circled three times (the correct number), and became a loaf. Amelia set the paper crown on the bureau; paste jewels winked at the moon.

"Tomorrow you'll accept congratulations at a reasonable hour," she told the cat. The huge eyes slid closed: *I accept tributes on my schedule.*

Amelia washed her face, grateful for a tap that squeaked on the second turn and a towel that smelled of lemon. She thought of Doris closing the café; Harlow writing reports no paper would print entire; Colby with contrition and lists. She thought of Benton, and her mind refused him. Not tonight.

She slipped into crisp sheets. Night air came gentle; in it rode thyme, a hint of smoke, and—unexpectedly—blueberries. Somewhere, someone had baked.

The house made faithful noises: the stair's third tread acknowledging itself; the radiator ticking by memory. Down the lane a wagon rattled; tomorrow someone would snug the bolt. "Thank you for today," she said into the dark. She meant Clara, Doris, Harlow, Colby, Mr. Larkin; glue-fingered children; the choir; the lake; a cat who'd put her body between rage and a woman she liked. She meant the town.

Sleep came like a neighbor who leaves soup, no fuss. There would be peaches in the morning; thunder might posture in the afternoon; someone would ask for a blanket in July and be gently handed one anyway; Clara would correct a label kindly; a child's crown would be filed under **Ephemera: Events (Joy)**; the cat would stage an intervention with a moth and accept applause.

Next door, Clara lay awake one minute longer, inventorying the archive as some count sheep—IOUs (A-3), ledger (sleeved; duplicate offsite), handkerchief (photographed; county holds original), children's poster (rolled; tube labeled). The list softened into lullaby. She almost reached for her notebook—she'd found a better verb than *kept*: *stewarded*—then trusted she'd remember. Trust was becoming a habit again.

Downstairs, the inn dreamed of tomorrow: tea in hands, suitcases thumped up by determined teenagers, a mop-and-bucket waltz, yeast frothing, lavender tucked in drawers. The house considered itself lucky.

Near midnight, cooler air slipped off the lake. It turned the paper crown's jewels into tiny stars. Somewhere a screen door thumped, then remembered its job and settled.

Lady Grey, vigilant even in sleep, opened her eyes to crescents, patted down the last ripple, and curled tighter. The kingdom—having crowned truth and eaten shortbread—kept watch the right way: with cats and quiet.

Tumblebrook exhaled. The lake breathed back. The night held.

Chapter 46

Epilogue: The Fork in the Garden

In the days after the festival, Tumblebrook settled into a rhythm it hadn't dared hope for. Market stalls returned like bright stitches; fishermen resumed ordinary complaints; the postman tucked gossip under stamps. The Inn filled—Duluth, Minneapolis, Chicago—guests drawn by quilts, lake light, and a town that had faced its shadows without dimming its welcome.

Amelia allowed herself slower mornings—tea on the porch, sleeves rolled, hair pinned any which way—watching the lake take its silver. From the kitchen came the buttery percussion of breakfast; from the parlor, Clara's measured voice, as neat with guests as with ledgers. Children asked if the Silver Queen paid for room and board. Lady Grey accepted tribute with grace and perfected the art of the official windowsill nap.

It was a golden run of days. Tumblebrook exhaled.

Still, quiet here was always a pause between chapters. At evening, with the garden amber in low sun, Amelia chose roses over riddles. In canvas gloves she trimmed spent blooms; bees shouldered past; birch leaves whispered harmless gossip. On the bench, Clara tapped her pencil over archive notes, a pale stripe on her wrist where paper lived.

"Records behave once they feel safe," she said. "Letters from flour tins, receipts from hymnals. Every time a timeline closes, someone brings a key."

"History deadheads so it can bloom again," Amelia said.

A robin bobbed approval. Then something pewter slid into light.

Lady Grey padded onto the brick path, ears intent. She sniffed the roses, then—unapologetically—began to dig. Damp earth flecked Amelia's boots.

"Lady Grey—"

A clear clink.

Clara's head snapped up. They let the cat work. She scissored forepaws with masonly precision until soil collapsed around a sliver of metal. Lady Grey stepped back, gracious as an archaeologist. Amelia brushed earth aside.

A blade, then—no: two tines, a shallow flare, balanced to serve, not slice. The handle lifted the last of the light: a crown above a three-masted ship.

"A fork," Clara breathed—reverent, wry. "Of course."

Amelia sat back, feeling the old echo—spoon, fork, lockbox, ledgers. Ordinary objects, unreasonable weight. Lady Grey wrapped her tail, whiskers proclaiming she had announced this all along.

Clara crouched. "We'll clean it, catalog it. Photograph, sleeve, accession. If we keep the town's story, we keep the muddy parts too."

Amelia turned the fork. Heavier than expected. "Do you suppose they hid a whole service?"

"If so, poorly," Clara said. "Or on purpose. Scattering forgets—and invites finding by episodes."

"I'd hoped for a season with nothing more dangerous than thorns."

"Thorns are dangerous," Clara said. "They're just polite." She glanced toward gathering lamplight. "We could leave it for morning."

"We could," Amelia said—and knew they wouldn't.

They carried the fork between glove and handkerchief, pausing at the gate as one does at borders: yard to house; present to record. "Mark the spot," Amelia said. "Coordinates, so we don't uproot Doris's thyme 'for context.'"

Clara folded a leaf of paper and wrote, clean as a map: *Inn garden, south bed, third rose from trellis, two bricks east. Fork (serving). Crest present. Cat insistent.* She dated it, underlined the last clause twice, and drew a lazy cat head in the margin.

Lady Grey nosed the note and brushed the gate to sign it.

In the kitchen the kettle purred; peaches confessed August; the wood held sugar forever in its grain. Amelia rinsed the fork until the water ran clear. Up close, the crown bore a nick; the ship's prow had softened. In a dish basin, the object that sent men to conspiracy looked like what it was: a piece of service.

Clara dried it with linen that remembered an iron. "The second fork," she said. "Imagine we hadn't believed the first."

"We might have invented a peace I wouldn't trust," Amelia said.

Lady Grey arranged herself to receive compliments as if by accident. Her fur made silver jealous.

"Keep finding pieces," Clara told her. "But perhaps...space them over a decade? For my heart."

The cat blinked: management noted.

They set the fork on the small table that bridged household and history. A clean journal waited—the same page that had hosted the handkerchief, IOU copies, a child's paper crown. Clara wrote as Amelia spoke: *Found by Lady Grey (Amelia present, Clara present). Condition: tarnish; crest legible; no blood; weight—* She looked up. "—more than a spoon, less than a burden."

"Quote me," Amelia said, resigned.

They sat with it a minute. The fork could wait another hour. Outside, first fireflies blinked. The house felt between chapters again, but not at a cliff—just a bend.

"Do you ever think the town chose us?" Amelia asked.

"It chose the cat," Clara said. "We are her unpaid staff."

Amelia touched her wrist. "I'm glad to be on duty with you."

"Likewise."

They settled the fork not on the mantel (mantels invite folly) but in a muslin-lined tray in the secretary whose second drawer stuck—enough to deter casual hands. Clara labeled it neatly: *Pending Accession: Garden Fork (Serving).* "Filed under *Artifacts, Silver (Local): Post-Recovery.* Subfolder *Unearthed by Cat,*" she added.

"That's a subfolder?"

"A category," she said gravely. "We have the data."

They put the room to rights—cups turned to dry, a book laid facedown with hopeful guilt, windows latched a quarter for sound without insects. The hall clock took its time about nine; the hour felt kinder than weeks ago. They detoured to the garden; roses were shadow, but Amelia saw the scuff where paws insisted. "We'll put a stone," she said. "Flat. The mower must forgive."

"Mr. Larkin will have a dignified orphaned paperweight," Clara said.

"Tell Doris tonight?" Amelia asked.

"She'll know by morning," Clara said. "Let her have one whole sleep without a crest."

They agreed without needing to and went inside. Lady Grey brushed Amelia's shin and led the ascent, tail flagging distinguished arrivals.

A draft from the landing window—no malice—lifted the curtain; the lake sent its report: calm now, a breeze promised around three. A single boat light kept its own orbit.

"'Tomorrow," Clara said, to the notion, "I'm bringing Colby's last list and county copies. Then I'll say no, kindly and in writing, to three people trying to buy their great-grandmother's scandal back."

"You say no beautifully," Amelia said.

"I spell it," Clara replied. "It holds better."

They parted like women who know where the other keeps her courage. In her room, Amelia found the bed properly made; the paper crown looked suddenly like a promise; lavender scented old linen. She thought of chairs tipped in cafés the world over—safety's ritual. Of Harlow writing reports no one reads in full and everyone keeps. Of Colby's line—*not choosing who forgets*—and how brave domestic sizes are.

Lady Grey audited: under bed (monsters: none); sill (moths: unbriefed); chair (pillows: satisfactory). She loafed.

"You're very good at your job," Amelia told her. The cat received the review as one whose performance has been consistent.

Sleep came without argument.

Morning swung its basket of light across the kitchen. Peaches ripened; the kettle sighed. At seven, a brisk triple knock. Doris stood in the back hall, apron on, hair pinned so fiercely no scandal could dislodge it, expression both apology and inevitability.

"I brought scones," she said, lifting a basket like a handshake. "And my trowel."

"We were going to tell you after breakfast," Clara offered.

"You were going to try," Doris said, not unkindly, taking a chair. "The roses told me. The bed's scuffed like a dance floor."

"It's a fork," Amelia said, offering truth as to a friend who knows how to hold it. "Serving piece. Crest intact."

Doris closed her eyes, then opened them. "The Finches," she said —neither bitterness nor apology. Only history. "May we never set a table with ghosts again."

"We won't," Clara said. "We'll set the archive."

"Good." Doris steadied herself with a sip. "And we'll plant thyme over every empty place where something could hide." She blew away gnats of feeling. "Enough. I brought jam."

They ate scones with intent—the sort of breakfast that mends. Then to the garden: three women and a cat with trowel, notebook, supervisory tail. They didn't rip up roses; they marked the spot with a flat stone from the shed, a respectable rectangle with a faint glimmer. Clara drew a neat map; Doris tucked a sprig of thyme under the stone and pressed it like a benediction.

"Let anything left down there feed the soil," she said. "Not the town."

Lady Grey refrained from editorial digging and sat with her back to the stone, approving the fence line.

Ordinary resumed: guests needed coffee; linens needed gossip; the lake, per Clara's margins, would attempt a breeze at three-fifteen. Mr. Larkin arrived early with archival sleeves and a paperweight with deer along the edge—exactly the weight guilt has once accounted for. "For the garden map," he said, and, to the cat, a length of gray satin. Lady Grey accepted it with weary nobility.

Before lunch, Harlow stopped by. He asked about business, sleep, and herbs, his hand lingering on a chair back in an apology large enough to stand on. By afternoon the square gleamed like clean linen. Children chalked crowns and ships into the cobbles—the crest turned back into a game. On the library steps, Colby sat like a gargoyle resigned to being human. They exchanged small salutes. Enough.

Toward dusk, honey light. Two cups of mint tea—Doris insists it cures thinking that thinks too far—waited on the bench. Lady Grey threaded the path and leapt up like punctuation.

"Will it always be like this?" Amelia asked. Not fear—curiosity.

"Like truth arriving late and muddy? Cats triumphant? Towns braver than their reputations?" Clara smiled. "I think so. Stories don't end. They slow. Sometimes they go to ground and wait for paws."

They listened to mint make its case against heat. Fireflies rehearsed. The robin declared the day done.

At the gate, Amelia paused, the fork now cradled in memory, not hand. She used to think an innkeeper's work was beds, tea, calm bread. Now she knew it was listening—to the house, the town, a cat. To the quiet that holds the next necessary sentence.

Lady Grey brushed her calf and slipped through the gate ahead—silver and certainty.

"The story isn't over," Clara said—neither warning nor promise. Just record.

"No," Amelia agreed, smiling into the hour when lamps take up posts. "But it is ours."

They went in. The door, content with its small, important job, closed behind them. Outside, the fork's stone cooled under thyme and sky. Inside, the inn took their footsteps and made them part of its peace.

Tumblebrook—secrets catalogued, joys unabashed, its stubborn, steady heart beating—readied itself for the next ordinary day. And if a cat found another glint under roses come autumn, there were sleeves, notes, and hands enough for that too.